Thomas Herbert Lewin

Progressive Colloquial Exercises in the Lushai Dialect

Vocabularies and Popular Tales (Notated)

Thomas Herbert Lewin

Progressive Colloquial Exercises in the Lushai Dialect
Vocabularies and Popular Tales (Notated)

ISBN/EAN: 9783742830951

Manufactured in Europe, USA, Canada, Australia, Japa

Cover: Foto ©Andreas Hilbeck / pixelio.de

Manufactured and distributed by brebook publishing software
(www.brebook.com)

Thomas Herbert Lewin

Progressive Colloquial Exercises in the Lushai Dialect

PROGRESSIVE COLLOQUIAL EXERCISES

IN THE

LUSHAI DIALECT

OF THE

'DZO' OR KÚKI LANGUAGE,

WITH

VOCABULARIES AND POPULAR TALES (NOTATED).

———— ◆ ————

BY

CAPT. THOMAS HERBERT LEWIN, B.S.C.,

Deputy Commissioner, Chittagong Hills.

———— ◆ ————

Calcutta:

CALCUTTA CENTRAL PRESS COMPANY, LIMITED,
5, COUNCIL HOUSE STREET.

1874.

INTRODUCTION.

THE 'Dzo' tribes inhabit the hilly country to the east of the Chittagong district in Lower Bengal; their habitat may be roughly stated as comprised within the parallels of Latitude 22·15 N. and 25·20 N., and between the Meridians of Longitude 92·30 and 93·45.

Under the term 'Dzo' are included all the hill tribes of this region, who wear their hair in a knot resting on the nap of the neck. The tribes further south and east, of whom little is as yet known, are distinguished under the generic title of 'Poi'; these wear the hair knotted upon the temple.

The 'Dzo' state that the Poi language is entirely distinct from theirs, and that they have no common medium of intercommunication. I am myself disposed to think that the two languages must have some affinity, but I have as yet no certain information on this point.

The term Kúkí is a generic name applied by the inhabitants of the plains, Bengalees and others, to all hill-dwellers who cultivate by *Júm*. The word Kúkí is foreign to the different dialects of the hill tribes, the nearest approach to it being the 'Dzo' term for the Tipra tribe, which is called by them *Tuí-Kúk*. (See Vocabulary).

The physiognomy, character, and traditions of the 'Dzo' people seem to indicate that they have sprung from the great Turanian stock of Central Asia. It would seem probable that at some previous epoch, more or less remote, they have come from the southern spurs of the Himalayan range. Our whole information, as to the tribes occupying the comparatively unexplored country between Bengal and China or Burmah, is however so incomplete that speculations as to their origin can be founded on no reliable data. I would invite attention, nevertheless, to the subjoined comparative list of words, which would seem to give strength to the theory above propounded; it at least, I think, gives reasonable grounds for considering the Lushai tribes, including the inhabitants of Munipoor, to have sprung from the same stock as the Ghúrkas and other Himalayan tribes (Mongoloid of Huxley).

English	Duo (Kostrian).			Gnoup or Nepalese (Himalayan).				
	Lushai	Hill Arracan, a part of Burmese.	Duo	Kuml	Thapp	Sibsh	Ban	Muniport
1 One	Pakat	Til	...	Ng'khi	Kat	Htis	Ksiag	Ama
2 Two	Pahnit	HaR	...	Hipi	Uuie	Hsa chi	Si	Aai
3 Three	Pa-thim	Thro	...	Brim	Gim	Sam-ini	Sim	Ohim
4 Four	Pali	Li	...	Pala	Bali	Li-ini	Bali	Mari
5 Five	Pa-ngd	Ngi	...	Pia	Bangd	Na-tui	Ri	Ma-nga
6 Hand	Kit	Lik	...	Ko-ok	Mi-hut	Hak	La	Kit
7 Nose	Hnir	Nakamg	...	Khao	Mi-ul	Nivohu	Kok	Naton
8 Eye	Mit	Myeui	...	Mi	Mi-mik	Mik	Mik-shi	Mih
9 Mouth	Mur	Hadp	...	Lebomg	Moudhep	Mim	...	Tehin
10 Ear	Beng	Na	...	Kano	Mi-taum	Nethbln	...	Nakong
11 Hair	Thum	Chymbang	...	Tehan	Mli-tik	Teb-beh-ta	Tehom	Tehum
12 Head	Li	Gomg	...	Li	Mli-tik	...	...	Kik
13 Tongue	Lei	...	...	Palai	Mi-lik	Li-eupa	Lem	Li
14 Belly	Pim	...	...	Kayenk	Mi-Ak	Sapdm	Hem	Pih
15 Sun	Ni	Ni	...	Kmi	Ni-khan	Nm	Kepiing	Ning shn
16 Moon	Tia	Li	...	Hlo	Giahni	Libn	Tiumi	Ta
17 Fire	Mal	Mi	...	Hmai	Mi	Mi	Mo	Mei
18 Water	Tui	Mi	...	Toi	Mi	Me	...	Labing
19 Earth	Li	...	...	...	...	Tmrait	...	Khim
20 Road	Lim	Lim	...	Lim	...	...	Lim	...
21 Fish	Nghah	Ngah	...	Ngo	...	...	Ngi	...

The 'Dzo' are divided and sub-divided into many tribes and clans, the chief among which are as follows :—

1. Lushai.	5. Hrang-tchal.	9. Boog.
2. Tchawtey.	6. Phantey.	10. Bongtchar.
3. Haltey.	7. Rukam.	11. Ngvatey.
4. Pailey.	8. Boila.	12. Dzongtey.

Nearly each separate clan has peculiarities of diction proper to itself; but the speech of the whole people is in truth but one language, the differences being those merely of local pronunciation, of special terms or provincialisms, affected by the different clans, in the same way that our English language is spoken differently by the country folk north and south in England. The dialect of the Lushai tribe is, however, common to, and understood by all, being the clan tongue of the great family from which all the chiefs are said to have sprung. The Lushai dialect is in fact the *lingua franca* of the country.

The clan-name Lushai probably means 'the decapitators,' being derived from 'lú' a head and 'shá' or 'shát' to cut; and it is undoubtedly the custom among this people to carry off as trophies the heads of enemies slain in battle.

The 'Dzo' language has hitherto existed only in the form of speech; it has never been reduced to writing, and to this cause may, I think, be attributed the confusing and infinite petty variations of speech among these people. I have not attempted here (nor, indeed, have I the ability) to construct a grammar of the language: starting in total ignorance of its structure or idioms, by slow degrees, the formation of thought and modes of utterance of the people unfold themselves in a manner that is altogether interesting, and that lures you on to continue the study; it is as if one saw unfolding the genesis of human speech.

It seemed to me that as this mode of learning had been to me not only easy but attractive, the course I had followed might advantageously be pursued in like manner by others, to whom, either from motives of scientific interest or from a necessity of communicating with the people, a knowledge of the 'Dzo' tongue might be desirable. I play the part here of a simple pioneer going forward into an unknown forest and blazing a path; it is for those who come after me to expand the track into a fair and well-engineered roadway for the good of all.

In reducing this language to writing, I have, as far as possible, followed the transliteration system of Sir Wm. Jones as adopted by the Indian Government. The Lushai tongue, however, is full of soft sounds and lingual euphonies, and

It is difficult to denote the various gradations in the expression of sound by the limited range prescribed in the Jonesian system; I have therefore been compelled in some cases to depart therefrom or find fresh combinations of letters to indicate novel niceties of pronunciation.

The system of literation which has been employed in this book is subjoined :—

Vowel Sounds.

n	...	as in the English	... 'can.'
á	...	as in the English	... 'ha ha.'
au or aw	...	as in	... 'cause.'
e	...	as in	... 'pen.'
é	...	has a sound like the a in case, or the a in ale.
ei	...	is not pronounced as in elder, nor as in either, but has two distinct sounds of é and i.
ey	...	is used as a final é.
ai	...	has the power of the Greek ai ai, alas! alas! alas!
i	...	as in the English word	... 'pit.'
í	...	sounded as a double ee, or as the ea in 'peat.'
ee	...	double ee or ie sometimes used as a final in place of í.
o	...	as in the English	... 'on.'
ó	...	ditto	... 'over.'
u	...	as in	... 'nut.'
ú	...	as oo in	... 'ooze.'
oy	...	as in	... 'coy.'
oi	...	as in Australian	... 'cuce.'

Sounds—Consonant.

There is the palatal t (marked thus ṭ), and the dental or ordinary t unmarked. The letters dz convey a sound like the j in the French, 'jour.' The sounds expressed by the letters ts, tse, and tseh, are not sibilant like our English s or ts, nor are they like the sh in shall; the sounds are intermediate between the two, and are pronounced and softened between tongue, teeth, and palate. There does not appear to be any sound in the language answering to our English th in 'them' or 'these.'

The 'Dzo' language possesses one peculiarity in common with Burmese, viz., the use of mute or final consonants; letters, that is to say, which cut or clip off the end of a word, which must be formed by the lips but the pronunciation be suppressed.

Such consonants are here denoted by a dot placed below; thus, the imperative affix or sign of the imperative mood in Lushai 'rok' is pronounced as in the french rôt. We find, also, a final sound of 'gh,' which has the powers of the Persian *ghain* as in the Lushai, "Ittir ahmun tlagh ey," Iron is useful.

The letter h in the Lushai language is always aspirated, whether it be prefixed, as in the word 'Hla,' for, or affixed, as in 'ngah,' fish.

· The consonants ng, prefixed or affixed, have the same sound as in the English 'bang.'

The language may be classed in the Altaic group of tongues, of which it possesses most of the characteristics. It is agglutinative, that is, the roots of words remain generally unchanged, inflections being arrived at by the use of particles suffixed to the root. In construction it is generally the reverse of our English language, the objective case generally preceding the verb, while the word governed by what is with us a preposition precedes the preposition.

In rendering the sentences given as exercises into English, I have purposely adopted a free mode of translation, in order that the student, by observing for himself the literal rendering of passages, may arrive at a more intimate and less parrot-like acquaintance with the structure of the language.

Vocabularies of all the words employed will be found at the end of the book.

There is in this small work much doubtless that requires correction, much to be modified. The need, however, for some manual of the sort is urgent, not merely to facilitate the intercourse of Government officers with the people, but also to pave the way for the introduction of education among the tribes at large.

It would be foolish to postpone an important journey from fear of stumbling by the way; and it would be false pride that would prevent me from putting forth this small compilation, because my successors may discover my many errors.

I would urge only that this book has had to be prepared under circumstances of considerable difficulty, owing to the absolute lack of any competent interpreter; thus to ascertain the meaning of a word or trace the origin or inflections of an idiom has often involved a search of many days.

I trust then that my readers will accord to me that indulgence which is so much needed.

THOMAS HERBERT LEWIN.

DEMAGREE,
LUSHAI FRONTIER.

PROGRESSIVE COLLOQUIAL EXERCISES

LUSHAI DIALECT OF THE KÚKI OR 'DZO' LANGUAGE.

EXERCISE 1.

Até or té, little; koyma, I; nungma, thou; koymani, we; nungmani, ye; ahé or hé, fatigue; dâm, health; hodm tachom, poverty; ûpa, elder, old; a-hté or hté, good; mé, man; hé-lam-hi, that, there; ashâng, tall, high.

1.	Koyma ka-té ey	...	I am little.
2.	Nungma í úpa ey	...	You are the elder.
3.	Koymani kan-hé-te	...	We are tired.
4.	Nungma í-dâm-loh emai ?	...	Are you sick ?
5.	Nungma í-hnam-tachom emai ?	...	Are you poor ?
6.	E-hi úpa oné-tem ?	...	Is he old ?
7.	Nungmani in-dâm-loh emai ?	...	Are ye sick ?
8.	Nungmani in-dâm em ?	...	Are ye well ?
9.	Mi hté eni em ?	...	Are they well ?
10.	Hé-lam-hi ashâng em ?	...	Is it high ?
11.	Koyma ka-hnam-tachom emai ?	...	Am I poor ?
12.	Koyma hashâng loh	...	I am not tall.
13.	E hi ashâng ey	...	He is tall.

(*Explanatory*.)—In the above exercise the following explanations are necessary :—' Ka' is the nominative prefix ; 'í,' the prefix of the second person singular ; 'kan,' of the first person plural ; 'in,' of the second person plural. The third person singular and plural is seldom used, but is expressed by a periphrasis. Thus, in sentence 6, they do not say, 'Is he old,' but 'that one is (he) elder or aged ;' again in sentence 10, the literal translation is not, " Is it high,' but 'that there high' (is it) ? 'em' being the interrogative affix. I have not been able to discover by what rules the use of the different interrogative affixes is regulated. In sentences 4, 5, 7, and 11, 'emai' is used ; in sentence 6, the uncommon form 'oné-tem ;' in others, simply 'em.' 'Ené-tem' and 'emai' would seem to be compounds of 'ené,' part of the verb to be, and 'em' the interrogative affix the ; in tem being added for euphony. The addition of a euphonic literal prefix we shall find, as we advance, is not unusual. In sentence 3, 'in' is the sign of the possessive. The phrase literally translated is, 'we fatigue have.' The word 'loh,' in sentences 4, 7, and 12, denotes the negative ; they have no word for sickness, but say, 'not well.' ' Hté,' good is sometimes used for 'dâm,' as in sentence 9.

Exercise 2.

Hlow, fear; achok, hardness, strength; aliaw, big; taaw, (demonstrative) that; tacbûh, (prohibition imperative) do not; ti, sign of plural number; tatacia, lazy; nen, with; ani, mother; fa, child; nowpang, boy.

1.	Hlow tacbûh	...	...	Do not fear.
2.	Hlow-tûr om-loh	...	...	There is no fear.
3.	Taaw aaháng ey	...	...	That is high.
4.	Koymani kan-chuk ey	...	...	We are strong.
5.	Koyma ka-lien em ?	...	...	Am I big?
6.	Koyma ka-lien ey	...	...	I am big.
7.	Hé mi-té tatacia	...	...	They are lazy.
8.	Hé-hi a-htá-loh ani-loh	...	...	He is not bad.
9.	Anú nen fa adám-loh	...	...	The mother and child are sick.
10.	Anú afá adám-loh	...	...	The mother's child is sick.
11.	Nowpang ani dam-loh	...	...	The boy's mother is sick.
12.	Hi fá a-htá em-aw a-hta-loh em-aw ?	...	Is that child good or bad ?

(*Explanatory.*)—Note in this exercise the inflection of ' ani' in sentence 9, part of the verb ' to be,' and the use of ' om,' to have, in sentence 2 ; in the same sentence, 'tûr' is the affix denoting the infinitive 'to.' In sentence 12, we find a new and very common mode of using the interrogative affix em—colloquially it becomes ' maw'—as ' a-htá maw ?' Is it good ?

Exercise 3.

Hé, this; hi, that; atar, old (in reference to age) ; a-hlui, old (in reference to condition) ; in, a house ; hmai-tacia, a woman ; hia, a village ; apá, father ; lo, a jum, *i. e.*, a piece of cultivated land on a hill side ; moeg, much ; tey, little.

1.	Hé in a-hta loh	...	...	This is not a good house.
2.	Hé in atar loh	...	...	This house is not old.
3.	Hé in ahlui ey	...	...	This house is old.
4.	Hi hmai-tacia afá a-htá loh	...	The son of that woman is bad.
5.	Hé hia a-htá ey	...	...	This village is good.
6.	Afá a-htá loh om-loh	...	...	The child is not a bad child.
7.	Kapá atar-tá em ?	...	...	Is my father old ?
8.	Kapá tar-tá ey	...	...	My father is old.
9.	In lo alien	...	...	The house and ' jum' are big.
10.	In a-hlui-loh-vey	...	...	The house is not old.
11.	In a-hlui moeg loh	...	...	The house is not very old.
12.	Hi lo a-htá loh emni ?	...	Is not this ' jum' bad ?
13.	In tey ani	...	...	The house is small.

(*Explanatory.*)—Roll the r in ' tar.' The i in 'in,' a house, is pronounced long, as if written with a double ee. The ' h' prefixed in ' hlui' (3), hmai-tacia (4), and ' hia' (1, 6, 12), must be clearly aspirated.

Exercise 4.

Eng, what; huing, name; bla, far; hnai, near; eng-tchongey, how much; kai, to go; hai-kong, path tá, who; tláng, a hill.

1.	Eng hming ngey?	...	...	What is its name?
2.	Eng tchongoy hlá?	...	...	How far is it?
3.	A-hnai tey em?	...	...	Is it near?
4.	A-blá ey	...	...	It is far off.
5.	A-hnai tey	...	...	It is near.
6.	Kui kong om em?	...	...	Is there a path?
7.	Kong om oy?	...	...	There is a path.
8.	Nungma tu-ngey?	...	...	Who are you?
9.	Nungma eng hmingey?	...	...	What is your name?
10.	Hé hmai-tacin a lá-tá	...	...	This woman is tired.
11.	Hi tláng asháng loh	...	...	That hill is not high.

(*Explanatory.*)—The affix 'ngey' is used in the interrogative form of all relative pronouns. The t prefixed in tey (sentences 3 and 5) would seem to be euphonic only.

Exercise 5.

A-liá-hlo, diligent; ajow, large, extensive; túkver, a window; kong-kar, a door; from hong, a path, and kar, to shut; dait, very; thukanga, wealth; Dzo-hlút, noun proper, masc.; ánao, relation; ú, elder brother or sister; nao, younger brother or sister; nú, mother; koya, where.

1.	Hi nowpang u-liá-hlo em?	...	Is that child diligent?
2.	A-liá-hlo loh...	...	He is not diligent.
3.	Hi lo ajow emni atey emni?	...	Is that '*jám*' big or little?
4.	Hé túkver kar-loh ani. Karok	...	This window is not shut. Shut it.
5.	Tsaw hting a-liá dait ani...	...	That tree is very good.
6.	Hi mi tankánga emni, hnám-tschom emni?	...	Is that man rich or poor?
7.	Dzohlúta ehú, ka-ánao ani ey	...	Dzo-hlút is a relation of mine.
8.	Hé nowpang ka-ú ani ey ...	...	This child is my sister.
9.	Nungma, koyma katien ani ey	...	You are my friend.
10.	Nungma i-lo, ajow-maw-ngey eul ey...	...	Your *jám* is extensive.
11.	Nungma nú koya-ngey?...	...	Where is your mother?
12.	Hé nowpang nungma nao emni?	...	Is that child your brother?

(*Explanatory.*)—Túkver is an opening cut in the wall of a house; kong-kar, literally translated, is the 'path-closer,' *i.e.*, a shutter to the window. The 'dz' in dait (sentence 5) must be softened almost to the sound of the French j, in jour. The word 'tankanga' (sentence 6) is of foreign origin, being derived from the Bengallee টাকা, a rupee. The emphatic 'ehú' (sentence 7) has, I believe, the same power as the particle *né* in Hindustani. Take care to harden the sound of the palatal t, in katien (sentence 9). In sentence 10, I think 'ajow-maugngry' should be written (see Ex. 3, s. 11); but I am doubtful about it. As to the *i* in *ti-lo* (sentence 10) see Ex. 1, ss. 2, 3, 4, 5, &c. The expression of relationships in the Lushai dialect is full of obscurity. *ü* is elder brother or sister, or cousin, and ' *nao*' applies to all younger relations of whatever sex. The terms father and mother are loosely used. . This subject requires further and minute inquiry.

Exercise 6.

Tokmwo, faithful; sbkhôr, a horse; hâm, your; tchem, a dao, a bill hook; tlem, few, small; heta, here; tûna, now; tatchia, lazy; Lai-jori, proper noun fem.; kul, to go; rok, verbal affix of imperative mood. -

1.	Koyma kutico tukmeo ani ey	...	My friend is true.
2.	Hé sokkur atey hrim emni?	...	Is this horse young?
3.	Hé sokkur akúm atlem ani ey	...	This horse is young.
4.	Koyma tchem koyangey?	...	Where is my *dao*?
5.	Nungma tchem heta hi	...	Here is your *dao*.
6.	Lai-jori túna kúm atlem emi ey	...	Lai-jori is still young.
7.	Túna kuhlrók...	...	Go now.
8.	Nungma nao a-tatchia emí	...	Your brother is lazy.
9.	Koyma jien a-htá-bto dait	...	My friend is very diligent.
10.	Koymani kan-pá a-htá ey	...	Our father is good.
11.	Ka-nú atey ey	...	My mother is little.
12.	Koymaui fâ alâm-luh	...	Our child is sick.

Exercise 7.

Ai-hi-un, than; tâm, much; dzawk, very; ahmél, appearance; ní, sun; tlâ, moon; hnaik, comparison bar, lead; hlir, iron; a-tfi, heavy.

The Burmese word for sun, day, corresponds with the Lushai *ní*.

1.	Hé mí nungma i-ú em em?	...	Is this man your brother?
2.	Hi hmai-tchin nungma hú em em?	...	Is that woman your sister?
3.	Dza-hlút nungma jien em em?	...	Is Dza-hlút your friend?
4.	Lai-jori nungmai i-ú em kuh	...	Lai-jori is not your sister.
5.	Koyma naó hó mí ai-hí-un ahta-hio	...	My younger brother is more diligent than he.
6.	Nungma hé mí ai-hí-un akúm atóm dzawk.	...	You are much older than he.
7.	Lai-jori a-hmél a-htá	...	Lai-jori is good looking.
8.	Hé mí koyma ai-hi-un at-chnk dzawk	...	He is stronger than I.
9.	Nungma fâ bè nowpang ai-hi-un akúm alleu.	...	Your child is younger than that boy.
10.	Tla, ni ai-hí-un atey ey	...	The moon is less than the sun.
11.	Nungma ú nungma ai-hí-un ahmél ahta dzawk.	...	Your sister is prettier than you are.
12.	Koymani hnaik-in nungma-ní tanka tam dzawk ey.	...	You are richer than we.
13.	Har hlir ahnaik-in arfi ey	...	Lead is heavier than iron.

EXERCISE 8.

A-hmaa, mo ; tla, to fall ; reg, what ; ang, like; al-in, than ; a-hlogh, expensive, dear.

1.	Hé hling tsaw hling ai-in atey dzawk.	This tree is smaller than that.
2.	Hé tchem auga tchem al-in ahtá dzawk.	This dao is better than his.
3.	Koymani lo amani lo al-in atey dzawk.	Our *júm* is smaller than theirs.
4.	Ili in ama in ai-in atey dzawk	...	That house is smaller than his.
5.	Hlir har al-in ahmûn tlagh	...	Iron is more useful than lead.
6.	Nuagma rogma hmûn tlagh loh	...	You are no use at all.
7.	Eng angey hmân ang ?	...	What use is it ?
8.	Eng angey reg ang ?	...	How is it, like what ?
9.	Koyma chú, ama al-in kúm allen loh	...	I am not older than he.
10.	Har hlir-tek al-in a-hlogh loh	...	Lead is not so dear as steel.
11.	Koymani hún tsaw mi-té húa ai-in allen ahtá tey oy.	Our village is bigger and better than theirs.

EXERCISE 9.

Alo, to lose ; hnên, along with, near ; hté, word ; tûk, true ; tla, for ; tûn-tlreg-la, till now ; par, flower.

1.	Nuagma tchem alo-tem ?	...	Is your *dao* lost ?
2.	Nuagma tchem aboia-emaw ?	...	Have you lost your *dao* ?
3.	Koyma ka-tchem nuagma hnênn om-em ?	...	Have you got my *dao* ?
4.	Dzo-hlûta hnênan atchem om	...	Dzo-hlût has the *dao*.
5.	Koyma htú tûk-tûk oul	...	I speak the truth.
6.	Koyma ka-fa-pa htú tûk eni-luh	...	My son's words are not true.
7.	Nuagma hnêna sûkhûr ley tchem om-om?	...	Have you a *dao* and a horn ?
8.	Hé tchem Dzo-hlûta tûa om ey	...	This *dao* is for Dzo-hlût.
9.	Hé in á-nú tûa om em ?	...	Is this house for your mother ?
10.	Nuagma i-pica hnêna tchem om em ?	...	Has your friend a *dao* ?
11.	Dzo-hlûta hnê'nan Ramoni hnê'nan tchem om em ?	...	Have Dzo-hlût and Ramoni got *daos* ?
12.	Nuagma pá tûn-tlong-la a-ú om em ?	...	Has your father still a sister ?
13.	Hé par koyma ka-fá atán a-om em ?	...	Is this flower for my daughter ?

EXERCISE 10.

Sciel, gayal, (bos gaural) ; nei, to get ; lei, to buy ; engtikengey, when ; anglangey, engtikangey, engey, langey, nian? for ; tk, to take ; tuchhr, to find ; hmd, to see ; en, to look ; vai, foreign ; lei, an earthen pot ; vaibel, a tobacco pipe.

1.	Hé silial koyangey nei ?	...	Where did you get that gun ?
2.	Nuagma pá bé sciel alal-tem ?	...	Has your father bought this gayal ?
3.	Engtikangey lei ?	...	When did he buy it ?
4.	Koyangey, lei ?	...	Where did he buy it ?
5.	Koyma sciel la-lei	...	I am buying a gayal.

6.	Koyma selel ka-lei-ta	...	I have bought a gayal.
7.	Nungma tchem engtangey hral?	...	Why are you selling your *dao*?
8.	Koyma vaibel nungma engeytangey i-bigh loh?	...	Why did you not take my pipe?
9.	Koyma ú nungma tchem atschür ey	...	My brother has found your *dao*.
10.	Nungma né kovmani kan-hmú-tá	...	We have seen your mother.
11.	Ili humi-tchia túna ka-hmu-loh	...	I do not see that woman now.
12.	Ilé humi-tchia endrok	...	Look at this woman.
13.	Koyma vaibel engey tangey lágh?	...	Why did you take my pipe?

EXERCISE 11.

Úi, *dog*; sillai, *gun*; hlo, *medicine*; káp, *to fire a gun*; koyatangey, *whence*; mi-hring, *a person*; tán *for*; tá, *belongs to*; lú, *head*; lú-dier, *turban*; hlo, *to mislay*; lál, *leader, chief*; boi, *a servant, retainer*.

1.	Ilé úi sukkur alei-tem?	...	Have you bought this dog and horse?
2.	Ili sillai koyma káp-luh	...	I did not fire that gun.
3.	Ili sillai-hlo sillai koyangey i-nei?	...	Where did you get that gun and powder?
4.	Sillai-hlo koyatangey i-nei?	...	From whom did you get the powder?
5.	Ilé sillai hi mi-hring ta eal ey	...	This gun belongs to that person.
6.	Sillai bé mi-hring tán kaleitá	...	I bought the gun for this person.
7.	Sciel nungmá ú alei emui?	...	Has your brother bought the gayal?
8.	Nungmá lú-dier ahlo emui?	...	Have you mislaid your turban?
9.	Nungma koymá vaibel tchem alagh-loh-maw?	...	Did you not take my pipe and dao?
10.	Koyma lál tún-tleng-in ka-hmú-lob-rey.	...	I have not yet seen the chief.
11.	Lál-nú n-ú ahmél ahtá loh	...	The Queen's sister is not pretty.
12.	Nungmá hi hmai-tchia i-ú n-om-em?	...	Are you the brother of that woman?
13.	Ilé bui-nú apá atkngtá-em?	...	Has the servant-girl's father arrived?

EXERCISE 12.

Pakat, *one*; pa-knit, *two*; pa-tam, *three*; pa-li, *four*; pa-ngá, *five*; parúk, *six*; pa-sari, *seven*; pa-riak, *eight*; pa-kua, *nine*; tchom, *ten*; ja, *a hundred*; tschang, *a thousand*; lei, *to buy*; pá-un, *cloth*; em, *basket*; savá, *a bird*; kél, *a goat*; föley, *a bag*; Muhlia *or* Motl, *noun prop., man.*

1.	Koymani úi ahotá	...	Our dog is lost.
2.	Ilé mi-hring fa-pa pakát far-nú pakát ahotá.		This person has lost a son and a daughter.
3.	Koymá ka-d tan, dier pakát kaleitá	...	I have bought a turban for my sister.
4.	Nungmá hi pá-un koyangey lei?	...	Where did you buy that cloth?
5.	Nungmá ú koymá em alagh-tá	...	Your brother has taken my basket.
6.	Nungmá sillai akáptá-em?	...	Did you fire a gun?
7.	Ili saváley káp-rok	...	Shoot that bird.

8. Amí kĕl a-htá tey ey	... Mother's goat is very fine.
9. Hé kĕl koyma neitá	... I have got this goat.
10. Apá afá abutá	... The father has lost his child.
11. Koymá kanú afá-nú abutá	... My mother has lost her daughter.
12. Koymá kapá in abráltá	... My uncle has sold his house.
13. Koymá kaní amá pú-un abráltá	... My aunt has sold her cloth.
14. Múktia amá ibicy aneitá	... Mui has got his bag.

EXERCISE 13.

Hrai, a sort of basket; tohemley, a little *dao* or knife; nopul, wife; engeylingey, engtingey, how; Hára, noun. prop. mase. ; nimina, yesterday; nahtá'n, to-morrow; apdsg, an assembly; ho, plural affix of number; tlung, to arrive; ang, sign of the future tense; nem or nen, with.

1. Lai-jovi ama pú-un a-tacbúu-tá	... Lai-jovi has found her cloth.
2. Hí mi-hring nem amá fápá ka-hmútá	I have seen that man and his son.
3. Koyma kaní amá hrai tohemley abutá	My mother has lost her knife and her basket.
4. Koyma ka-ú ama alú-dier ala-ta	... My brother has taken his turban.
5. Nungmá i-pa ka-hmútá; ama hnáman túna sukkar a-om-em?	I have seen your uncle. Has he now got a house?
6. Hé mi-hring a-nopui abuta	... This man has lost his wife.
7. Engeytingey abo?	... How (was she) lost?
8. Kára amúntá	... Kara caught hold of her.
9. Koyma kaní ama fá-pá átán sciel pakal aleita.	My aunt has bought a guyal for her son.
10. Hé mi-hring nimina kahmutá	... I saw this man yesterday.
11. Hé mi-hí uhulus ailengtá	... He arrived yesterday.
12. Mi-púng-ho nuktúka amleng-angey ...	All the people will arrive to-morrow.
13. Hé hmaitchla a-ú ka-om-ey	... I am the sister of that woman.
14. Ka-u hrai i-lá-tem?	... Have you taken my sister's basket?
15. Kapá kĕl i-hmú-té-em?	... Have you seen my father's goat?

EXERCISE 14.

Hrí, to know; ley, plural affix; tachéng, inside; adzeagey, which, what; bá, rice.

1. Hí boinú tpá kan-hrier ey	... We know the father of this slave girl.
2. Koyma ibicy túngey la?	... Who has taken my bag?
3. Koyma ka-lá	... I have taken it.
4. Taaw mí alá	... He has taken it.
5. Hé mi-tey alá	... They have taken it.
6. Engey-tangey lagh?	... Why did you take it?
7. Englikangey alagh?	... When did you take it?
8. Hé mi-tachúnga angey nei?	... What did you get in it?
9. Hé ibicy koj atangey i-nei?	... Where did you get this bag from?

10. Nungma enlingey kul? ... How did you go?
11. Nungma engtingey l-kul-ang? ... How will you go?
12. Ibiey pa-bnit-la adzengey lagh? ... Out of the two bags, which did you take?
13. Bú engjangey om? ... How much rice is there?
14. Engtchengey mi an-om? ... How many men are there?
15. Nungma engtikangey kul? ... When did you go?

Exercise 15.

Tiem, to know; pul, great; pui-tiem, exorcist; hon, to open; bunglai, a room.

1. Hé mi-brhg pui-tiem a-ú eni ey ... This man is the exorcist's brother.
2. Hé hmai-tchia lel nó a-ú eni ey ... This woman is the sister of the chlst's mother.
3. Hé nowpang abol-nú afu-pá eni ... This child is the son of the slave girl.
4. In kong-kar hon-loh ani-ey. Hongrot ... The house door is not open. Open it.
5. Pui-tiem afu-pá afaná koyma ka baidta ... I have seen the son and daughter of the exorcist.
6. Lál kél koyma ka-hmai-tá   ... I have seen the chief's goat.
7. Kau-lal aboinú pui-tiem a-ú ani ... Our chief's slave is the exorcist's sister.
8. Bunglai kong-kar engatangey shon?... Why is the room door open?
9. Hé pui-tiem afapá koymani kan-brier ... We know the son of this exorcist.
10. Kau-lal úl tûk ani ... Our chief's dog is faithful.
11. Hé nowpang ami atlongta ... This child's mother has arrived.
12. Hi nowpang adier koyma kancita ... I have got the turban of that child.
13. Koyma pá aboinú nungma emni? ... Are you my uncle's slave girl?

Exercise 16.

Lalsheva, n. p. masc.; Ratong Poi, noun prop. masc.; Denkaia, noun prop. masc; Belkai, name of place; kawnbul, agent, man of business, deputy; dzawtey, a cat; pá, affix masc.; ud, affix fem.; thas; lien, a friend; lien-pa, a male friend; lien-nú, female friend; boi, a slave; boi-ud, a female slave.

1. Nungma Ratong Poi mi emni? ... Are you Rutton Poia's man?
2. Nungma Ratong Poi in-a om emni? ... Are you son of Rutton Poia's house?
3. Nungma Batong Poi ú-nao emai? ... Are you a relative of Rutton Poia's?
4. Koyma Belkaia anui kani ... I am a man of Belkai.
5. Koyma Benkuia kawnbul kani ... I am Denkaia's agent.
6. Nungma ú tchem a-htá dait eni ey ... Your brother's *dao* is very good.
7. Nungma ú dzawtey ahta-loh ... Your sister's cat is bad.
8. Koyma kani a-in alien dzit ani ey ... My aunt's house is very big.
9. Lalsheva ama pa asillai almtá ... Lalsheva has lost his father's gun.
10. Lai-jovi ama ú tchem ancitá ... Lai-jovi has got her sister's *dao*.
11. Lai-jovi ama ú tchem atachûrtá ... Lai-jovi has found her sister's *dao*.
12. Nungma pá lo bé lo si-in ahtá daawk emn? ... Is your father's *jum* better than this?

13. Nungma gien-pá afá adior kancitá   ...   I have got the turban of your *friend's* child.
14. Koyma nú pú-aa pakát alaitá   ...   My mother has bought a cloth.

EXERCISE 17.

Tchaw, a meal, food.

1. Hé dier pui-tiem até cni   ...   This turban is the exorcist's.
2. Nungma-té ani   ...   It is yours.
3. Nungma tán cni ey   ...   It is for you.
4. Koyma gien pá anú a la cni   ...   It is the house of my friend's mother.
5. Koyma gien-nú a-la ani ey   ...   It is my sweetheart's house.
6. Koyma gien a-la ani   ...   It is my friend's house.
7. Koyma ú apé-an nungma ú agien apé-tá   ...   My sister has given her cloth to your brother's friend.
8. Koyma pá aillai pakát lál fá apé tá   ...   My uncle has given a gun to the chief's son.
9. Hi nowpang tchaw l-pé-tem ?   ...   Have you given that child food ?
10. Hé hmul takhta pú-aa pakát nungma l pé-tem ?   ...   Have you given a cloth to that woman ?
11. Hé lo lál lo venni ?   ...   Is this *jám* the chief's ?
12. Lál lo ani-luh ama ú lo ani   ...   It is not the chief's ; It is his sister's *jám*.
13. Koymani aciol koyma pá atiena hmén an-hrálta.   ...   We have sold our gayal to our uncle's friend.
14. Hé pú-aa, hé boinú tá ermni taw bulnú tá ?   Does this cloth belong to this slave girl or that ?

NOTE.—Sentence 11, the v. in venni is euphonic only.

EXERCISE 18.

Pár, a flower; pi, grandmother; ṭing, speech, language; chey, to say; Choog-ringi, a. p. loa. ; khduagal, to love ; tchí, caste, clan ; Tuihút, Thra (the name of a Hill tribe).

1. Koyma tchem koyma d agien ka-pé-tá...   I have given my *dao* to my brother's friend.
2. Koyma draawtcy koyma ú agien ka-pé-tá.   I have given my cat to my sister's friend.
3. Hé pár koyma ka-nao nungma l-pé-tem ?   Did you give my younger brother this flower ?
4. Hé lo koyma ú alo ani   ...   This field is my brother's.
5. Hi aillai nungma nao-té ani luh   ...   That gun does not belong to your younger brother.
6. Hi tchem nungma nao tá-agey nungma ú atá em?   Does this *dao* belong to your younger brother or your sister.
7. Ramoni ama pá i-hmú-tem ama ná i-hmú-tem ?   Has Ramoni seen his father or his mother ?
8. Hi aciol koyma gien a-kuéna koyma hmcita.   I got this gayal from my friend.
9. Hé in nungma ú a-hnéna ka-leitá   ...   I bought this dog from your sister.

10. Lal-jovi tehem pakát ama pá a-bnenan   Lal-jovi has received a *dao* from her father's
    aneitá, adáng pú-un pakát ama pí   elder brother, and a cloth from her grand-
    ahnénan aneitá.   mother.

11. Tsaw in ley tsaw dsawtey kyoma kan-   I speak of this dog and of this cat.
    tong.

12. Nungma ú atong ka-shoy enl-ey   ...   I speak of your brother.

13. Choigvángi ama pá ley anin an-kho-   Chongvángi's uncle and aunt love her.
    ngai-ey.

14. Hé púitiem hmaltebia ama afá-pá tán   The wife of this exorcist has got a cloth for
    pá-un pakát aneitá.   her son.

15. Daohlúta tahi Tai-kúk anl ey   ...   Daohlút is a Tipra.

EXERCISE 19.

Htá-tlen, a promise; min, me; tl, to do; ar, fowl; a-dza, all; tahri, a tiger; mai, an elephant; htar,
strength; dá, to place, put; ahón, into.

1. Múktin Tai-kúk ú-nao anl ey   ...   Moti has Tipra relatives.

2. Koyma ka-kultúr, htn katiem-tá   ...   I promise to go.

3. Koyma min hmú-tírok   ...   Show it to me.

4. Min tlamrok   ...   Promise me.

5. Min pérok   ...   Give it to me.

6. Koyma min brítá   ...   He told me.

7. Hé ar atey oy, adza-ai-in atey ey ...   This fowl is a small one; it is the smallest of
                                            all.

8. Chongvángi ahnél ahtá dait, an-dza   Chongvángi is pretty; she is the prettiest of
    al-in a-htá dzawk.   all.

9. Táuka htlv ahnalk-in ahrudn tlagh lob ... Silver is not so useful as iron.

10. Sakel aai ahnaik-in htar anci loh   ... The tiger is not so strong as the elephant.

11. Hi pá-un bí drok   ...   Put it in this cloth.

12. Tsaw io-a alaín kukdrok   ...   Go into that house,

13. In techinga kukdrok   ...   Go inside the house,

14. Héta hi-uu ora   ...   Here it is.

15. Koyma adza-in min pé-tá   ...   He gave me everything.

EXERCISE 20.

Tirn, tirn, to promise; htr, very, extremely; d, imp. affix; ley, also.

1. Amaní mí andsa-in kultúr-in min   He promised me to come with all his people.
    tiemta.

2. Andza-in koyma bnenan kultúr-in min   He ordered all of them to go with me.
    tiem-tá.

3. Koyma bnénan lo-kal-túm-in min   He promised that all of them should come
    tiem-ta.   with me.

4. Ramoní Múkin ai-in ahtá dzawk ey ...   Ramoni is more diligent than Múkti.

5. Dzohlúta andza-ai-in a-hté-hto dzawk ey.   Dzohlút is the most diligent.

6. Koyma kanao hnaïk-in í-patchia-loh ...   You are not poorer than my younger brother.

7. Hé mi-hring taw kúa a-chon, andza-al-in a-pa-tchia bér ey.   That man is the poorest in all that village.

8. Lokul tirok   ...   Tell him to come.

9. Kuidrok ú, tirok   ...   Tell him to go.

10. Koyma ú hnéman adza-al-in lo key tchem ahtá bér ka-pétá.   I have given my brother the best *jum* and the best *dao*,

11. Túngey om?   ...   Who is it?

12. Pul-tiem om   ...   It is the exorcist.

13. Hé hmaltchia túngey?   ...   Who is that woman?

14. Lál nopui ení   ...   It is the chief's wife.

15. Koyma ú aboinú ení ey   ...   It is my brother's slave girl.

EXERCISE 21.

Hril, to speak ; htei, to be able.

1. Nangma tchem túngey-i-pék tágh?   To whom have you given your dao?

2. Koyma náo ala pá kapétá   ...   I gave it to my younger brother's son.

3. Nangma engatangey i-pék?   ...   Why did you give it?

4. Nangma ú a-ui túngey ahrál?   ...   To whom have you sold your brother's dog?

5. Koyma jien a-ú arney koy-tangey ansi?   Where did my friend's sister get the bird ?

6. Hé hmaltchia apá ahnéman ansitá   ...   She got it from this woman's father.

7. Nangma dzeugey i-lei-tagh?   ...   What have you bought?

8. Koyma ú atan tchem pakat leisitá   ...   I have bought a dao for my brother.

9. Nangma engey i-lagh-tagh?   ...   What have you taken?

10. Koyma engma ka-lá-loh   .   ...   I have taken nothing.

11. Nangma tú-zong-ngey ishey?   ...   Who are you talking about?

12. Nangma engey i-shey?   ...   What do you say?

13. Koyma pakat ajong-ma ka-shey-loh   ...   I was not saying anything.

14. Ka-hril-loh; ka-shey-htei-loh   .   ...   I did not speak. I cannot say.

EXERCISE 22.

Ton-htá, a tale, story ; nen, with ; lah, a band ; hla, a song; sa, to sing.

1. Nangma ton-htá-shey tiem om?   ...   Do you know a story?

2. Ton-htú shey-rah   ...   Tell a story.

3. Koyma ton-htú ka-shey ey   ...   I am telling a story.

4. Koyma ton-htú ka-shey-tá   ...   I have told a story.

5. Hlá sarok   ...   Sing a song.

6. Nangma ú koyangey?   ...   Where is your sister ?

7. Ama lo-va a-om-ey   ...   She is at her *jum*.

8. Nungma ú koyangey ? ...	Where is your brother ?
9. Ama jien a-hnéna a-om-ey ...	He is with his friend.
10. Nungma pá pawna em-a-om ? ...	Is your father outside ?
11. Puitiom nen a-om	He is with the exorcist.
12. Nungma bé pú-un i-lei-tem ? ...	Have you bought this cloth ?
13. Nungma hi tchem flagh-taw-em ? ...	Have you taken that dao?
14. Ili tchem ahtá em ? ...	Is that dao a good one ?
15. Hé mi-hring a-kút-a taw pú-un i-nei tem ?	Did you receive that cloth from the hands of this man ?

EXERCISE 23.

Roa, an auxiliary verbal prefix ; ape or mel, fire ; ti-ang, a stick, staff ; amoy, pretty.

1. Hé hnaitchia in-a hi-un lei ar nungma i-roa-lei-tem ? ...	Did you buy this bird in the house of this woman ?
2. Roa-larak	Come and take it.
3. Mel roa-púruk	Come and give me a light.
4. Hé in-a hi-un nungma trbem abotem ?	Did you lose your dao in this house ?
5. Nungma ú tú-nen-ngry akul ? ...	With whom did your brother go ?
6. Nungma tchem túngey fpék-tagh ? ...	To whom did you give your dao ?
7. Ili ti-ang abotem ? ...	Have you lost that stick ?
8. Hé mi-hring taw lo avatá ...	This man cut that júm.
9. Koyma hnéna úi pakat ani, hé atey dzit ani oy.	I have a dog ; he is a very small one.
10. Koymani hnénan dzawtey pakat a-om, hé amoy tey-ey	We have a cat ; she is very pretty.
11. Koyma pá in pakat aleita, ahtá dzit eai ey.	My father has bought a house ; it is a very good one.
12. Koyma anú pú-un pakat aleita ; nungma fhmú-tem ?	My mother has bought a cloth ; have you seen it ?
13. Nungma ú tchem pakat abota nungma i-tschür-em ?	Have you found the dao which your brother lost ?
14. Nungma ni sciei abril koymani kan-hmútá, ...	We have seen the gayal that your aunt bought.
15. Nungma pú-un-nei koyangey ? ...	Where is the cloth you got ?
16. Hé tchem ka-ni fá-in aleita bé tchem koyma ka-lá-tá	I have taken the dao which my aunt's son bought.
17. Hi brzai-tchin nen, hin kan-ahoy kan, i-hmú tem ?	Have you seen the woman we were speaking with ?

EXERCISE 24.

Khá, that ; adaag, another, separate, additional ; in, to drink ; ei, to eat ; dzú, to imbibe ; dza, hers ; rak-dra, spirits.

1. Hi rai-hlo hi ama nao aneita ...	His younger brother got that tobacco.
2. Hé nowprug akút-an tchem om-khá i-hmú tem ?	Did you see the dao that was in the child's hands ?

3. Kelma ui kepa ui ai-in, ui tuk ani ...	My dog is more faithful than my uncle's.
4. Kan-bainú nangma boi ai-in biar ane' dzawk.	Our slave girl is stronger than your slave.
5. Koyma in koyma ļien in ai-chú-un alien dzawk.	My house is bigger than that of my friend's.
6. Ilé nangma ftiey eni-loh, koyma ú ftiey ani.	This is not your bag; it is my brother's.
7. Koyma ło adang koyma ļieu-pa ło bļú ka-shoy eni.	I speak of my *jum* and of my friend's *jum.*
8. Laijovi ama pú-un adang ama nú pu-un abota.	Laijovi has lost her cloth and that of her mother's.
9. Koyma bú adang koyma ú bá l-ei-ta?..	You have eaten my rice and my brother's rice?
10. Adang ei-rok ...	Eat some more.
11. Koyma vai-hlo ka-ú vai-hlo ai-chú-na, abié dzawk.	My tobacco is better than my brother's.
12. Vai-hlo l-dzú-doa-em? ...	Will you smoke?
13. Koyma dsú ka-dsú-loh ...	I do not drink beer.
14. Rak-dzu l-dzúk-ang? ...	Will you drink some spirits?
15. Koyma nowpang ły-ta ka-in-loh ...	I have not drunk from a child.

EXERCISE 25.

Dú, to wish; tschaw-hmét, condiments, vegetables; ehá, meat; tui, water; ļiou, a little; darkleng, plate; fi-au, spoon; tuel, salt; ai, to be salt; ley, also.

1. Rák-dsú agey l-in-dú dad agey l-in-dú?	Do you wish to drink spirits or beer?
2. Dsú-agoy l-dsdk-ang, rákdsú agoy l-dsúk-ang?	Will you drink beer or spirits?
3. Koyma rák-dsú ka-in-dúloh ...	I do not wish to drink spirits.
4. Tschaw-hmét ļiem-tey, ahá ley tái min pérok. ʃang?	Give me a little vegetable and some meat and water.
5. Darkleng ley fi-un koytangey ka-nei-	From where shall I get platter and spoon?
6. Darkleng koyangoy nei? ...	Where did you get the plate?
7. Bú loy tái béta a-om-ey ...	Here is rice and water.
8. Koymaní dsú ļiemtey kan-in-tá ...	We drank a little beer.
9. Nangma ahá ļiemtey Járok tschaw-hmét ļiemtey darok.	Put by a little meat and vegetables.
10. Nangma tschaw-hmét taci a-ul-tam? ...	Have you sufficient salt with your food?
11. Taci a-ai-tá ...	There is salt enough.
12. Ilé hmai-tchin dsú ļiemtey pérok ...	Give a little beer to that woman?
13. Nangmaní in-an dsú biá a-om em? ...	Have ye good beer in your houses?
14. Koymaní lál a-hodaan bú ahté dzawk ..	Our chief has good rice.
15. Hé dsú ai-lú-un dsú biá min pérok ...	Give me better beer than this.

The Leahais are very simple eaters. As among most orientals, the staple of their food is rice—*bé*; or, in its cooked form, *tarhaw-fikh*. Whatever else they may eat, to give a relish to the rice, be it pork, dried-fish, yam, or what not, is known by the name of *tarhaw-bawk*. The *tach* in *tarhaw* is an attempt to represent, in writing, a sound that is not *ch*, nor *sh* or *tsh*, but is intermediary, partaking of all three.

Exercise 26.

Tachúm, to cook, dhúll; chátl-je, so much; chiti-rbé-an, but, however; váh, pig; tal, to kill; vol, a time; pilang, a bottle. probably derived from the Burmese ⟨ ⟩ ⟨ ⟩ ⟨ ⟩, tsang, bread; rvng, remain; húla, always; rúl, outside; rúl stúm, hungry; húl, to burn; tal shúl, thirsty; paw, moreover; bah, indeed; volas, to-day.

1. Koyma in-an dzé-tachúm-já nangma in-an a-om-em ?
   Have you as much beer prepared in your house as I ?

2. Koyma in-an chit-já omloh, chitchtú vák tmntoh ka-tal-angry.
   I have not so much, but I will kill many pigs.

3. Bú tachúm-rok ... Cook the dinner.

4. Koymani dsé voi-túm kan-fatá ... We have drunk beer three times.

5. Tui pilang hat koyma min pérok ... Give me a bottle of water.

6. Nnagma tsang Hé-don-em ? ... Will you take some bread ?

7. Koymani bnénan tsang ley ahd ahtá om-ey.
   We have good bread and flesh.

8. Nangma in-an dsé ahtá dalt kanei-rvng-húm-ey.
   One always gets good liquor in your house.

9. Hé bé tsaw patscior tsaw pérok ... Give that rice to that poor man.

10. I-rúl stam em ? ... Are you hungry ?

11. Koyma karil stam loh ... I am not hungry.

12. Aril stam-a toi paw ahúl ey ... I am both hungry and thirsty.

13. Koyma karil stam-bah-ey ahál-bah-ey... I am very hungry and thirsty.

14. Nnagma min pék-chul-un dsé ka-in-angry. Volas koyma blé-mk-a ka-hul-ey.
   I will drink spirits, if you give me some. I have travelled for to-day.

Exercise 27.

Hming, name; tchoy, lift, raise; yu-tu-fen, petticoat; ashey, long; Ulpám, name of a hill; Samata, Kaaalong (name of place) ; Barhhel, ditto.

1. Koyma ú hming Mákia sui ... My brother's name is Múktee.

2. Koyma boinú afnad a-hming Laijovi úal ey.
   The daughter of my female slave is named Laljovi.

3. Nnagma Dzohlúta nao ngey Mákia nao ?
   Are you the younger brother of Dsohlút or Mukee?

4. Laljovi loy Dzo-hláta koy-ang-ey ? ... Where are Laijovi and Dsohlúl ?

5. Tui tchoya ahul-ey ; anmátí nan Karé akulta.
   They have gone to draw water. Kara went with them.

6.	Nungma tchem Dzo-hlúta í-pé-tem ?	....	Have you given your dao to Dzohlút ?
7.	Hé par Laijovi túngey péä ?	...	Who gave that flower to Laijovi?
8.	Laijovi ama par tangey apéä	....	To whom has Laijovi given her flowers?
9.	Pú-un pakat Dzo-hlúta bu-nan kanel-ta		I got a cloth from Dzohlút.
10.	Múkti a-d, tey tuk ani ey		Múkti's sister is very short.
11.	Hmúnjovi pú-un-fra, ashey duit ani ey.		Hmunjovi's petticoat is very long.
12.	Koyma kaní ín Úpúina a-om-ey		My aunt's house is on Úhnim.
13.	Koyma é ín Belkaia aul ey	...	My brother's house is at Belkai.
14.	Koyma zien Sazsata a-kul-ey		My friend has gone to Kazalong.
15.	Múkia Burkhal-a at leng ta	....	Múkti has arrived at Burkhal.
16.	Itatong Poi nungma í-bumí-tem		Have you seen Itatton Poia?

Exercise 28.

Darpuichongi, noun, prop. fem. ; tey, plural, affix ; duong, collective, all ; enghim, everything ; duáng-búin, a ring ; thaw, to work.

1.	Laijovi ama nd non a-om	...	Laijovi is with her mother.
2.	Darpuichongi ama nao nen akulta		Darpuichongi has gone with her brother.
3.	Nungma é koyma zien a-ói aloíta	...	Your brother has bought my friend's dog.
4.	Itatong Poia fa-pa tey-dzong au-dam-loh.		All Itatton Poia's children are sick.
5.	Koyma ka-oí sukkor nen dzawtey nen í-hmu-tem?		Have you seen my aunt's horse and cat?
6.	Koyma é pú-un tungey la?	...	Who has taken my brother's cloth?
7.	Nungma pú-nu-lal koyangey?		Where is the cloth you bought?
8.	Pai-tieu afa-pa ahnénen hí artey ka-oeíta.		I got that bird from the exorcist's son.
9.	Nungma tchem adza-in an-buinú tey hapék-ta.		I have given your *dao* to the servant girls.
10.	Hilr eng-kim-a ahmun llagh ey	...	Iron is in every way useful.
11.	Engkim btá shoy-rok-á	...	Say anything you like.
12.	Hé ul-tey tuk ani-ey	...	These dogs are faithful.
13.	Nungma é pai-tieu fa-pa-tey nen pawna om ey.		Your brother is outside with the exorcist's sons.
14.	Dzo-hlúta key Múkia an-zientey btó, an-shoy-ey.		Dzohlút and Múkti are talking of their friends.
15.	Dzo-hlúta key Múkia an-dzúng-bdn aloíta.		Dzohlút and Múkti have lost their rings.
16.	Nungma pá ama lo atlaw loh	...	Your uncle has not cleared his *júm*.

Exercise 29.

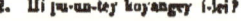

Ké-pa, foot ; nrar, white ; akhua, perspiration ; nshú, hot ; nhrelah, come out ; aldu, warm.

1.	Hí pú-un-toy koy-a-tangey í-lei ?	...	From whom did you buy these cloths?
2.	Hí pu-un-tey koyangey í-lei ?	...	Where did you buy these cloths?

3.	Ili tcham-toy-bi koyangey i-nei? ...	Where did you get these daos?
4.	Koyma hé-pá atey dait ani oy.	My foot is very small.
5.	Koyma ú ama daúng-búm aboté ...	My brother has lost his ring.
6.	Koyma tieu-tey hotman hé hting ka-neité.	I got this timber from my friends.
7.	Hé hting taaw hting aishon ashang daawk.	This tree is taller than that.
8.	Ilé sava-tey adaa-in ahla oy	These birds are all fine ones.
9.	Ilé boinú-tey-bi an-tatacla dait	These servant girls are very lazy.
10.	Koyma dier-tey-bi túna i-hmú-tem? ...	Did you see my turbans just now?
11.	Darí pú-an Laijorí pú-un al-zbú-un avar oy.	Darí's cloth is whiter than Laijorí's.
12.	Nuugma há avar-loh-ey	Your teeth are not white.
13.	Koyma kút aklan ashé dait oy ...	My hands are very hot.
14.	Koyma kút alúm dait ey, klan atscfuak ey.	My hands are very warm ; the perspiration has come out.
15.	Ni ashé dait ani ey	The sun is very warm.

Exercise 30.

Láng, to stroll ; tlán, to run ; tlá, to fall ; haw, (part of verb, hong,) to come ; chong, to gather up ; hné, leaves ; dashkalang, a mirror ; dulang-bun, a ring ; dzang, a finger ; bla, a circle ; daow, (naz. verb), to complete, falah ; rín, rain.

1.	Nungma now-pang-tey koy-angey? ...	Where are your children?
2.	Koyma now-pang-tey pawna aknita, k'ug-a aknita.	My children have gone out ; gone out for a walk.
3.	Anmani tieutey antkeng-tá	Their friends have arrived.
4.	Tláu-rok hí now-pang ailáta	Ilan, that child has fallen down.
5.	Nungma tchaw túna i-ai-don-ogey? ...	Will you have dinner now?
6.	Nungma tchaw túna el-don-loh? ...	Will you not eat now?
7.	Nungma tchaw tuna el-loh vempni? ...	Have you not eaten yet?
8.	Ilé pú-an-hí adaá aahzng-túr tángey haw?	Who has come to take away all these cloths?
9.	Ilé pú-un adza hí-un tángey lei? ...	Who has bought all these cloths?
10.	Darí hé tcham adaa-in aboté ...	Darí has lost all those daos.
11.	Ilé ín adaa-in kan-hmuté ...	We have seen all these houses.
12.	Nungma lal ín i-hmú-tem?	Have you seen the chief's house?
13.	Koyma hné tángey la? ...	Who has taken my leaves?
14.	Ilé now-pang-tey anmani dier aboté ...	These children have lost their turbans.
15.	Ili dar-kla-lang Múkla pérok adang dzáng-bun Laijorí pérok.	Give that looking-glass to Múkil, and the ring to Laijorí.
16.	Ilé hting-hné adaa in atla-daow-tá ...	The leaves of that tree have all fallen.
17.	Tui atlá-ta ...	The water is spilt.
18.	Rúa atlé ...	Rain is falling.

EXERCISE 31.

Hriaw, needle; roa-tachin, to bring; tar, old; hlat, new.

1. Koyma zien ama artey zhrál-daow-tem?   Has my friend sold all his fowls?
2. Pui-tiem ama hriow aron-tachin-ta   ...   The exorcist has brought his needle with him.
3. Koymani tan bú ley tchem pakat tachindrok-d.   Bring rice and a *dao* for us.
4. Ilé hriow-tey koyangey alei?   ...   Where did you buy these needles?
5. Ilé kúa in ad-za-in abia ey   ...   All the houses of this village are good.
6. Nangma ú alo-tleng loh   ...   Your brother has not arrived.
7. Dzohlúta ley Múkia ú-nao tak tak an[1] ey.   Dzohlút and múktí are own brothers.
8. Koymani nú-tey lal lo shaulta   ...   Our mothers have seen the chief's *jám.*
9. Koyma fá-tey kazien alo aleita   ...   My children have bought my friend's *jám.*
10. Sotel-tey sakei al-chú-an alien daawk...   Gayals are bigger than tigers.
11. Koyma kút avar em?   ...   Are my hands clean?
12. Nangma pú-an ahtar em?   ...   Is your cloth new?
13. Koyma pa in patúa lo palnit om   ...   My father has three houses and two *jáms.*
14. Ilé mi-hring fa únao pangá farmi pali an-om-ey.   This man has five sons and four daughters.
15. Koyma zien a-ú-tey pasari an-om-ey ...   My friend has seven sisters.
16. Koymani tchem panga kanelti   ...   We have got five *daos.*

EXERCISE 32.

Ngai, v, to desire; ngai a, a sweetheart; tla, a moon, a month; ley, sign of plural (-lóng, a boat; hi, to fell; túk, to hollow out; tanka, rupees; sôhong, cow; kin, a cow; tui, water; daú-bei, a beer-pot; tleng, to arrive; dog, a hole; pur, a flower; vúk, a pig; púlr, to burrow; hlí, beads; hruí, a rope, string; darrua, a sort of basket; hadam, cut, kind; tú, to weave; blei, to be able.

1. Ilé kúa hi-un pui-tiem tachom-hnít an-om-ey.   There are twenty exorcists in this village.
2. Koyma ngai dzawtey pahnít aleita   ...   My sweetheart has bought two cats.
3. Koyma nao kúm tachom ley kum sari tla hnít anl-ta.   My younger brother is seventeen years and two months old.
4. Koyma nú bú-fai hrai-hnít pú-an parúk aleitá.   My mother has bought two baskets of husked rice and six cloths.
5. In-a boitey húing patúm an-kítá alang lóng pahnít an-túktá.   The house slaves have cut three trees and two boats.
6. Ili ní-sari tanka tachom-hnít, só-hong pahnít kanelta.   This week I have got twenty rupees and two cows.
7. Múkia bú-fai kin-tám a-eitú, daúbei pangá túl a-intá.   Múktí has eaten three seers of rice and drunk five pots of water.
8. Dzohlút atleng ní túm anítá   ...   Dzohlút arrived three days ago.
9. Kongkar-a óng pa-hnít a-om-ey   ...   There are two holes in the door.

10.	Boi koyma fa-tey par pahait a-pé-tá ...	The slave gave my children two flowers.
11.	Koyma kani sé-luong patúm aleité ...	My aunt has bought three cows.
12.	Ilé mí nopai nei hí-no-in tanka tschom ley pasarí rák pahoit apéta.	This man gave seventeen rupees and two pigs for his wife.
13.	Til mí hnémau koyma hi kin tschom-hnit ley kin kát koymą kapúktá.	I borrowed from that man twenty-one score of rice.
14.	Koyma bit brúí-hat, daúngbún pakat ka-meitá.	I got a string of beads and one ring.
15.	Ilé kúa hí-un koyma lien pakátma amloh.	I have not a single friend in this village.
16.	Koymaní durrun bním-túm-in kan-tá-hítei-ey.	We know how to weave three sorts of baskets.

Bál, to fight, to die; bít, to die; daw, to complete fialah, entirely; bíní, heart, mind; fáréng, s. p. maa.

1.	Tlá ráltá ...	The moon has disappeared (between new and full).
2.	Bú adzá-in ahti ríl-dzowjá ...	All the rice is dead.
3.	Koyma rál-bía-túr hím a-om-loh-vey...	I have no mind to fight.
4.	Taaw mí taaw ahtí tá ...	That man is dead.
5.	Hting ahti dzowtá ...	The tree is completely dead.
6.	Tlá arnlatá ka-bmú khátí-chro ka-bmú-vey ngai loh.	I saw him last month; since then I have not seen him.
7.	Khovar tika-ta hé-hí ka-bmú loh ...	I have not seen him since early morning.
8.	Nangma engtíka-ngey í-kul-don? ...	When are you going ?
9.	Koyma fa-kul-chro ata koyangvoy í-om?	Where have you been since I went ?
10.	Savúng kúa min prik, kha-tichm atá ka-dá.	I have kept it since you gave it me at Savúnga's village.
11.	Savúng trúa kan-la-tawg khatíchon atá kan-tawg-loh.	I have not met him since we met at Savúnga's.
12.	Koyma tníkongą ka-tawg ...	I met him on the road.
13.	Fa-tey í-nei-tem ? ...	Have you any children ?
14.	Nangma pa, bting a-lei-tem ?	Has your father bought a tree ?
15.	Koyma nao hnénan, drú a-om dalt-ey, tam-tak aní.	In my younger brother's house there are much bees ; a great deal.
16.	Koyma lal hnénan af hong ley ar om-ey.	My chief has cows and fowls.

Samat, s. p.; Rah-matla, n. p.; dil, to want; tlo, to clear; hámfaa, this year; mímloa, yesterday.

1.	Húr ley tanka ahmán tla-gh drit ...	Iron and silver are very useful.
2.	Samát ley Ráh-matla kúá alien dait ...	Kossalong and Rangamati are big villages.
3.	Kan-dná-in Dzó kani ...	We are all Kuokies.

4. Nungma engey t-lil? ... What do you want?
5. Koymani lo kan-thó-tá ... We have weeded the *júm*.
6. Edminan lo bú tum-tuk suey ey ... This year the crops are good (plentiful).
7. Koyma nüminan ka-knltn ... I went yesterday.
8. Kan-bai-tey ta-a par atnm dzit ... There are many flowers in our above' houses.
9. Kan-lal bnénan tanka atnm dzit ani, Our chief is very wealthy; he has many
   aclel ánga dzit. gayals.
10. Dzohldta Múhi al-in fá angá loh Dzohlút has not so many children as Muti.
11. Hé büng-a hi-an savatey tnoi tnk ka' I see many birds in that tree.
    hmú-ey.
12. Nungmani hüa hi-nn-in pai-tlem eng* How many exorcists are there in your village.
    jangey om?
13. Hé hting tsaw bting al-in ahná atlem This tree has fewer leaves than that.
    dzawk.
14. Hé lo bú tum-tuk ani-lon ey ... This *júm* will bear plentifully.
15. Koyma nopui pú-on pakni atátá ... My wife has woven a cloth.

(*Explanatory.*)—The terminal *n* in *kndzon*, *kúminan* (sentences 6, 7, 9, and 10) would seem to be an abbreviation for *ánína-in*, *kimínan-ín*. The *tey* in *savatey* (sentence 11) denotes the plural number. This affix has previously been made use of (see sentence 15 of preceding exercise). I am at a loss to explain the word *angá* in sentences 9 and 10.

EXERCISE 35.

New, *soft*, *fine*; Long, *a cubit*; hmen, *a dhoti*; moy, *pretty*; Kor, *Bengali*; bar-sai, *a corruption of* 'burra sahib.'

1. Nungma bnénan vak engjangey om? ... How many pigs have you?
2. Hé pú-on anén ani ey; tanka-in tóng That cloth is fine (in texture); how much a
   engjangey t-loi? ... cubit did you pay for it?
3. Túng kai engjangey t-pét? ... What did you give a cubit?
4. Túng engjangey t-lagh? ... How many cubits do you take?
5. Hren pakai chú-on ani-loh-vang-ey ... It will not be enough for a waist cloth.
6. Hé nowpang-tey bnénan hú amoy dzit Those children have pretty neck-laces.
   om-ey.
7. Koymani bnénan jientey tuk-tuk ani ey We have faithful friends.
8. Hé Korbnénan hú moy-dzit t-nol-ang-ey You will get pretty beads at that Bengali's.
9. Bar sai húa almui tey a-om-ey ... It is near the station.
10. Koyma tchom-htá túng ka-eloy-ey ... I speak of a good *dao*.
11. Hé mi-hring ahti-tá ... This person has died.
12. Hi dui ahtá dzit ... That beer is very good.
13. Koyma naopang koyangey? ... Where is my child?
14. Koyma pá tánka tam-dzit ani ey ... My uncle is very wealthy.
15. Dzohúta pá tar pakai a-om ey ... Dzohlút's father is an old man.
16. Hé nowpang tán bú-htá a-om-loh- Is there no good rice for this child?
    vomni?

D

Exercise 36.

Reng, to remain; btla, always; baa-tawk, work; btawk, to work; bmai-taci-tey, an abbreviation of bmai-tocia-tey, a little woman, a girl; bimnfan, this year; tachdan, goods; tacbor, to forge (iron); bhó-ngai, to love; rang-mi pók, no one; kawakal, a deputy or agent; bêl, potatoes; ti, to do (used sometimes, as in French, for the verb 'to say'); pom, to obey, carry out; adib, proper; adib-lab, improper; bonda, use, service; koy, crumbed; tlagh, to fall.

1. Hé mi-bring béta ka-hmd-reng-hŭu-ey.   I always see this man here.
2. Koyma ú pawna akul-btci-loh, bo̱ biawtár a-om.   My brother cannot go out; he has work to do.
3. Tána ashík ey   ...   It is cold now.
4. Mukia mowpang abtá ani-ey   Mukia is a good child.
5. Laijorí bmai-taci-tey amoy-ley-ey   Laijoví is a pretty little girl.
6. Tsaw anú abtá-mk-ey   ...   That mother seems good.
7. Kúmina koymani Kur tachran tamtak ahralú.   This year our Bengaã has sold much merchandise.
8. Ka-dá mong-lob-rey   ...   I don't care much about it.
9. Jlé mi-bring tchera-btá atachér-loh   ...   This man does not make good dam.
10. Koyma ka-shey-btei-ey   ...   I know how to speak.
11. Mî tá-tacia eng-mi pók-in ankbó-ngai-loh.   No one cares for the lazy man.
12. Lal-btá mî andea-in ankbó-ngai ey   ...   Every one loves a good chief.
13. Hé bmai-tacia pa-tacia a-fé-tey tan bd om-loh.   This poor woman has no rice for her children.
14. Jlí kawnbal pa-taci-mí bal tam tak a-pó-ey.   That *kavbart* gives many potatoes to poor people.
15. Moy-dait nála-tey-bók ka-ngai ey   ...   I like pretty girls.
16. Jlé pá-un-btá-loh koyma ka-hmd-moy-loh.   I do not like that ugly cloth.
17. Koyma in aangma nen a-moy-loh-rey   My house is not worthy (fit for) of you.
18. Lal-in atir-chd-on btá pom adik-ey   ...   It is proper (fit) to obey the chief's order.
19. Jle tchem engma hman tlagh-loh-vey ; akoy-ey.   This *dao* is not fit for me; it is bent.

Exercise 37.

Bá, fruit; ahama, gold; mi, my, mine; pa, tatea, afila; rokhtae, youth, young; dzah, ahama, modesty; ahrol, big, large.

1. Hé ní citár abtá lob   ...   This fruit is not good to eat.
2. Koyma ú shoza daáng-bán voina ka-naiá.   I got my brother's gold ring to-day.
3. Shoza daáng-ban koyma ú voina anelta   My brother got a gold ring to-day.
4. Lalahéva anao nen pawna akulú   ...   Lalahéva has gone out with his younger brother.
5. Jlé mi-pá, rol-btar apa pof-tiem ani-ey   This young man's father is an exorcist.
6. Jlé tarná afa-mí adám-loh-vey   ...   This old woman's daughter is sick.

7.	Hí dzú-htú nungma í-in-tem ?	...	Have you drunk of that good beer ?
8.	Ilé rá n-hta hí nungma tlemtey í-lá-dou-em ?		Will you take a little of this nice fruit.
9.	Nungma eug daruna agoy í-lagh ?	...	What basket have you taken ?
10.	Koyma a-brol ka-lá	...	I have taken the large one.
11.	Koyma adzá alien ka-lá-tá	...	I took the biggest.
12.	Nungma eng-lóng-agey í-hrál ?	...	What boat have you sold ?
13.	Nungma hé lóng í-hrál tem ?	...	Have you sold this boat ?
14.	Nungma hoy-lóng-ngey-í-hral ?	...	Which boat have you sold ?
15.	Koyma até-bér ka-hral-tá	...	I have sold the smallest.
16.	Dzohlút tam-tuk-in a-dzak-ey	...	Dzohlút is very modest.
17.	Koyma tien ama in a-hraltá	...	My friend has sold his house.
18.	Nungma túna hí-no-in lál í-hmú-tem ?...		Have you seen the chief just now ?
19.	Tsaw nuogma ú ani, nungma í-hmú-tem ?	... ...	There is your brother, do you see him ?
20.	Nungma í-hmú-loh-remai ?	...	Do you not see him ?

EXERCISE 88.

Kúm, year; ring, to believe; ngui-tda, to consider; ril-rú, to ponder; taw, about; en, very; dzaw, finish, complete; hôk, plural affix.

1.	Nungma kúm eugjaugey eui-tá?	...	How old are you ?
2.	Nungma nao kúm eugjaugey eui-tá ? ...		How old is your young brother ?
3.	Koyma kúm tschom ley kúm búit eni-tá		I am twelve years old.
4.	Koyma kúm tschom ley tla rúk kanitá		I am ten years and six months old.
5.	Tla-htár-in kúm tschom ley kúm rúk ani-aug-ey.		I shall be sixteen years old next month.
6.	Nungma ka-hmú-chú-en kúm eng-ja-tí ka-hré-loh.		I should not take you to be so old by your appearance.
7.	Nungma kúm tum tak eui-in ka-riug-ey		You seem to me to be very old.
8.	Koyma ka-ngai-tua nungma kúm tam tak ani-aug-ey.		I think you are very old.
9.	Hé mihríug atar ey.	...	This man is old.
10.	Nungma pá kúm eugjk-ngey ani-tagh ?		How old is your uncle ?
11.	Kô-rua ngai-tua-in kúm tschom rúk ani-taw-ang-ey.		I think he must be about sixty years old.
12.	Kúm tschom riek ai-in atôm-tá atar-tá-em-ey.		He is more than eighty, he is very old.
13.	Chiti-Jaa-maw ani-tá? Ot-karéyo! ...		Is he as much as that ? Good heavens !
14.	Tar a-huai-tá	...	He is getting old.
15.	Koyma kúm tschom ley kúm ngá tlá rúk kanitá.		I was fifteen years and six months old.
16.	Koyma ka-dzaw-loh-chú-en ka-dzak-ey		I am ashamed of my incapability.

In sentences 1 and 2, tá would seem to be the possessive affix.

17. Nungma lo koyma lo ahoaik-in alien-loh.   Your *júm* is no bigger than mine.

18. Koyma fá-pú nungma fú al-in a-biá-lito-dzawh.   My child is more diligent than yours.

19. Dzohlút koyma tchom-em alagh-tagh ama tchom-em alagh-tagh?   Has Dzohlút taken my *dao* or his own?

20. Koyma ú-bik nungma ú ai-in acowpang dzawh-ey.   My sisters are younger than yours.

(*Explanatory*).—The interrogative affix *ewm* in sentence 13, is an abbreviation of *em-aw*. In sentence 19, the re-duplication of the final sound in *tchem* would seem to be euphonic only. The same custom is common in colloquial Hindoostani.

EXERCISE 39.

Tchoy, to lift, raise; bid, a word; shih, solid; hrd, hrif, to know, comprehend, hear; hrú, to tell.

1. Koyma ka-kal-htei-loh ...   ...   I cannot go.

2. Koyma ka-in-btei-loh ...   ...   I am not able to drink.

3. Koyma kailzow hwi lob ...   ...   I am not capable of it.

4. Koyma ka-dzaw-tir htei loh-vang-ey, ka-hrú-loh.   I do not know whether I can complete it.

5. Koyma ka-hré-btei-loh ...   ...   I am not able to understand.

6. Koyma ka-teboy-htei-loh...   ...   I cannot lift it.

7. Htú aboy-túr ka-htei-loh chú-on ka-dzak-ey.   I am ashamed at not being able to speak.

8. Koyma jien-tey nen nungma jien-tey nen bid kamaboy-ey.   We are talking of our friends and yours.

9. Vot-hát ka-aboy-tá rol-hnít ka-aboy-loh-vang-ey.   I have said it once, and I will not repeat it.

10. Múkta ama pú-on ka-pú-lob-vang al-ey.   Múktí says he will not give his cloth.

11. Koyma ka-aboy-btei-loh ...   ...   I cannot say.

12. Múkia shéb jong aaboy-htei-ey   ...   Múkri knows English.

13. Koyma pá bid pahnit patim a-tiem-ey   My father knows two or three words.

14. Koyma pá jong huuón bait badin tán a-tiem.   My father knows two or three languages.

15. Ka-aboy-btei-loh   ...   ...   I cannot say it.

16. Ka-hril-btei-loh   ...   ...   I cannot tell.

17. Nungma koyma tchom-tey f-lá-tá chú-mi bid aul-ey ka-aboy.   I was talking about my knife which you have taken.

18. Nungma engry l-aboy? ...   What do you say?

19. Tap tachuh, koyma hton btú ka-aboy-angry.   Do not cry, I will tell you a story.

20. Nungma nowpang abtá cal chu-an, lina-btaw abtá chú-an, koyma hton-btú ka-aboy-angry.   If you are a good boy and work well, I will tell you a story.

EXERCISE 40.

Kîr, again; lo, an intention or auxiliary of the verb to come; min, me; hreng, near; ngai, to listen, to be quiet; dil, to want, ask for; du, to wish; lier, a coat; shen, red; rieng, forcible; dai, gentle.

1.	Eng htû ngey ashoy?	What does he say?
2.	Htû hmûn hmût shoy-tûr om-loh	There are not two ways of saying it.
3.	Nungma, hmûn eng jangey om, i-shoy-htei-em?	How many sorts are there, can you tell?
4.	Hmûn engia-ti-in tatuk-in ka-shoy-htei-loh.	I cannot say exactly how many sorts there are.
5.	Engtî-ka-ngey a-lo-kîr-ang, nungma i-shoy-htei-em?	Can you say what time she will return?
6.	Pawna akul-chû-an koyma min hril-in akul-loh; koya emaw akul, ka-shoy-htei-loh.	She does not tell me where she is going when she goes out. I cannot say where she has gone.
7.	Ka-kienga, lô-hawrôk; koyma htû pakat shoy-tûr a-om-ey? ngoiruk-û	Come near me I have something to say to you, listen.
8.	Nungma engey i-dil?	What do you want?
9.	Koyma, nungma ka-hril-dû-ey ...	I wish to speak to you.
10.	Koyma, nungma ka-hiel-tchey 'ni-ey ...	I am speaking to you.
11.	Koyma nungma ka-hril-loh-tchey ...	I am not speaking to you.
12.	Koyma engma ka-shoy-loh	I said nothing.
13.	Nungma korahon jong i-hrier em? ...	Do you understand Bengali?
14.	Koyma jong tlemtey ka-hrier-ey; ashoy-kîr ka-tiem-loh-vey.	I understand it a little, but I cannot speak it.
15.	Itû ring-tuk-in shoy rok ...	Speak loudly.
16.	Ring tuk-in shoy tachuh dzoi-tuk-in shoy rok.	Do not speak loudly; speak gently.
17.	Nungma hé htû koyma min hril-don-loh-vemni?	Did you not tell me that?
18.	Nungma tangey shoy?	Who told you?
19.	Hé mî-tey koyma heti-hû-an min hril ey.	They told me so.
20.	Nungma engey i-shoy-dû? ...	What do you want to say?

EXERCISE 41.

Nui, to laugh; Pldatey, Leshai, names of Kûki clans; ahâr, difficult, hard; a-ol, easy; hâng, car; lûth, to sit; om-dûh, meaning; hé-tachh-ri, footstep; twei, quick.

1.	Nungma nao akul-tem ka-hre-loh; voina, akul-chû-an ahtá-ey, ni-htá-lui-la.	I do not know whether your brother has started to-day, but it is well if he does in this fine weather.
2.	Koyma mi jong tum ka-hré-loh-vey, htû dik-loh-chû-un, nui-tachûh-û	I do not know much of the language, do not laugh if I make mistakes.
3.	Ili htû adik em?	Is that correct?

4.	Vui-tschom-knit shoy rok ...	Say it twenty times.
5.	Nungma lo-hawrôk ti-in ka-shoy nung-ma koyangey I-om.	When I told you to come where were you.
6.	Phratey tong shir ey, Lmshai tong a-ol dzawk ani.	The Phratey dialect is difficult, but the Lmshai tongue is very easy.
7.	Koyma biú shoy I-ngai-loh chd-un I-bré-loh-rang ey.	If you do not listen to what I say you will not understand.
8.	Tsink-in I-béng-a ngai-loh chn-un I-bré-loh-rang-ey.	If you do not listen attentively you will not understand.
9.	Ngoi-reng-in tuhrdk.	Sit quiet.
10.	Tána I-ngoi-loh chd-nn ka bril-dú-loh-rang-tchey.	If you are not quiet I will say no more.
11.	Tú hril atán-ngey dú?	Who do you want it told for ?
12.	Tú-ngey bril-vey-ang? ...	To whom will you tell it ?
13.	Koyma eng-hiu-ngey ka-shoy, nuugma I-brí-em ?	Do you hear what I am saying ?
14.	Nungma ka-hid I-brí-em ?	Do you understand what I say ?
15.	Koyma hiú-shoy I-hrier-ey i koyma om-dula I-hrier-ey i adza-in I-hriev i hal-taw-rok.	You have heard what I say, and you understand my meaning, and now you know all about it. Go.
16.	Ké-taeéb-rí I-bré-loh-vemni?	Did you not hear his footfall ?
17.	Hé-mí-tey eng shoy pók ka-hré dzowth	I heard whatever they said.
18.	Koyma engey ka-ti-don ka-bré-loh ...	I do not know what to do.
19.	Híí boinú ajs kan-hrier-ey ...	We know that slave girl's father.
20.	Nungma I-hrier-twei-chd-un koy-pót ka-dú-ey.	I also wish you to know quickly all about it.

Exercise 42.

Khd, that or this ; Mirang, a Burman ; hmana, formerly ; hié-nghã, to forget ; bil, to die ; pang-tchrng, pride ; pum, observe ; kin, every ; hti-rá ul, advise ; hman-kai, alike ; reng, to remain ; ang, like, resemble.

1.	Koyma bé ka-il-khá nungma engtingey I-hriet ?	How do you know I did this ?
2.	Nungma I-hré-loh vemni ? ...	Do you not know ?
3.	Nungma ú-in a brí-ang-cm ...	Will your sister know ?
4.	Nungma lám I-tkm-em ? ...	Do you know how to dance ?
5.	Nungma Mirang tong I-tiem-em? ...	Do you know Burmese ?
6.	Hmán-lai-chd-un ka-tiem-ey túna ka-hié-ngbil-tá.	I knew it formerly, but have forgotten it now
7.	Koymani kamlza-in kan-hrier-ey, vofkst chd absí-ang-ey.	We all know that we shall one day die.
8.	Anmani htín-htá anj-ey ...	They are good-natured.
9.	Hé mí hí a-pung-tschung i mí htú angal-loh-rey, pom-loh-rey.	He is very proud; he neither desires nor follows any one's advice.

10.	Híú-tin a a-hríer	...	He knows every word.
11.	Tú-tin an-hríer	...	Every one knows it.
12.	Nangma Saipola i-hríer-em ?	...	Do you know Saipola ?
13.	Chiti-chú-un ka-hré-loh, ka-hmn-cini-un ka-hré-áng-ey.		I don't exactly know him, but should recognize him if I saw him.
14.	Aluning chd ka-hríer-ey, chiti-chú-un ka-hré-loh.		I know him by name, not otherwise.
15.	Koyma eng-pók hid min hril koyma ka-hríer.		Whatever is said to me I understand.
16.	Nangma hil-rú-nt koyma ka-hríer-ey ; nungma híú tnmtnk ka-pom-ey.		I am listening to your advice, I attach importance to what you say.
17.	Nangma koyma híú i-en-chú-un hé hná-bzawk dzaw-chú-un ahíá ey.		If you mind what I say, it will be well to have done with this business.
18.	Hé mí pakat hid ashoy, tsaw mí híú dang ashoy ; nungmani híú hmún hat ani-loh.		This man says one thing, and that man another. Your words do not agree.
19.	Koyma min hríer em ?		Do you know me ?
20.	Ka-hríer-ang-rung	...	I think I know you.

(*Explanatory*).—This verb hrd, and its parts hríer, hrí-ot, hrí-ey, is very obscure ; it seems to have more than one meaning—to know, to understand, to hear, to listen—are all comprised within its scope.

Exercise 43.

Lem, happy ; mi-ah, a fool ; hmú-hríot, recognition ; eng-la, something ; eng-ma nothing ; sahim-hnns presently ; tzmn, no one ; hid er hiow, to rise, get up ; tun-tleng-in, until, now, yet.

1.	Koyma pá pók i-hríer em ?	Do you know my father also ?
2.	Tsaw mí tsaw hríer-ti-in koyma min hril-loh-vemi ?	Did not that man tell me he knew it ?
3.	Koyma ka-hmi-chd-un ka-hríer-ang-ey	I shall know him if I see him.
4.	Koyma tong hríer-in nongma ú koyma min hríer-ey.	Your sister recognised me by my speech.
5.	Hé now-pang-tay tún-tleng-in koyma min hré-loh-rey.	Those children did not know me just now.
6.	Koyma ka-hríer-chd-un lom-dzit-in ka-shoy-hlei-ang-ey.	If I know it I should be very happy to tell.
7.	Hé mí koyangey a-om nnngma i-hríer em ?	Do you know where that man lives ?
8.	Koyma eng hid-egoy ka-ngai-túm i-hríer-em ?	Do you know what I am thinking about ?
9.	Hí roi-htar ahtá-loh-vey, mi-ah hid a-shoy-fo-rey.	That young man is no good, he is always talking foolishly.
10	Hmú-hríet i-nei-em ?	Do you know him by sight ?

11. Koyma i-hména eng-lo shoy-tár om-ey | I have something to say to you (that I would say).
12. Nungma koyma hném engey i-shoy-lú? | What do you wish to say to me?
13. Nungma koyma engma ka-shoy-loh ... | I said nothing to you.
14. Koyma hném shoy-rok, mi dang pahal hném hril-tachnh. | Say it to me, do not tell any one else.
15. Koyma nakin-huna ka-shoy-ang-ey ... | I will speak presently.
16. Nungma hném hiú ka-shoy-khá tú-ma hném shoy-tachnh-ang-chey. | You must not speak of what I told you to any one.
17. Nungma hném hiú ku-shoy-khá kanao hném shoy-tachnh-ang-chey. | You must not tell my brother what I told you.
18. Nungma taaw-taaw engey a-shoy-ta ?... | What did he say to you?
19. Tún-tlong-in koyma ka-hió-loh nungma bé-hi shoy-tachnh-ang-tchey. | Do not tell him that I have not yet got up.
20. Hé mi-hi hiú-shoy-khá engey i-ti? ... | What do you say to what he says?

EXERCISE 44.

Ang. like : tdh, to sit ; dzir, to learn; dzir-tir, to teach; adang, different ; hi, tongue ; nghil, straight; tytuka, abb. of ; tuk-tak, a táktka, abbreviation of táktákta.

1. Mi-ab ang-reng-in, ngol-reng-in, túh-tachnh. | Don't sit there like a fool, saying nothing.
2. Nungma ka-hril-loh-remni ? ... | Did I not tell you ?
3. Túna koyma min hril tachnh ... | Do not tell me now.
4. Tún-tlong-in koyma hném a shoy-lub-rey. | You have not yet told me.
5. Nungma tú-nen-engey htú i-shoy? ... | Who were you talking with ?
6. Koyma tong min dzir-tiró ... | Teach me the language.
7. Koyma dzir ka-du-ye ... | I wish to learn.
8. Nungma i-dzir-chú-da ahtá-ang-ey ... | It is good for you to learn.
9. Nangma koyma min dzir-tir-chú-an nungma tán ahtá ang-ey. | If you teach me it will be good for you.
10. Nungma ka-dzir-tir ang-tchey ... | I will teach you.
11. Koyma ka-dzir-ang-ey ... | I will learn.
12. Koyma ka-dzir-ta ... | I have learnt.
13. Koyma ka-dzir-dzowta ... | I have finished learning.
14. Nungma dzir-túr túm-túk a-om-ey ... | There is much for you to learn.
15. Nungma tong dzir-tir-tu túm-túk an-om-ey. | There are many to teach you.
16. Adang htú nen min hril-tirok ... | Make me understand in other words.
17. Nungma ták-ták-a dzir-tir-tú ani ... | You are a first rate teacher.
18. Koyma kia htú táktka ashoy hrei-loh-chú-an nungma ani-tuk-in min hril-rok. | If I pronounce a word wrong you should correct me.

19. Koyma hid adik-loh atí-chú-na nungma ahuy-nghil-ruh.

    If I do not speak correctly do you correct me.

20. Hé táng chú, ahar ey; koy-ma kadzir hisi-loh-vang-ey.

    This language is very difficult; I shall not be able to learn it.

EXERCISE 45.

Láng, heart; úr, to anger; ol, to believe; ke, a *jám*; lo-rat, to cut *jám*; hee, to abuse; ngal, to desire; lai, time.

1.	Lúng ni-loh-vin om-tachúh	...	Do not be perverse (obstinate).
2.	Lúng ni-loh-taclúh	...	Do not set yourself against it.
3.	Húin úr-tachuh	...	Do not be angry.
4.	Taaw mi taaw hísa-úr a-lām-ey	...	That man is very bad tempered.
5.	Ama d-tey an-lúng a-ol-ey	...	His sisters are well dispositioned.
6.	Nungma lo ahtá-loh-vin l-vá-tá; lal-in ahmd chú-na a hún a-úr angey, a-bao-vang-tebey.		You have cut the *jam* badly; if the chief sees it he will be angry and abuse you.
7.	Nungmani hnéna ka-pá chá-un kuldrok atí koyma ka-ol-loh.		I do not believe that my father said I was to go.
8.	Nungma hná l-htawk loh-va lal-in nungma ahúa-tebey.		You do so work, the chief is justly angry with you.
9.	And ahtá dzil omloh emni?	...	Is not the mother comfortable?
10.	Taaw mi khá lúng a-ol-loh-rey	...	That man is not contented.
11.	Nungma lúng oi-em?	...	Are you content?
12.	Nungma hmaik-lu ka-lúng ka-ol-ey	...	I am more contented than you.
13.	Koymani taaw mi-tey ai-in tankangu-loh, chiil-chian koymani húin ahtá-daawk.		We are not so rich as those men, but we are more happy.
14.	Nungma eng lúng in-oi?	...	What is your desire?
15.	Dzohlúta nen Mukla and Ahota; en-mani a-lúng ngai-dzit.		Dzohlúta and Moti have lost their mother; they are very sad.
16.	Hé mi-bring a-láng-ngal-ey ama nopúi a-hti-ta.		This man is said; his wife is dead.
17.	Hé nen kan-in-ngel-dzit ani-ey	...	We are great friends with him.
18.	Now-mag-lal-in hula ahtá kani-ey	...	I was happy in my childhood.
19.	Koyma ka-ngai tin roina hna-htaw-túr om-loh.		I don't think I shall work to-day.
20.	Hman-lai-in l-lo-kal-loh chú-un koyma ka-lúng ngai-ey.		I was anxious formerly because you did not come.

(*Explanatory*).—In sentences Nos. 1 and 2 the negative and affirmative should be remembered, thus, ni-ey or eni-ey is used for 'yes' and, ni-loh for no, in the Lushai dialect.

EXERCISE 46.

Tlám, sweet ; dawt, falsehood ; lo, again ; lom, joy.

1.	Nungma ka-hmŭ-loh chu-un ka-om-btri-loh; ka-ngai-oy tchey.	I cannot remain out of sight of you, I grow anxious.
2.	Nungma engey-tingey (-Hang-ngai; nungma engey ti-tangey-ley ?	Why are you so sorrowful, what is the matter ?
3.	Ráh-dzd ahtá dzit ka-ngai-ey.	I like good liquor.
4.	Hotichen ka-bmŭ-loh chú-un ka-ngai-ey.	I have not seen you for so long, I grew anxious.
5.	Koyma ka-ngai-tŭa voina tclaw-hmót abta-loh-rang-ey.	I am afraid the dinner will not be good to-day.
6.	Hoti-ang daú tlum ka-in-rey ngai-loh-rey.	I never drank such sweet beer.
7.	Dzohlŭta engtikama dzáng-bdn unei-ngai-loh.	Dzohlŭt never had a ring.
8.	Hman-lai-in heta ka-haw-rey ngai-loh-rey.	I have never been here before.
9.	Hmán-kat-el (-hmŭ-rey ngai-em ?	Did you ever see him any where ?
10.	Ka-htŭ-ldng om-ta-loh	I do not remember.
11.	Ka-ngai-tŭa-in ni heti-chen ani-in a-lo-tleng angey.	I think they will arrive when the sun is so high.
12.	Koyma kangai-tna ka-jien túna akulŭ	I think my friend left just now.
13.	Koyma ka-loog-ngai-ey adang bld shoy chú-un dawt ati-ang-ey.	I fear if he says any more he will fall to lying.
14.	Hé hna-htawk-tár ti-in (-tiun-ta, ka-ti ril-ru-a ngai-tŭa-in ahtawk-htci-ang, ati.	My sister hopes you will do the work you promised to do.
15.	Mŭkta Lai-jovi ngai eni-ey	Moli is Lai-jorí's sweetheart.
16.	Nungma om-loh-vio kan-ngai-tna-ey	We remembered you in your absence.
17.	Nungma ka-tho-ngai-ey tch-ey	I love you.
18.	Nungma ka-lo-hmd-lé-a ka-lom-ey	I am glad to see you again.
19.	Puitlem hé lrla hi-un antci-al-in a-lom té-ey.	The exorcist is the happiest man in this village.
20.	Eugey-tingey nungma lom-lo (-om ?	Why are you joyful ?
21.	Koyma pá voina atleng-ang-ey ti-in ka-lom-ey.	I am glad because my father will arrive to-day

NOTE.—The translation of these sentences into English is purposely rendered in as idiomatic and colloquial a form as possible. To find out the exact literal translation and trace the formation of the sentence in Lushai is the essential part of the student's task.

EXERCISE 47.

Tieng, a stick, staff; sili, to snap in two ; adi, to laugh; enginhel, any thing; dan, custom ; ma, even ; pek, also ; tama, no one; pal, to throw away ; pam, to observe, obey ; hān, period, time ; hming, name ; fo, (verbal aff.) always.

1.	Nuagma tia-brier-chú-un oi-luh-vang-ey.	If he knew you he would not believe.
2.	Ama a-lo-kal ka-oi-loh-vey	I do not believe he will come.
3.	Hé htú kat-lōñ asi ka-oi	I believe this only.
4.	Eng-htú-pōk aboy chú-un l-oi htin-ey...	You always believe whatever is said.
5.	Eng-ti-trang pōk aboy chú-no ka-oi-túr	I believed everything he said.
6.	Nuagma koyma tien, engey-tíngey ka htú i-oi-loh koyma mia ring-loh taebúh.	I am your friend, why are you suspicious of me? Do not disbelieve me.
7.	Tiung silfek-la ka-ring-loh	I don't believe it will break.
8.	Koymani kan-oi-loh, ka-nao pōk-via a-oi-loh.	We do not believe it, and our brother also does not believe.
9.	Nuagma i-oi-em ?	Do you believe ?
10.	Koyma ka-oi-chú-un nuagma i-nui-ang-ey.	If I believe, you will laugh.
11.	Koyma hé htú tiamtay-ma ka-oi-loh-vey.	I do not believe it one bit.
12.	Heti-ang htú ta-ma an-oi-loh vang-ey.	No one would believe such a thing.
13.	Nuagma i-hmú-chú-un koy-ma ka-oi-angey.	If you saw it I will believe.
14.	Hé mi-tey an-oi-loh-vey	They do not believe it.
15.	Koyma engtingey ka-oi-ang-ley ? ...	How should I believe it ?
16.	Nuagma nao englo-tul aaboy chú-un koy-ma ka-oi-ey. Htú tāk aaboy-htin-ey.	Whatever your brother says I believe. He always speaks the truth.
17.	Nuagma htú tūk i-aboy-ey, i-htú ka-oi-ang-ey, kapom-ey. Hé dēn ahtú-loh-ka-pai-taw-ang-ey.	You may truly I believe and will observe what you say. The custom is a bad one, and I will abandon it.
18.	Koyma ka-ngai-tua tuhaw-fāk a-hún-taw-ang-ey.	I believe it is about noon, (i.e., about lunch time).
19.	Ama hming koymani ngai-tná-fo-vey...	We always remember him.
20.	Koyma engtikma ka-hmú-loh-vey ...	I never saw it.

EXERCISE 48.

Mé, to recline. Fo down ; hbd-ni-la, always; anda, to seize; tuagini, a room ; tri, land, earth ; háha, tribute, revenue ; húleg-hrúng, timber ; la, to take ; allal, a gun ; taa, for ; ron-tain, ron-hos, hen, to bring; hang, to open ; hong, hse, to cause ; hás, to shut; vāb, pig; dll, to ask for, demand, express a want.

1.	Nuagma koyma ngai-tña-fo-vey, nuag-ma tarú koyma mia ngai-tña-loh-vey.	I always remembered you, but you did not remember me.

2.	Vángí a-lokul-á allongtá hid hluí a-shoy-ey. Ama hid nlai-in oi-tár ani-loh.		Vangee has arrived talking (mock) of old matters. All the says is not to be believed.
3.	Ili bná koyma ka-hiawk-a nuagma-in í-ci-loh-remni?		Do you not believe that I did that work?
4.	Nuagma jong ka-oi-ey	...	I believe you.
5.	Nuagma í-oi-fo-vey	...	You are always eating.
6.	Nangma í-ei-fo-ve, í-mú-fovey	...	You are always eating and always sleeping.
7.	Nuagma koyma nao í-rei-fovey, mí bid-loh oai-ey.		You are always beating my younger brother. You are a bad man.
8.	Nungma, hdm khú-ai-in, ka-khóngai-ang-tchey.		I will always love you.
9.	Koyma ó ama bd amán a-ei-ey, koyma-hl amán a-ei-ey?		Has my sister eaten her own rice or mine?
10.	Nuagma in bangbl ama bnaglai ai-in alien ngey atey?		Are your house rooms larger or smaller than his?
11.	Pnitiem ama lei ha aron-tain-tem?	...	Has the exorcist brought his tribute?
12.	Ilting-bring valaruk ati-terd	...	He said go bring timber.
13.	Tmw silai beta ron-bon drók	...	Bring that gun here.
14.	Koyma ú blín-hta áni ey ama nopmia tan bid moy-drit a-ron-lei-tá.		My brother is a good fellow, he has bought and brought for his wife, pretty necklace.
15.	I-lo-tma-in, ron-tainadrok	...	Bring it when you come.
16.	Nuagma í-lo-kul-chú-an ron-hóng-rúk.		Open it when you come.
17.	Nungma í-lo-kul-chú-an ron-tain-drók...		Bring it when you come.
18.	Nungma í-lo-kul-in koyma in hong-kar bon-ché í-ron-bmú-em?		When you were coming did you see my house door open?
19.	Kong-kar hon-teni ha-bmú-loh vák-kong-kar terd ka-busú.		I did not see the house door open, but the pig sty done I saw open.
20.	Hán-dil-ang, bán-hondrók	...	Ask for and bring it.

(*Explanatory*,)—This exercise presents more than usual difficulties. The inflections of the verbs to come, to go, to bring, and to open, are very obscure, and require further amplification and study. The subject is pursued in the next exercise, but much still remains to be elucidated. *Han* and *ron* (8. 18-20) would seem to be verbal prefixes merely.

Exercise 49.

Kul-pal, send; twei-twei, quickly; dren, night; dmnim, evening; bin-deng, blacksmith; roina, to-day; dulang, early; aui-tika, to-morrow; Timbonga, (n. p) Demagree; phil, to permit.

1.	Ama adam-loh, a-haw-hlai-loh	...	He is sick, he cannot come.
2.	Tmw-tmw béta ron-kul-pairók-d	...	Send him here.
3.	Hán-kul-pai twei-twei-rók-d	...	Send quickly.
4.	Boi, koyma pd-an i-ron-tain-tem?	...	Slave, have you brought my cloth?
5.	Tdna ka-tain-loh-vey, dmnim a-ron-tain-angrey.		I have not brought it now but will bring it this evening.

6.	Hétú lo-hawrók	...	Come here.
7.	Hír-deng ína ka-lo-hong-ey	...	I am come from the blacksmith's.
8.	Voina dzinga bon-kong ahta-loh	...	The road we came this morning was bad.
9.	Díla ka-lo-kul-ey	...	I am come to beg.
10.	Ka-hóng-btei-loh, tobern pakat hon-drók.		I cannot open it, bring a daa.
11.	Nagma koyangey kul?	...	Where are you going?
12.	Nagma farnú hudea voina dzinga koynngey í-kul?	...	Where did you go this morning with your sister?
13.	Koymani pai-tiem hía kan-kul-ey	...	We went to the exorcist's house.
14.	Koyma farnú ama farnú en-in a-kul-ey	...	My daughter is going to see his.
15.	Nuktúka Tbúnga í-kul don-lom?	...	Are you not going to Demagree to-morrow?
16.	Koyma pá koyma kul a-pbál-loh	...	My father will not permit me to go.
17.	Nungma tún-ileng-in í-kul-don-em?	...	Are you going just now?
18.	Rowídle túna a-kul-loh-váng	...	Rowidle will not go now.
19.	Koyma ka-kul-ták-ták-ang-ey	...	I really will go.
20.	Túna í-lo-haw-ta-loh	...	You do not come now.

(*Explanatory*).—In sentence 15, *lom* would appear to be a colloquial contraction of *lud-enund*.

Exercise 50.

En, a description of basket; apiong, no; eng-lo, whatever; dínloa, yesterday; laíshú, a writing; Lien-tschdteg-badnga, proper name; Tsamat-dora, Kásamlong; hoy-lamangey, whence; evn, to agree, fraternize, to el peace; ichoy, to raise; tú, to fall.

1.	Ilé em Kára a-tsin-htsí-ang?	...	Can Kara take away this basket?
2.	Ili tehem a-kul-pai chú-un koyma pá-in min liáo-vang-ey		If you take away that *deo* my father will abuse me for it.
3.	Nuagma eng-lo rá í-dú apiong ka-hon-angey.		I will bring you whatever fruit you like.
4.	Koyma ka-hrier-chú-un ka-ron-hon-tá?		If I had known I would have brought it.
5.	Nimina Rámatey laishui pabnit patám a-ron-hon-tá.		He brought two or three letters from Rangamatee yesterday.
6.	Nuktúka Lien-tschdteg-badnga ama fá sron-hon-angey.		To-morrow Lientschdteg-badnga will bring his son.
7.	Asmani Tsamat-dóra-tá, ani sn-hon-ey.		They are bringing their seat from Kásamlong.
8.	Nungma thoy ndla-khé, nungma hæma ron-bon-pai-lang ahta-ta-ldr.		It would be well to bring with you the girl you mentioned.
9.	Nungma koylam-angey i-lo-hon?	...	Whence do you come?
10.	Ní ahtá-chú-un koymani bnéna tchaw-ei-tár-in Múkía lo-baw-don ali-ey.	...	If it is fine, Múktí said he was coming to dine with us.
11.	Nuagma, tchaw a-hon-don í-ti-em?	...	Did you tell me to bring dinner?
12.	Túí tlemley ron-bon-twei twei-rók	...	Bring a little water quickly.
13.	Ama a-lo-hong-chú-un kul-tírok	...	Send him when he comes.

14.	Iléta lo-haw-tachob-ú; omrók-ú ...	Stop, don't come here.
15.	Nungma Múkia l-kul-tir ani-ang-ey ...	You sent Múktí here I think.
16.	Nungma min poi-don-em ?	Will you help me ?
17.	I-bmún-phia-khá bmún-phia, kul-pui-lang pairók.	Take away the broom with which you have swept the house and throw it away.
18.	Tioutey-bók khá-pui-a an-bla-ey, an-rem-ey.	It is an amicable and good thing to assist one's friends.
19.	Iló mi-bring allú-ey, tehoy-pui-rók-ú...	That man has fallen, help to lift him up.

(*Explanatory*).— As far as I am able to ascertain *kul-tírók* (S. 14-16) means 'to send'; the employment therefore of *kul-pairók* (Ex: 47, S. 2-3), in a similar sense requires explanation. Kul-tírók literally translated, would mean make go, or come; (kul, to go; ti, aux. verb to make) and kul-poirók might in the same way mean to help or assist, go or come, (kul to go; pai aux. verb to assist), but we find the latter constantly used in the sense of *take away*, remove. See also here as to *take away*, sentence 1, of this exercise. The *ts* in tain must be softened almost to the sound of the English sh in *shin*. On the use of the auxiliary verb *tí, to do* (as in kul-tírók) see next Exercise.

Exercise 51.

Atleng, to arrive.

1.	Taaw tlang angey atí?	...	What is the name of that hill ?
2.	Engey li tangey ley ?	...	What is the ado ?
3.	Iló lo koyma min bmú-tir-tá	...	The field was shown to me.
4.	Lo-kul tirok	...	Tell him to come.
5.	Hongrók-ú, tírok	...	Say, come.
6.	Nungma angey l-tí-ley ?	...	What are you doing ?
7.	Koyma ka-tí-htei-loh	...	I cannot do it.
8.	Koyma min briei-tírok	...	Explain it to me.
9.	Koyma min bá-tir chú-na ama ka-há-tir-angey	...	If he troubles me I shall trouble him.
10.	Koyma ka-tí-angey	...	I will do it.
11.	Min hmútírok	...	Show it to me.
12.	Túb tírok, ei-tírok	...	Let him sit, let him eat.
13.	Tchut-tírók-ú	...	Let him go. (*i.e.*, loose or release them).
14.	Koyma ka-tí-htei chú-na ka-tí-angey	...	If I can do it I will.
15.	Iló atí btei-loh-rang-ey	...	This cannot be done.
16.	Nungma l-tí-btei-ang-em ?	...	Will you be able to do it ?
17.	Nungma l-tí túr engey em?	...	What have you to do ?
18.	Iló-tí-ang-bí tírók	...	Do like this.
19.	Ama pá atleng-tá atí-in pék-loh	...	He will not give it because his father has arrived.
20.	Nungma á atleng-tá atí-in min shoy-ey.		He told me your brother had arrived.

EXERCISE 52.

Mateilovin, certainly; hman, leisure; reng, to remain; bad, work; htawk, to perform.

1. Nungma d-hók mateilovin a-ti-angey... | Your sisters must do it.
2. Nungma d engey aií? | What is your sister doing?
3. Túna koymani engey kanti-ang? | What shall we do now?
4. Nungma engtingey í-tí? | How do you do it?
5. Nungma dam-loh-tí ka hrier, a-en-tdr-in ka-lo-kul-ey. | I have come to see you, hearing you were ill.
6. Nungma nao nimina ka-enté nohidka ka-lo-hul-angey ati-ey | I saw your younger brother yesterday, he said he would come to-morrow.
7. Hé dzéng-bún nungma htá í-ti-em? | Do you think this ring a good one?
8. Engey ka-ti-ang? | What shall I do?
9. Engtingey ka-tí? | How do I do it?
10. Amei-engey ti-chd-na karil-rd-ey | I think he will get it.
11. Eng pót nei-loh-vang-tí í-hriei-chu-na dil-tachob ang-tr'hey. | Do not ask for what you know you will not get it.
12. Koyma hé ka-ti-khá nungma engtingey í-hriei? | How do you know I did this?
13. Hé mi ahman a-ti-a in-a a-mei-reng ey. | Having nothing to do he is asleep in the house.
14. Hé tángey tí koyma ka-hré-twei-angey | I will soon know who did this.
15. Voina hly-tama engey a-ti-don? | What shall we do this evening?
16. Nungma koy-engey ati-don? | Where are you going?
17. I-hna-htawk abté-loh | Your work is bad.
18. Nungma hna-htawk-rók | Do your work.
19. Nungma dzengey í-htaw? | How much have you done?
20. Hna htaw-túr a-ore | He has work to do.

EXERCISE 53.

Htoy, to sacrifice; kúavang-tí, to worship; rel, delay; hém, hot; aghil, straight; ahil, to build, cut; hún, time.

1. Hé mi-hring-té-haík tám-ták hna an-htaw-tá. | These men have done a great deal of work.
2. Koyma hé hna ka-htawk-htei-angey ... | I shall be able to do this work.
3. Nungma hna-htaw-túr, nungma í-ti-htei-loh-vemni? | Cannot you do your work?
4. Hé hna túngey htawk-ang? | Who will do this?
5. Hé mi engtingey ka-tí nungma í-hri-em? | Do you know what I am doing to this man?
6. Kún-té-mi htoy-túr-in koyma ka-ti-ta... | I told the people I would offer a sacrifice.
7. Kún-tí-mi kuavang tí-tdr-in ka-ti-ey... | I promised the people I would sacrifice.
8. Túi húm í-ti-taw-em? | Have you heated the water?
9. Rei-tak om-a ka-kúl-tír-ta ... | I sent him some time ago.

10.	Nungma engry i-ti?	...	What are you doing?
11.	Mel hü-tiruk	...	Put out the light.
12.	Ti ngbil rök	...	Put it straight.
13.	Koyma fa-pa engoy aii?	...	What is my son doing?
14.	Nungma hna raga-tangey i-htaw-loh?_		Why do you not work?
15.	Koyma tön-tleng-in hna ka-htawk adang ka-htawk loh-vang.		I have worked until now, but shall do no more.
16.	Hna a-htawk-ey	[tem?	She is working.
17.	Nungma tün'a hi-un-in in i-ahi-daow-		Have you finished the house by this time?
18.	Koyma in ka-ahi	...	I am building a house.
19.	Naktüka nungma heti-hün-in in i-ahi-daow-vang-em?		Will you be able to finish the house by this time to-morrow.
20.	Koyma in htar nungma i-hmü-tem? ...		Have you seen my new house?

(*Explanatory*).—The word *Ahi* (S. 19 *et supra*) means literally ' to cut." The language contains no word to build, nor indeed is there a synonym for the idea in the Lushai mind. All their houses are built of bamboos, and the work is one of cutting from first to last.

EXERCISE 54.

Tsäw, hair.

1.	Hi dzünglük moy-tok-tey-hi koyma-tangey i-uei?		Where did you get those pretty rings?
2.	Nungma dier koyangey?	...	Where is your turban?
3.	Nungma pü-un-fen koyangey?	...	Where is your petticoat?
4.	Koymani kan-tleng-in koyangey i-om?		Where were you when we arrived?
5.	Heti-ang tchem koyangey a-lei-htsi-ang?		Where can one buy a *dao* like this?
6.	Koyma Samata ka-lei		I buy them at Kasalong.
7.	Koyma tchem tü hmena-ngey?	...	Who has my *dao*?
8.	Koyma tchem-in tüngey hna-htawk?...		Who has used my *dao*?
9.	Koyma nungma tchem-in hna ka-htawk-loh, nungma ü i-hna-htawk ...		I have not used your *dao*, it was your brother who used it.
10.	Koyma bü ka-nei, dem-tey-tal nungma i-ei-tem?		Have you eaten any of the rice I got?
11.	Nungma hnëna tchem htä om-ey, koyma ü hna-htawk-tür tkom pé-bri-rök.		You have a good *dao*; lend it to my sister for a little to work.
12.	Om-bri-rök	...	Stay a little.
13.	Heta eng tsäw ngey?	...	What hair is this here?
14.	Nungma ül koyangey?	...	Where is your dog?
15.	Koyma pa üi a-hralta	...	My father has sold it.
16.	Koyma pü-un-tey i-ron-twin-tem?		Have you brought my cloths?
17.	Puithem beta a-haw-tem?	...	Has the exorcist been here?
18.	Heta a-hong-loh	...	He did not come here.
19.	Nungma, ni eng-jangey Samata i-om?		How long were you at Kasalong?

EXERCISE 55.

Hmda, a part; tsem, to divide; hten, to separate; in-bú-an, to fight; daíng-an, an assemblage; hmá-shá, in front; hndnga, in rear; tlaw, a kick; tlín, to run; shón, in; tanklem, on top; ler, to climb; táwn, ascend; tih, to sit; ding, to stand; híem, to rise.

1.	Koyma bú hrai tschom ley brai nga koyma ní hmána kansítá.	I have received fifteen baskets of rice from my aunt.
2.	Tschom ley pariek hmda rúk kan-tsem ílang, hmda túm-a a-rúwal-in a-om-ey	Eighteen divided by six gives three.
3.	Hé-rá tsem-rók	... Divide this fruit.
4.	Tsaw mí-tey htandrók-d, in-bú-un lír-tschúh-d.	Part these men, do not let them fight.
5.	Tlá kat-a hmda lí in-tsemílang ní tsarí a-rúwal-in a-om-ey.	The fourth part of a month is seven days.
6.	Hé-hi aríwal-in tsaw-ta shón darík-d	Put them together in that place.
7.	Kúm kat-a tschom ley pahnít in-tsem -ílang, tla kat-a aríwal-in a-om-ey.	The twelfth part of a year is a month.
8.	Nungmaní daíng-an túngey htel, eu-rók, tsaw á-shón atlang hmá-shá tanka túm ka-pó-ang-ey; au-dza hndnga a-om-chú koyma ka-tlaw-vakangey. Tlandrók.	See which is the best among you; whoever arrives first at that place I will give him three rupees, but I shall give the last man a kick. Run.
9.	Koymaui-bok-vin á-kul-ang, tsaw mí tsaw ama tchang-in, ahrang-in kuldrók twy.	You will come along with us, but let that fellow go by himself.
10.	Nang hmei-tacin mí, nungua tchang-in réma kai ahtá-luh.	You are a female, it is not good that you should go alone through the jungle.
11.	Hmá-shá-a kuldrók	... Go in front.
12.	Tsák-láma kuldrók	... Go up there.
13.	Híé húng léra lawndrók	... Climb that tree.
14.	Ina lo-lawndrok	... Come up into the house.
15.	Dzíng-a htó rók	... Got up early.
16.	Túhrók; dingrok; htowrók	... Sit down; stand up; rise.
17.	Tsáka dárók	... Put it on top.
18.	In tscá-nga lawndrok	... Get on top of the house.
19.	In tschánga lo-kuldrók	... Come inside the house.
20.	Hndnga omrók	... Stay behind.

(Explanatory.)—In reference to the word *daínga* in sentence 8, it is as well to add the following words in elucidation; mao-daínga, a bamboo-thicket, or clump of bamboos; húng-daínga, tree jungle; mí-hring daínga, a crowd.

F

EXERCISE 56.

Tláng. underneath ; alai. middle ; huáo, brinre ; hman-lai-ín, formerly ; abáng. a part.

1. Tlángu l-kul-chu-un omrók   ...   Go underneath and stay there.
2. Alai-a darók   Place it in the middle.
3. Hmá-shá-á ni-tin-in í-lo-hon, túna í-lo   Formerly you used to come every day, you
   haw-ta-loh.   do not come now.
4. Nowpang lai-in hún-htn kani-ey ;   I was happy in youth for I was strong, but
   koyma biáh kanei, tán-lai-in kaíat-   now I have grown old and am not as
   tá koyma hman-lai-ang-in kaní-ta-loh.   heretofore.
5. Koyma abáng kái min pé-ma-shá-rák   First give me half.
6. Koyma lo-rá-tur ka-bman-loh   I have no leisure to *jám.*
7. Hman-lai-ín an-in-ra-a mí-bring tum   In former times many people died in battle.
   tuk an-hú-tá.
8. Túna he-bman-loh, hnáuga ka-pé-ang-   I have no leisure now, but will send it
   tchey.   presently.
9. Hman-lai-ín anmaní lai an-khóngai-ey·   Formerly they loved their chief, now it is
   tán-lai-chú-un an-khóngai-loh.   not so.
10. Hman-lai-ín, nowpang lai-ín, in-lom-   Formerly when I was young I wished to
    lem ka-dú-ey ; tán-lai-chú-un nopuí   sport, but now I am married I have no
    kanella ín-lom-lem ka-dn-loh-rey,   mind to play ; It is work I want.
    hna-htawk eni ka-lú.
11. Nungma hman-lai-ín í-latacía, hna-htaw   You were wont to be very lazy and had no
    htin a-om-loh-rey.   mind to work.
12. Voína chú-un ka-mú bmáahá-dou-ey :   I shall go to bed first to-night, to-morrow
    nuktuka daínga lo-vá kul-tur eni-ang-ey   early I have to go afield.
13. Hmá-shá-a kuklrók, hnúng-lam-a eri-   Go in front, do not stay behind.
    tschúh.
14. Dzoi-tuk-ín kuldrok hmá-shá kul tachub   Go easy, do not go in front.
15. Koyma ka-llán blei-loh   ...   I cannot run.
16. Túna chú-un mí pabnít a-rúwul-in kul-   From this time forth send two men together.
    tirok-n.
17. Koyma pí-un ley nung-ma pé-un a-   My cloth is as good as yours.
    rúwul-kai alítá-tey-ey.
18. Nungma hman-lai-ín ka-khóngai-tchey   Did you not know that I loved you formerly?
    nungma í-bré-loh-maw ?
19. Hé rá apúna ka-nei-loh chú-un ka-dé-   If I do not get the whole of that fruit I do
    loh-rey.   not want any.
20. Hmána-chú-un nungma hna-tawk-a   Formerly you showed great diligence in
    taíma ka-tí-chey, túna engma í-tawk-   your work, but now you do nothing. I
    loh-rá, nungma bíva (bíva, from hao,   have a mind to abuse you.
    to abuse) ka-ríí-rú-ey.

Exercise 57.

Dán, habit ; tui-pui, river ; tanh, up ; tlang, down ; tuchúng, inside; tuvúnga, on top; hnoya, beneath ; tlang-un, uader; in-kót, house platform ; mhlna, presently.

1.	Tún-ang-in tchaw oi a-om-ey	...	He is now eating his meal.
2.	Tún-tlong in tchaw oi-lob-vemni ?	...	Have you not yet eaten your meal ?
3.	Nungma túna tchaw ei-in i-taw-tá ?	...	Did you eat before coming ?
4.	I-lo-hoa hmá-in tchaw ei-dzow-vin i-bong-emni ?		Did you finish eating your meal before coming ?
5.	Túna ka-ei-loh-rey, hndnga ka-nao non ka-nei-angry.		I have not yet eaten ; I shall do so presently with my younger brother.
6.	Tchaw-ták-húna tchaw-ei ka-dán eni-cy.		I am accustomed to eat at noon.
7.	Koyma ka-kul-tangey ; ka-hma-hiawk-túr atúrn em-cy.		I am going now, I have much to do.
8.	Koyma pót ka-kul-ang-ey, nnngma hnúng-láma.		I also will go along with you.
9.	Koyma hnúngma ka-en-angey	...	I will see afterwards.
10.	Koyma hnúng-láma ka-en-angey	...	I will look behind.
11.	Nungma hnúnga endrók	...	Look behind you.
12.	Koyma tashlam ka-en, in tuvúnga ka-en-ta.		I saw it up there, on the top of the house.
13.	In kawhi-an vák a-kultá	...	The pig has gone under the house.
14.	In tuchúnga ka-kul-dón	...	I am going into the house.
15.	Vák, in hnoya a-om-ey	...	The pig is beneath the house.
16.	Nungma tlang-un darók	...	Put it under you.
17.	Pú-un hnoya om-ey	...	It is under the cloth.
18.	Tui-pui tlang-láma ka-om-ey	...	I live down the river.
19.	I-ei hmal-in rak-lxvi tlemtey indrók	...	Before eating drink a little spirit.
20.	In-kót-hmaia ar attm-oy	...	There are many fowls in front of the house.
21.	Nakina ahtá-ang-chí	...	You will be well presently.

(*Explanatory*.)—Sentence 7. *Ka-kul-tangey* is an abbreviation of *ka-kul-taw-angey.* See exercise 58. In the same manner in sentence 0 *Anúnga-in* is contracted to *hnúngan.*

Exercise 58.

Tobiara, to prepare ; tám, to dance ; in-hui-ua, to interlock, to wrestle ; in-bú-al to bathe, to immerse ; in-tleng, to interchange ; in-ngvi or in-ngui, to asissn ; in-biua, disjoin, separate.

1.	Nungma i-kul-don-taw-em ?	...	Are you about to go ?
2.	Koymani adz-vin tchiem-dzow chú-un kul-taw-ang.		We shall be going when we have got every-thing ready.
3.	Nungma kul-túr-in i-tchiam-dzow-taw-em ?		Are you about ready to go ?

4. Adang om-chú ka-hún-láng om-ta-loh,   I won't stay any longer, I shall go, (am
    ka-kul-taw-angey.   about to go).

5. Koyma ka-ngai-túis tchaw fák a-bún-   I think it is about noon.
    taw-ang-ey.

6. Ilé hasitacia nulla pa-bnit, ni-dzasa   These two girls were to have danced last
    slám-dén-taw-a, alám-ta-loh.   night but they did not.

7. Ka-kul-taw-angey ; tlem-tey om-brí-   I am just going, stop a bit.
    rók.

8. Nungma tú-nen-ngey in-bú-m-dón ? ...   Who will you wrestle with ?

9. Nungma tú-nen-ngey in-bú-an ?   ...   Who are you wrestling with ?

10. Pú-an in-tleng-ang   ...   We will change cloths.

11. Múkis ley Dzohlúa an-in-bú-an angey   Mutse and Dzohlú will wrestle together.

12. Koyma ka-bú-an-lob-raug   ...   I will not wrestle.

13. Nungma túi l-in-bú-ul-tem ?   ...   Have you bathed ?

14. Kul-lang, in-bú-ulrúk   ...   Go and bathe.

15. In-bú-un dzaw-in túi in-bú-ul-nan   It is good to bathe after wrestling.
    abiá-ey.

16. Hé mi nen kan-in-ngai-loh   ...   We do not agree with this man.

17. In-htendrók-ú, nungmaui dang lai-ey... Separate—you are different.

18. Koymaní in-tchium-in kan-kul-ey   ...   We are ready and going.

19. Lai in-tchium-loh chú-un engey-tang-   What is the use of going when the chief is
    ey kul-ang ?   not ready.

20. Nungma í-in-tchiem-taw-em   ...   Are you nearly ready.

(*Explanatory*.)—The language seems to have no measure of time, as hours, minutes, &c. ;
they divide their day by the height of the sun,—or say, as in sentence 5, for noon, simply
" the hour of food."

EXERCISE 59.

Teng, to visit, mort ; bao, to shun ; la-hao, to quarrel ; af-tis, daily, hetichen, thea much ; i-tiou,
ingratials, to become friends (tai, to kill, slay ; ahin, to dos, put on ; tleng, to change ; kai, wear ; ewem, to
wish.

1. Vaína tchaw-fák-bún-in in-taw-a lo-   Come and visit us to-day about noon.
    hawrók.

2. Koymaní kan-in-jen chú-an htí daug   I will tell you differently when we separate
    ka-sboy-angey.   from them.

3. In-tchiem twei-tweirók   ...

4. Kullúr-in lai-in htí min tium-tá   ...   The chief promised me to go

5. Volna bly-lama in-om-lem-a í-kul-don-   Will you go to play this evening ?
    em ?

6. In-om-lem-ang.   ...   I will play.

7. Kanao nen t-in-bao-fo-vey   ...   You are always quarrelling with my brother.

8. Hé mí la-hao-fo-mí ani-ey   ...   He is a very quarrelsome man.

9. Nungma engey-tangey túi in-bú-ul-loh?   Why have you not bathed ?

10. In-bú-al ka-dn-ey, tái ka-nel-loh-vey...   I wished to bathe, but there was no water.

11. Koymaní ní-tin-in kan-in-bú-na-chú-an hta-tak-in kan-in-ba-na bíei-angey.   If we wrestle every day, we shall be able to wrestle well.

12. Voina mi andsa-in, an-kul-angey Sama-ta, In-btoy-túr.   To-day every one is going to Kamalong to offer sacrifice.

13. Múkia búo ahtá-loh-chú-na-in hotí-ohen kan-in-giam btel-loh-vang-ey.   If Motse were bad dispositioned we should not be such good friends.

14. Dsanina bó vák kan-talaaga, nuagma tchanja-in koyma ka-tchan-angey.   To-night we will kill this pig; my share will be equal to yours.

15. Hmáshá tchiem-cha-in ka-dá-túr, koy-ma pú-na shín-in ka-om-ey.   I should have got it ready before but was putting on my cloth.

16. Koyma hmána ka-tahinon-dzow-tá-túr, bad ka-hiawk-a, hren ka-kal-tleng-ani.   I should have prepared it before, but was changing my waistcloth after work.

17. Hé mi shoy tak-tak-túr ani-angey, nuagma ang kani-chú-un, ka-shoy tak-tak-túr.   You ought certainly to tell him; were I in your place I should do so certainly.

18. Koyma ka-hman-chú-an aníwul-in ban-kai-túr.   If I were at leisure we would both go together.

19. Koyma hódzá hma-hiawk-túr om-loh-chú-an ní-tin-in ka-lo-haw-túr.   If I had not so much work to do I should come every day.

20. Nungma í-nwum-em í-hména ka-shoy-túr?   Do you wish that I should tell you?

(*Explanatory.*)—I cannot ascertain the meaning of the root *tchan* in sentence 14. The constant irregularities in the verb to prepare, make, ready, from *tchiem* to *tchiem*, are very puzzling.

EXERCISE 60.

Chíti-vang-in, for this reason, on this account; shem, to divide, parcel out; reng, to remain.

1. Andsa-in an-hrior-ey, chíti-vang-in shoytúr ahtá-loh.   Every body knows it, therefore it is no good telling.

2. Nungma pá nímína koyma min hríltá amá la hraltúr.   Your uncle told me yesterday he would sell his house.

3. Koymaní hmena lo ava-chú-an í-nang-reng-in ka-shem-túr.   If you had joined with us we should have shared with you.

4. Nungma min khóngai-chú-an nuagma pók ka-khóngai-túr-tchey.   If you had loved me, I also should have loved you.

5. Hé mi koyangey a-om, koyma min hríl-chú-an nuagma tanka pakát ka-pé-túr tchey.   If you had told me where that man was, I should have given you a rupee.

6. Koymaní há-tachnh-í-lang nuagmaní hména kan-hon-túr.   If we had not been so tired we should have come to you.

7. Koyma hmona tanka om-chú-an pú-un lei-in ka-loh-haw-túr.   If I had had any money I should have come to buy cloth.

8. Koymani pā lािलmri ka-nel-loh-chú-un
   túa-ebam-iu han-lo-tleng-loh-rang-ey.
   | If we had not received our father's letter we should not have arrived so soon.

9. Koyma pā bman-lai-la lo dzow-tāk
   ava-chú-na túna hi-un koymani min
   hral-loh-rang-ey.
   | If our father had formerly cut big *jám* we should not now have been sold (as slaves).

10. Koymani taaw-mi-tó al-in tankanga
    loh-chiti-chú-un koymani húin ahiá-
    daawk.
    | We are not so rich as that man, but we are more happy.

11. Chiti-chú-un min luil   ...
    | He told me so.

12. Chiti-chú-un ka-shoy   ...
    | Thus I say.

13. Ili lo ahiá-tó-ey chiti-chú-un koyma
    ú lo adza al-in ahiá ey.
    | That *jám* is good, but my brother's *jám* is the best of all.

14. Koyma sciel tum-tuk-in asháng chiti-
    chú-un hé-sclel-hi ashang daawk, chi-
    ti-chú-un koyma ka-nú a-sclel adza-
    al-in asháng-ver-ey.
    | My guyal is very tall, but that guyal is taller, however my mother's guyal is the tallest of all.

15. Nungma, koyma tchom i-ki-tem chiti-
    chú-un koyma d tchem em, i-lagh?
    | Have you taken my *dao* or my sister's *dao*?

16. Nungma lal túa i-kul-tem?   ...
    | Have you been to the chief's house?

17. Ka-kul-loh-vey   ...
    | I have not been.

18. Koymani Mūkla a-lo-vá kan-kul-in par
    túin-tāk kan-ncltá.
    | We got many flowers going to Moti's field.

19. Daohlúta lo-vá juik par om em?   ...
    | Are there flowers also in Daohlút's *jám*.

20. Koyma ú btin btá ani-ey, ama nopnl-a
    tan htí moy-dait a-ron-lci-tá.
    | My brother is very kind-hearted, he has bought and brought for his wife a pretty necklace.

Exercise 61.

Tát, to cut; bew; blow, fear; tán, to chop; daal-tehdm to saw, cut by sawing; ahi, to incline; hd, leg; ai-hér, a sore; hi, to fell; tcahám, north; hiá, to fall; ahál, dirty; búh, overeat; ljp-np.

1. Voina ama pā pen ard-wal-in akulá;
   koyma Laljika hún ka-hmú.
   | To-day he went along with his uncle; I saw them in Laljika's village.

2. Koymani tla-rúk khatá kan-om-ey   ...
   | We were there six months.

3. Nungma sag-tik-angey i-lo-hon-ang?
   | At what time will you come?

4. Koyma pā hnan-lai-la tankanga aal   ...
   | My father was formerly rich.

5. Ilé limai-tacia, ulla-lai-chú-un ahmél
   ahiá tey engey.
   | This woman was very pretty in her youth.

6. Koyma d-tey nimína an-dám-loh-va
   om-ey.
   | Your sisters were ill yesterday.

7. Nungma i-pa ína om-lai-in húm enjan-
   gay eal-tagh?
   | How old were you when you were at your father's house?

8. Nungma tángey tát-htei-ang-key? Ilow
   tachah.
   | Who can cut you down? Do not fear.

9.	Pakát-ma-in nungma an-tát-htái-loh-vung tschúh.	No one will be able to cut you down.
10.	Koyma táh-tár ka-dú-ey ...	I want to cut it.
11.	A-lá tándrok ...	Cut off his head.
12.	Nungma i-tsám i-dzai-tchúm-tem ? ...	Have you cut your hair ?
13.	Ka-kút ka-aht-ey ...	I have cut my finger.
14.	Nungma koyma pá-nn i-dzai-tá	You have cut my cloth.
15.	Nungma ké atscher a-tám am-ey ...	That is a bad sore on your leg.
16.	Húing a-ki-chá-nn tschím-láma aild-angey.	If you cut down that tree it will fall to the south.
17.	Tsaw mi tsaw an-tsat-tchik-dzowta, ahtí-loh-rey.	That man is wounded, he is not dead.
18.	Kúmina lo i-vá-tem ?	Have you cut him this year ?
19.	Koyma ka-tlá-a, ka-pú-na abái-hlo-ta-ey.	I have fallen down and dirtied my clothes.
20.	Hé-mi-hí búkangey, i-tlá-angey ...	That will upset and you will fall down.

(*Explanatory.*)—For example of the employment of hé mi, that thing. (S. 20 above) See sentence 8, Ex. 14.

EXERCISE 62.

Affng. wisdom.

1.	Koyma ka-kal-chen a-tá nungma eagey i-htaw ?	What have you done since I went ?
2.	Volum nungma Laijovi huena ani-tem ?	Were you with Laijovi to-day ?
3.	Koyma voiu-in dzinga ka-om-ey, khá-tíehen ka-hmú-loh.	I was with her early to-day, but have not seen her since ?
4.	Nungma uowpang lai-a-ta tatsoia eni ey.	You have been lazy since you were a child.
5.	Koyma sliru ka-lo-kal-in nungma hna-htaw i-dzow-htái-loh-vemui ?	Have you not finished your work since I came ?
6.	Nungma i-lo-kal-tir-in ka-hmú-loh-tchey.	Since you came I have not seen him.
7.	Koyma lo-bou-kan-in nungma pawu-a i-kulta.	When I came you were out.
8.	Koymad a-dick ahlo-rin khá-lai-in nungma i-hmú-em ?	Did you see when my brother lost his turban.
9.	Kha-la-rok ...	Take that.
10.	Koyma sillai ka-kap-kan nungma i-hmú-em ?	Did you see when I fired the gun ?
11.	Mukia hnáma-chn-na koyma nao nen an-la-tien-ey.	Motl was formerly a great friend of my younger brothers.
12.	Hmél ai-in ang-loh ...	He does not resemble him.

13. Dzobldtu a-bjilu, nowpang altá aoi,   Dzoblát is dead, he was a good lad and wise,
    ama afing oy ; andzu-in akhóngai-oy;   every one liked him; we constantly used
    ama ló va koymani kan-kul-fo-vey.   to go to his júm.
14. Nungma i-mi-fo-vey   ...   You are always lying down.
15. Ama haéna hman-lal-in pd-un tam-luk   He formerly had much cloth.
    a-om-oy.
16. Ama od ley pé chiti tanka howkmloh   His mother and father although not rich
    chiti-chu-un lo adzow an-vái-oy.   are great cultivators.
17. Koyma nimlu ka-dám-loh, ka-kul-   I was sick yesterday and not able to go.
    btoi-loh.
18. Túo-lleng-in nungma hna-htawk i-   Have you not yet finished your work ?
    dzow-loh-remni ?
19. Koyma ka-dzow-loh. Koyma nao   I have not finished. My younger brother
    khá-lai-in hna htaw-dzowla. Koyma   had finished them. I have not done.
    kati-dzow-loh.
20. Koyma ka-ti-btei, chiti-chú-un koyma   I can do it, but my younger brother cannot.
    nao ati-btei-lob-vey.

Bto, a fly ; dear, to settle, alight ; dé, wish ; dil, want ; rogma, anything ; doong, to search for ; engpóh,
whatever.

1. Hto min daár, ka-om-htei-loh   ...   The flies are very troublesome. I cannot
                                             stand it.
2. Koyma in ka-dá   ...   I want to drink.
3. Dzawt-rók   ...   Ask.
4. Dzawlang, lo-kuldrók   ...   Ask then come.
5. Engey i-di ?   ...   What do you want ?
6. Nungma adil-ehú-un, i-dil-btei-angoy;   You may certainly ask, but you will not get
   engma i-wei-loh-vang-oy.   anything.
7. Engma omloh   ...   There is nothing.
8. Koyma engma ka-dil-loh   ...   I do not want anything.
9. Nungma engoy en ?   ...   What are you looking for.
10. Kan-kul-don-in nungma nao ama   When we left your brother was searching for
    tchem adzong-oy.   ...   his dao.
11. Nungma nimlu adzong-td hlir-deng   The blacksmith you were looking for yester-
    bá-ta om-oy.   day is here.
12. Baipoia kla koymani kan-om-lal-in   When we were at Baipola's village we
    arúwul-in hai kau-htawk-oy.   worked together.
13. Bá dil-nau ahtá-loh   ...   It is bad to want food.
14. Nungma eng-loh i-dil fo-vey   ...   You always want something.
15. Koyma ti-tár engma om-loh   ...   I have nothing to do.
16. In-tár eng-loh-tál min pé-rók   ... Give me something to drink.
17. Hé-ml-téy engoy an-dil ?   ...   What do they want ?

18. Nuagma treboag pakat lei í-dú-em ? ... Do you want to buy a cow ?
19. Nuagma dzáng-bán brái í-dú-ey ... You want to sell your ring.
20. Eng-púit í-dil, lá-lang ei-rók ... Whatever you fancy take and eat.

EXERCISE 64.

Pi̇, grandmother ; tá, to weave ; táp, to weep ; wáí, to laugh ; vaíhlo, tobacco ; vaí-bol, a pipe ; vei, foreign ; hla medicine, a drug ; béi, a bowl, receptacle ; hor, a cent ; shen, red ; kershen, a Bengalee ; vanci, good fortune.

1. Nungma tchemtey koyma min pérók ... Give me your knife.
2. Koyma ka-pé-htci-lob-tchey koyma d I cannot give it you, my sister has taken it
   ashintá. away.
3. Nungma koyma pí bú í-pé-tem ? ... Have you given rice to my grandmother ?
4. Nungma ni koyma d huéna í-hral-tem ? Have you sold your dog to my sister ?
5. Koyma ni koyma bé-mí ka-hral-lob ... I did not sell it to her.
6. Ka-hral-tá-lob I have not sold it.
7. Voina ka-tí-htci-lob, nak-túka ka-tí- I cannot do it to-day, I will to-morrow.
   angey.
8. Koymani hé pd-un kan-tá-htci-ey ... We can weave this cloth.
9. Koymani kaa-táp-in nungma í-nui-ey, When we were weeping, you were laughing
   í-lam-in í-om-ey. and dancing.
10. Hé mi-tey nunmani ló an-vát-htci-lob, These men cannot cut their *jáms,* they have
    aamaai hséaa tchem om loh. no *daos.*
11. Nungma d engtiszgey a-om ? ... How is your brother ?
12. Koyma laí ina kor buéuan hstiang One can get a *dao* like this from the
    tchem mei. Bengalee at the chief's house.
13. Koyma, vaíhlo tlemtey nungma min Will you give me a little tobacco ?
    pé-ang-em ?
14. I-vaíbel koyma min pérók ... Give me your pipe.
15. Nungma d ama tchem koyma ni hnit Will your sister lend me her *dao* for a couple
    bméaa, min pé-ang-em ? of days ?
16. Hí hmai-tocia-bók pú-un lei an-díl ... These women wish to buy cloth.
17. Koyma ang-in vanci pakat-ma an-om- No one is so fortunate as I am.
    loh.
18. Nungma engy í-in-dú ? ... What would you like to drink ?
19. Túi-ngey in-ang, rák-dzú ngey í-in- Will you drink water or spirits ?
    ang ?
20. Nungma min pék-ebú-un dzú ka-in- I will drink spirits if you give me some.
    angey.

EXERCISE 65.

Mí-hríang, a person ; ra, fruit ; hral, big basket ; em, small basket ; htpa, to seal, cause to be conveyed ; tlow, to weed, clear of weeds.

1. Nungma aao koyangey ? Koyma ní Where is your younger brother ? I have
   ama ka-hraltá. sold him my dog.

e

2. Hé mí-bríng tankanga aoi, roí-lien aoi, scíeí adaa-in ama-té aoi.	That man is rich, he is a powerful man ; all those goyal belong to him.
3. Nongma túagey vel tebey ? táp-tachídb.	Who has beaten you ? Do not cry.
4. Nuagma aí-in mín vel... ...	Your aunt beat me.
5. Koyma nopúi túa-tíeng-in koyma pú-an a-taú-loh ; ama túaa atsú-angey.	My wife has not yet washed my cloth, she will wash it now.
6. Koyma, aangma, íd hrai tachom-bnit ka-hraltá chiti-chú-aa nongma koyma tanka mín pé-loh.	I sold you twenty baskets of rice, but you have not paid me.
7. Koyma tíen mín khú-ngai-a abera em kat mín htow-ey.	My friend has kindly sent me a basket of fruit.
8. Nongma túa-tíeng-in ka-tchem mín pé-loh.	You have not yet sent me my *dao*.
9. Nuagma koyma mín agai-túa-em ? ...	Do you remember me ?
10. Hé tchem koyma nao tchom aoi ; ama mateilovia pék aoi ang-ey.	That is my brother's *dao*. You must be sure to give it to him.
11. Engey-tíngey apéh-loh ...	Why does he not give it.
12. Lal badaa mateilovia aboy aaí-aag-ey.	You must certainly tell the chief.
13. Hé lo hta-tak-in aa-tlow lah-vey ...	You have not well cleared this *jám*.
14. Koyma paaal a-tan pú-an pakní ka-tá-ey.	I am weaving a cloth for my husband.
15. Dzohldta koyangey om, aangma í-ahoy-htei-aag-em ?	Can you say where Dzohldí is ?
16. Ama Samata om ey ...	He is at Kamalong.
17. Nongma pé hnéna em í-om ? ...	Were you with your uncle ?
18. Koyma ama haém ka-om-loh ...	I was not with him.
19. Nongma Belkaia em í-kal ?	Are you going to Belkai ?
20. Ahtá apíang roo-taia-aag-tchey	You may bring it if it is good.

Exercise 66.

Hál, to set on fire ; apíung, as, whatever ; maaí, his own ; eag-kím, everything ; amda, prise ; ahár, difficult.

1. Mí apíung híín blé andaa-in aa-khú-ngai-ey.	Every one loves a good-hearted man.
2. Koyma lo vn apíung em í-hal ? ...	Did you burn the *jám* I cut ?
3. Nongma í-dú apíung kha-larók ...	Take whatever you like.
4. Nongma í-dú apíung aboy-rók ...	Say whatever you like.
5. Nongma í-bral-dú apíung bral-rók ...	Sell as you like.
6. Nongma í-dú apíung in, í-kal btei-aagey, í-baw btei angey.	You can come and go as you like.
7. Nongma í-dú apíung tírók ...	Do as you like.
8. Mí apíung maní tanka hta-tak-in bral-chú-aa hé mí híín ahtá ey.	The man who spends his money freely is good.

9.   Nuagma eng-lo rá í-dú apinag ka-hoa-angey. | I will bring you whatever fruit you like.
10. Kan-tchem lei apinag ai-chú-oa bé tchem hi ahtá daawk. | This dao is better than the one we have bought.
11. Ka-pú-an lei apiung koysngey ?   ... | Where is the cloth I bought ?
12. Eag-pók í-dil lá-lang eirók,   ... | Take whatever you fancy.
13. I-dú-tchin larok   ... | Take what you like.
14. Koyma engma kawsi-ta-loh   ... | I have got nothing.
15. Hé núla koyma htá ka-tí-lob-vey mi a-hao-fo-vey. | That girl is no good, she is always abusing people.
16. Koyma ama tchem vol-kat-ma min pó-loh. | He never gave me his dao.
17. Koyma ama-hi eng-kim ka-pey-ey   ... | I give him everything.
18. Hé nowpang-té-bók an-dm-in avel-ey. | All the boys beat him.
19. Pá-na roa-hi tmbúh amóa ahar ey ... | Do not buy cloth, it is too dear.
20. Nungma d ama tchem voins ahraltá ... | Your brother sold his dao to-day.

Exercise 67.

English, at no time ; táing, bread ; roiktar, youth ; rdi, intoxication ; dmno, a cup ; ahaldey-dm, a bottle ; rdak, to empty.

1.   Nungma engey í-ia ?   ... | What are you drinking ?
2.   Koyma dzú ka-in-ey   ... | I am drinking beer.
3.   Koyma pók-dzú ka-in-dé-ey | I also wish to drink beer.
4.   Koymani arák-dzú engma kan-in-loh, eng-tikma kan-in-loh. | We drink no spirits, we never drink.
5.   Koyma tchaw ka-ei koyma nao tsáng a-ei-ey. | I am eating rice, my brother is eating bread.
6.   Koymani rák-dzú themtey kan-in-angey. | We will drink a little liquor.
7.   Nungma ins in tir engma om-loh-remni? | Have you nothing to drink in the house ?
8.   Koyma dzú ka-in-loh, rák-dzú ka-in ... | I do not drink beer, I take spirits.
9.   Koymani túl kan-in-fo-vey, koyma nao dzú a-in-ey. | We always drink water, my brother drinks beer.
10. Nungma engma in-loh ; ka-lawh-ang-tchey. Indrúk. | You are drinking nothing, I challenge you. Drink.
11. Ka-roi-btar lai-in tui-lob-tecüb engma ka-in-ta-loh. | I drank nothing but water in my youth.
12. Hé mi tum-tak la a-rang-in themtey araí-tá. Mú-ta kai-tírok. | That man is a little drunk from much liquor. Let him go to sleep.
13. Tumtak-chú a-ei-loh chiti-chú-an tum-tak a-in-sy. | He does not eat much but he drinks a lot.
14. Koyma dzúno-vin túngey in-tá ? | Who has drunk out of my cup ?

15. Nimim arák-dud kaa-in-chú bétin shtá tí kan-bré-loh ; mánĭ-in shaidoy úm-kat, kaa-ĭn-ey.	The liquor we drank yesterday was so good I cannot tell you, each of us drank a bottle.
16. Nongma dzuo hat rúsk-laag min pérók.	Empty your glass and give it to me.
17. Tús-tleng-in ĭ-dzúno a-kat arúsk-loh : nongma rúsk-rók, ĭn-dzaw-rók.	You have not drunk a single glass yet. Drain it, drink it up.
18. Hú durrun arúsk ani, atsúnga engma onloh.	The basket is empty, there is nothing inside it.
19. Nungma ĭ-rúi-loh-vem ?	Are you not drunk ?
20. Nungma tlomtey-um ĭ-ei-loh-vey.	You have eaten scarcely any thing.

Exercise 68.

Bil, entrails ; bring, a morsel ; hai, to set fire ; khom, a measure, a flagon.

1. Naagma ĭ-ril a-tam-em ?	...	Are you hungry ?
2. Ei-chú-un ka-ei-btei-ey	...	Yes, I might eat a bit.
3. Koytha tam-tak ka-ril atam-ey	...	I am very hungry.
4. Tlam-tey eirók	...	Eat a little.
5. Nungma engey ei-dú ?	...	What would you like to eat ?
6. Nungma ĭ-ei-dú-em ?	...	Do you feel inclined to eat ?
7. Nungma engey ĭ-ei ?	...	What are you eating ?
8. Nungma ĭ-ei-loh	...	You do not eat.
9. Nungma ĭ-ei-doo-loh-vemal ?	...	Will you not eat ?
10. Koyma tam-tak ka-ei-tá	...	I have eaten much.
11. Adang bráng-kát eirók	...	Eat another bit.
12. Koyma adang ka-ei-btei-loh-vey	...	I can eat no more.
13. Nungma ĭ-túi abál-em ?	...	Are you thirsty ?
14. Nungma túi abál-loh-vem ?	...	Are you not thirsty ?
15. Koyma túi hál-in ka-hil-don-tá	...	I am dying of thirst.
16. Koyma lu-túr tlomtey min pérók	...	Give me a little to drink.
17. Nungma dzúno-kát thi ĭ-in-dú-em ?	...	Will you drink a cup of water ?
18. Rákdzi no-kát indrók	...	Drink a cup of liquor.
19. Adang no-kát in-lé-rók	...	Drink another cup.
20. Dzú khom-kát indrók	...	Drink a measure of beer.

Exercise 69.

Sha or tea, Soeh ; Gangham-mâ, pumpkin seeds ; shtan, fat ; par-vé, pigeon, tchhâm, to cook.

Ann tchaw ei-don-em ?	...	Will he eat ?
2. Kan ei-túr a-om-ang-em ?	...	Have we anything to eat ?
3. Koymanl hatma ei-a om-ang-em ?	...	Will you stay and eat with us ?
4. Koyma ka-om-btei-loh.	...	I cannot stay.

5.	Voica ni engichen ani-in tebaw ci ani-ang?	What time are we to dine to-day ?
6.	Ni tchaw-fák a-bún-ehú-un kan-ei-ang-ey.	We will eat at noon.
7.	Mi-dáng pakát-al koymani huén tebaw ei-túi a-hon-ang-em?	Is any one coming to eat with us ?
8.	A-haw-loh-vangey ...	No one is coming.
9.	A-hon-om-loh-vey ...	No one will stop to eat.
10.	Ki-túr engey om? ...	What is there to eat ?
11.	Sha-nghá rang-in i-kui-tir-em? ...	Have you sent for the fish ?
12.	Vák-tai ka-ei-ang-ey ...	I will eat pork.
13.	Engey i-en in-lang cirúk ...	What are you looking at, take—eat.
14.	Tlemtey fanghma-mú i-tá-don-em?	Will you take some pumpkin seeds ?
15.	Tlemtey abian hirók ...	Take a little fat.
16.	Nungma teá tlemtey ka-pé-dú-ey ...	I wish to give you a little meat.
17.	Eng tza ngey i-lagh-don? ...	What meat will you take ?
18.	Ilé par-vá-tai hrang-kát koyma min pé-ang -em?	Will you give me a bit of pigeon ?
19.	Adáng koyma ka-ei-htei-loh.	I can eat no more.
20.	Nungma tehaw-tehhúm koyma tum-tuk ka-ei-ey.	I have eaten plentifully of your cooking.

EXERCISE 70.

Atlúm, sweet ; hlong, platter ; ni-bliep, an umbrella.

1.	Duú-túi atlúm em ? ...	Is the beer sweet ?
2.	Atlúm dait ey.	It is very sweet.
3.	Hlong kan-tarang him-loh-vang-ey ; a-dang pahuli patúm hondrók.	There will not be enough plates for us ; bring two or three more.
4.	Ading voi-kat i-shoy-chú-ún ka-hri-angey.	If you will say it once again I shall under-stand.
5.	Eng-tikangey a-lo-kir-ang ? ...	What time will she return ?
6.	Nungma voi-duána lo-kir-htei-ang-em ?	Will you be able to return to-night ?
7.	Nungma i-lo-kir-chú-un i-far-nú ron-hondrók.	When you come again, bring your daughter.
8.	Nungma btei kir-shoy katiem-loh-vey.	I do not know how to reply to you.
9.	Koyma engtikangey a-lo-kir-ang ?	At what time will my father return ?
10.	Rowláila túua akai ahir-ló-tá.	Rowláila has just been and returned.
11.	Nungma ni-bliep ashin-khá a-pék-kir -taw-em ?	Have you returned the umbrella you took away ?
12.	Miu khúngoi-lang koyma tchaw min pé-hirók-á.	Be so good as to return my dao ?
13.	Khá-lai-in koyma tebem pé, min pé-hirók-á.	Give me back the *dao* I then lent you.
14.	Adang-tám shoy-ló-rók.	After that, speak again.

15. Nungma bta-tok-a om-loh-chú-no i-tlá-lé-ang-ey.   If you do not take care you will fall again.

16. Alá si-lé-angey.   He will eat again.

17. Nungma engtingey i-shoy-kir-loh ? ...   Why did you not speak again.

18. Nungma ni-bleip suktúka ka-pé-kir-ang-tobey.   I will return your umbrella to-morrow.

19. Nungma htú adang-dang-in i-shoy-a, Nungma htú engma i-hré-fia-loh-vey.   Your words are contradictory, there is no reliance on what you say.

20. Hi-isi-chow-loh vey.   There is no certainty.

EXERCISE 71.

1. Koyma tlanval-lal-in hétey loa ka-om-ey.   I used to live in this house in my youth.

2. Engtingey nangma hna-hudoga i-om ?   Why are you behind-hand ?

3. Nungma i-kul-htei-em-ey   ...   You are a good walker.

4. Nungma i-kol-htai em emol ?   ...   Are you a good walker ?

5. Nungma ii dzdog-bán moy dzit alei ahonlá, nongma tán adza-ai-in ahtá-bér atláoga adá-ey.   Your sister has bought some pretty rings, of which she has kept the best for you.

6. Nungma koyma ai-in bná i-btawk-htei-ey chiti-chú-on nangma ai-in koyma lám ka-tiom-daawk-ey.   You can work better than I, but I know how to dance better than you do.

7. Nungma koymani oan i-kol-ang-em ?   Will you go with me ?

8. Min khóngai-lang bú brai-hét min pé-rók.   Kindly give me a basket of rice.

9. Voism htú min tiom-chú-on lal lo kan-tlo-vang-ey.   To-day if ordered we will clear the chief's *júm.*

10. Voina hna blaw-dao-em ?   Shall we work to-day ?

11. Hétá lo-koldrók-ú now-paog-bók, in-há-tang-ey.   Come here children, you will be tired.

12. Hétí-ang tchem ka-dú-ey   ...   I want a *dao* like this.

13. Aumani dnao ahmél ah-angey   ...   The brother and sister are much alike.

14. Hé par adza-in Laijovi hné-nan om-tai-lang a-iom-angey.   [hmú-ey.   If you give all those flowers to Laijovi, she will be very pleased.

15. He khaw-htar hi-on andza-in tar ka-   In this new village they are all old people.

16. Nakin-hnúa ka-pé-ang-tchey túna chú-on eni-loh.   I will give it you, presently, not now.

17. Nungmani-hók hétá lo in-vá-dzaw-chú-on koy-ang khaw-btar i-chá-don ?   When you have exhausted the *júm* land here, where will you build your new village ?

18. Nungma bná i-btaw-loh-vá lal-in nang-ma ahda tobey.   You do no work, the chief will be angry with you.

19. Lo nimiua ka-vá tchium tá-ey   ...   I cut a great deal of *júm* yesterday.

20. Anal-ta-tchium-ey   ...   He laughed consumedly.

EXERCISE 72.

1.	Nimina lal-bŏk tarhier an-inam-ey ...	Yesterday the chiefs took the oath.
2.	Nangma kuldrŏk, in-bú-ni-rŏk chiï-loh-chü-un hnduga chü-un nangma i-kui-htei-loh-vang ey.	You go and bathe, else you will not be able to go.
3.	Aw! kasú túna koyma ka-kui-ang-a, ka-in-bú-ni-angey.	Yes, my mother, I will go now and bathe.
4.	Nangma engeytiangey i-nüi? ...	Why are you laughing?
5.	Nangma engey i-hmú-a i-nüi? ...	What are you laughing at?
6.	He khing-kat béng-bey tanka bnít eni-ey; hé lám khing-kát béng-bey tanka túm ani-ey; khing-bnít in tanka sgá mán ani ey.	One earring cost two rupees, the other three, both together cost five rupees.
7.	Nangma i-mit-a i-bmd-loh chá-un mi-dang htú-ahoy ka-oy-loh-vey.	If you had not seen it with your own eyes, I should not have believed it.
8.	Hing-tak-in shoy-rŏk	Say it from the beginning.
9.	Túna ka-kui-túr-ang-tzbey nangma tiy-lama kna i-htawk-dzow-vang-em?	If I let you go now will you finish the work by the evening?
10.	Koyma ka-hman-chú-un ka-lom-in ka-htawk-túr.	I shall do it with pleasure if I have leisure.
11.	Túna nangma i-bto-don-loh-vemni? ...	Have you not got up yet?
12.	Nangma i-rei-em i-hto-don-loh-vemni?	It is so late, have you not yet risen?
13.	Koyma ka-dám-loh voina ka-bto-htei-loh-vey.	I am sick I cannot get up to-day.
14.	Voina ni ahtá-em-ey, pawna kui ka-'dú-ey.	The day is so fine I wish to go out.
15.	Kong kirók	Shut the door.
16.	Kong-kar-hóng rŏk	Open the door.
17.	Nangma nao ni-tin kong hon-mi-in adai-ey.	Your younger brother leaves the door open every day.
18.	Voina pawna i-kng-dú-loh-vemni? ...	Do you not want to go out to-day?
19.	Voina ka-kui-loh-vang-ey ...	I shall not go to-day?
20.	Koyma ú ni-kát-a pawna vei-bnít a-kui-ey.	My brother goes out twice a day.

EXERCISE 73.

Trbá, to communicate; ahil, to put on; long, abbreviation for loh eang; hud, to win; di, to forbid; vok, entire; potet, to tear; pai, to abandon, throw away; khém, to bind on; dám, blank; tachém, things, goods; pik, to borrow.

1.	Koymapá atlengta, btú-btá min tchá-a.	My father has arrived, he has brought good news.
2.	Voina pá-on htar ahil-drok-ú, lál a-lo-tleng-ang-ey; btú ahoy-túr eni-ang-ey	Put on a new cloth to-day, the chief has arrived and will have something to say to us.

3.	Nungma eng-ting-ey em ?	How are you ?
4.	Rei ka-om-long-ey, ka-lá-hman-loh-vey	I will not be long, I am not at leisure.
5.	Voim i-om-dun-ngey, i-kul-dou ?	Are you going or do you stay to-day ?
6.	Volna nungma i-in-bú-un-ang-em ?	Will you wrestle to-day.
7.	Voina chú-en han-in-bó-un-long-ey, koyma ka-haé-loh-fo-vey-tchey.	I will not wrestle to-day, I always lose.
8.	Nungma blá i-btawk-chú-un-in i-hné-ang-ey.	If you work with a will you will win.
9.	Nungma nú a-öi-em ?	Has your mother forbid it.
10.	Hé nowrang shíd-loh, ama dier apótoi-vek-ey.	This is bad boy, his turban is all torn.
11.	Potei-lang, peirok	Tear it up and throw it away.
12.	Dier-dúm khim koyma dán eal	I am accustomed to wear a black turban.
13.	Hé-tiang tachúm pák-chú-un-in pék-kir-lé shta ey.	If you borrow things like this it is good to return them.
14.	Koyma nowpang-tey i-in-om-lena in-hong-terani ?	My children do you come after playing together.
15.	Héta io-hawrók, eng-lo ré ka-pé-ang-tchey.	Come here I will give you some fruit.
16.	Ka-ahem-ang-tchey	I will divide it.
17.	Ni-loh, ka-ahem daw-té	No, it is already divided.
18.	Engatangey nungma kong i-kar-rek-ley ?	Why have you shut all the doors ?
19.	Samat dora kulidr ka-braan-loh-vey	I have no time to go to Kassalong bazaar.
20.	Volna koymani hea htawk-tdr tam-luk a-om-ey.	We have much work to-day.

Exercise 74.

Ashú, hot ; ná, pain ; hrót, trouble ; vún, shy ; evar, clear ; páng, body ; pún, wound ; htak, to itch ; ltíp, to smart ; vandéai, unfortunate.

1.	Hé in túogey ahé ?	Who built this house ?
2.	Koyma ka-ríl-rú-a ka-en-in Mukia aha-hani-om-ey.	I believe it has been built by Moise.
3.	Nungma engjangey i-rei-tá ?	How long did you stay ?
4.	Nungma lai hodua ni eng-jangey i-on rei-tá ?	How long did you stay with the chief ?
5.	Ni atlagh hmá-in koyma ka-pang ashú-tey.	Just before sunset my body became hot.
6.	Koyma hea-htawk aium em-a ka-dám-loh-rey.	I am ill from working too much.
7.	Ama pé lua om-lai-chú-en ahté-lo a-om-ey.	She was very well when she was staying with her uncle.

8. Nungma ka-hmü-tir-chau i-hlin eng. How have you been since I saw you?
   tingey a-om?

9. Lom-dait-in ka-om-ey ... I have been flourishing.

10. Voina ka-hto htel-loh, ka-tá and ey ... I cannot get up to-day, I have a headache.

11. Nungma dám-loh-pók eul-loh-vey, nei- You are not sick, you are in no pain, you
    pók ná loh, nungma hun i-hrot-vung- are too lazy to go.
    ani.

12. Lo-hto-lang, lenga lo-knldrók. Itei-tuk Get up and come for a stroll. Do not delay.
    om-tscúh.

13. Vän avar om, ni ashá ey ... The sky is clear, the sun hot.

14. Ni a-lo-tscúak-tá. ... The sun has come out.

15. Ni atscúak-tá. ... The sun has risen.

16. Ni atlá-tá. ... The sun has set.

17. In pawns tscúak ilrúk-á ... Put him out of the house.

18. Koyma páng tum-tuk a-shá-ey ... My body is very hot.

19. Ka-pán ahták em, ahtip em ... My wound burns, pains.

20. Nungma vamlúal ani-ey, eug-kim blo You are very unfortunate no medicine can
    pók-pók-in abtá-loh-vang-ey. cure you.

EXERCISE 75.

Hǎag, a thorn; tchúla to sprat, pierce; hpul, to extract; achik, cold; tán, to lead; tscúm, to puff; hrt, a cold; hǎng, to burn; draw-tuk, exactly; iái tir, to force, compel.

1. Illo ei-dou-in hta-tuk ahrict ei-a ahtá-ey. It is proper to be cautious in the use of
   medicine.

2. Eng-tikangey ná-tá-túm? ... Since when did it begin to pain?

3. Eng-tika-khangey anát ... Since when did it pain?

4. Eng-tik-húna-ngey anát? ... When does it pain?

5. Ka-kút-a bling in a-tchún, hpuirúk ... I have run a thorn into my hand, take it out.

6. I-tsám pakat ka-hpol-augoy ... I will pull out one of your hairs.

7. Ka-há olúl-in, ahtlon-in aná ey ... It hurts to extract, to wrench out my tooth.

8. Túi lúm ani ka-aol ... I wish the water to be hot.

9. Túi-tchoy-khá ahoy-rúk-u, daing-a tui Tell the water-drawer to draw water early;
   tchoy-rók, ti-in ni asháng-chú-un tni if the day grows old the water will grow
   slím angey. hot.

10. Túi-lúm ka-tchum-dzow-tá I have made ready hot water.

11. Ashik em ey, koyma ka-hri-tlang-ey ... It is very chilly, I have caught a cold.

12. Túna ka-khin-ahik ey; roina ashik em I am cold now; it is very cold to-day.

13. Koyma ka-lo-hun-in nungma eng-ti- What were you doing when I came?
    lngey-om?

14. Mei ka-tiu-oy, mei ká-tscúm-ey ... I was lighting the fire, blowing it up.

15. Mei hta-tuk-in aking The fire burns well.

16. Adzaw-tuk-in kap-rok Fire exactly on the place.

17. Koyma túi lúm ka-dil-ey ... I have asked for hot water.

R

18. In ama-in akang tchop ani   ...   The house was burned down by accident.
19. Ama htú-in ani akul   ...   He went of his own accord.
20. Koyma htú-in ani ka-shoy, tdiná in   I am speaking of my own accord, no one
    min shoy htú-tir-loh; koyma min   forces me; do not be suspicious.
    ring-loh-tacúih.

Exercise 76.

Dzanlai, midnight; mút-hnúa, sleeping place.

1. Ama-in shoy-rók-tchoy   ...   Let him speak for himself.
2. Koyma ka-ni em min bton tún-tleng-in   I have not yet looked into the basket my
   ataing ka-en-loh-vey.   aunt sent me.
3. Koyma ú blíng parík ashá-tá   .   My brother has cut six trees.
4. Núi-tár htú a-om-loh-vey ndt-tachúh-d.   It is no laughing matter. Do not laugh.
5. Koyma bnén pawna í-knl-dú-maw? ..   Do you wish to go out with us?
6. Koyma htú min tchá-hhá abtá brilidr   I have some good news to tell, which has
   a-om-ey.   been communicated to me.
7. Kul ahún-tey .   ...   It is time to go.
8. Eng pú-na agey ka-kai-don?   ...   What cloth shall I wear.
9. Túna om-brí-rók koyma kong hon ka-   Stop a moment I want to open the door.
   du-ey.
10. Ama htú briét-chow loh-vey   ...   There is no depending on her word.
11. Nangma a-ret-tuk-in í-nú-a, í-btn-ra;   You always get up late; this is a bad custom
    í-dán ahtá-loh-vey.   of yours.
12. Itúthtar-lai-in dúinga hto-a ahta-ey,   When one is young it is good and proper to
    adik-ey.   rise early.
13. Nangma koyma nen í-nú-don-em?   ...   Will you sleep along with me?
14. Eagtingey key í tún-tleng-a í-mut-key í   How! what still sleeping! are you not
    Hetiang rei-tuk-a mút í-daak-loh-   ashamed to sleep so late?
    vemni?
15. Hétiang rei-tuk mút dzong adzak-tlegh-   I am ashamed much of sleeping so late.
    em-ey.
16. Tlai-lana ka-mú-twei-a, rei-tuk-in ka-   It is my custom to sleep early and rise late.
    hto-va koyma dún rni-ey.
17. Nangma koymani ai-in tkm-tey mú-ey   You have slept a little longer than we have.
18. Koymani rei-tuk kan-mú-ey   ...   We have slept late indeed.
19. Nimin-dsána bta-tak-in í-nú-loh   ...   You did not sleep well last night.
20. Tumtnk ka-mú-ta-loh, tú-na dzánlai ani-   I have not slept much and it is now mid-
    tá, koyma mút-hnuina ka-kul angey.   night; I shall go to bed.

Exercise 77.

K'tdi, to comb; talem, diligence; rána, jungle; bpi, to wash face; tawh, to wash; drú-drú, a frost.

1. Koyma hajien avandúni-a, anó ley apá   My friend is very unfortunate, his father
   pahnit shti-tá.   [hong-ey.   and mother have both died.
2. Nangma em ka-ron-tachin-in ka-lo-   I went to bring your basket.

3. Tún-tleng-in hren a-kai-loh-venmi? ... Have you not put on your waist cloth yet ?
4. Nungma pú-an shildrók ... Put on your cloth.
5. Túma koyma hren ka-kai-angey ... I will put on my waist cloth now.
6. Ru-i-tuk om-chu ka-ril-rú om-loh-vey... I do not wish to delay any longer.
7. Koyma hren nangma ka-kai-ang-ichey. I will give you my waist cloth to wear.
8. Túna koyma ka-shil-ang-ey, tlemtey om-hri-rók. I will put it on directly, stay a little.
9. Nungma tàm engey-tangey khui-loh? Why have you not combed your hair ?
10. Ilna-hiawk-túr a-om-a ka-khui bman-loh-vey. I had work to do, so had no leisure for hair-combing.
11. Nungma hétía taima chai-un ka-lom-ey. I am glad to see you so diligent.
12. Aui-loh. Nungma btú túk anl-loh; ka-nao hréta om-loh-vey, amani rima nimína akultí. No ; you do not speak the truth ; my brother is not here he went away yesterday to his own country.
13. Koyma htú adík ey, nimína ka-hmú tuk ey. I speak correctly, I certainly saw him yesterday.
14. Engeytangey túi ‡-roa-tchoy loh ley?... Why have you not drawn water ?
15. Il mai ka hpí-loh-vey ... I have not washed my face.
16. Pú-an tsawb-rók ... Wash the cloth.
17. Koymani Saipoia kúa kan-kul-in dsú-dsú kan-hmd-ey. Wo saw a festival as we were going to Saipoia's village.
18. Nungma farnú hía reng-in a-om-em?... Is your younger sister well ?
19. Tlai-lama koyma ka-kul-angey ... I will go in the evening.
20. Naktúka dsínga ka-lo-hong-ang-ey ... I will come to-morrow early.

EXERCISE 78.

Reng, to remain ; naktípa, day after to-morrow ; ngoi, silent, quiet ; mú, to repose ; nghil, forget ; mú-nghil, to sleep ; hév, to slant.

1. Hétichena ‡-om-roi l-lo-kul-loh-va; en-gey-tingey om reng ? You have not been to see us for so long, how is this ?
2. Naktípa tleng-túr-in ka-lo-hong-angey. I will come the day after to-morrow.
3. Nungma ‡-ahoy-fo-vey túna agol-reng-rók ka-mú-nghil-du-ey. You are always talking, be quiet a little I want to sleep.
4. Voina koyma hlá-tuk-a ka-kul-ey ... I have gone far to-day.
5. Nungma ú heyláma a-hong-angey ... Your brother will come this way.
6. Kúm eng-jang-ey eul-tá? ... How old are you ?
7. Tún-tleng-in koyma tchaw ka-ei-loh-vey I have not yet eaten.
8. Ni abértá, ka-kul-túr ani angey ... It is past twelve, I must go.
9. Ama ahon-tagh ka-ring-loh ... I do not believe he will come.
10. Voina nungma hlá-tuk-a emmí lo-hon? Have you come far to-day ?

11.	Tehaw airók aboy tachúh ...	Eat your dinner and don't talk.
12.	Tlailama eng-tik-húna ngey tehaw ol ...	What time do you eat in the evening.
13.	Lien-ngora kúa ka-kul-angey mí tam-dáit-in a-púng-ang-ey.	I will go to Lien-ngora's village, many people will be assembled there.
14.	Lien-ngora kúa ka-kul-angey mí tam-dáit-in ka-pún-tír-angey.	I will go to Lien-ngora's village and assemble many men there.
15	Lien-ngora kúa kul-túr vang-in mí tam-tuk ka-pún-tír-angey.	I will assemble many men to go Lien-ngora's village.
16.	Tum í-táp-onni ...	Were you crying just now?
17.	Ka-dám-loh-va, ka tap-ani ...	I was crying because I felt ill.
18.	Nungma hid cul ché-na ka-léng-ang-ey.	With your permission I will go for a stroll.
19.	Hao-rók, in-a kul a-hún-oy ...	Get up it is time to go home.
20.	Voina ka-mú-twei-ang-ey, ka-há-dait ...	I shall go to bed quickly to-day, I am very tired.

Exercise 79.

Bálagh, harvest; rám-taviah, to hunt; tchúm, cloud, mist.

1.	Nungma tlentey í-léng-lon em? ...	Will you take a short walk?
2.	Ni eng-tingey em? ...	What sort of day is it?
3.	Voina ni abid-in ka-hmú-ey ...	It seems fine to-day.
4.	Itis ashúar-loh-chú-na ka-léng-angey...	If it does not rain, I will take a stroll with you.
5.	Nimina al-in voina ni a-hté ey; bú alan abia ey.	To-day is a finer day than yesterday, good for the corn.
6.	Rúa-shúar-alon-chú-na abid-loh; rúa-shúar-lai-in mí anbá-in dím-loh-rey.	The rains are not healthy, at that time every one is ill.
7.	Nungma kul-lai-in rúa ashúar-loh-vey.	When you went it was not raining.
8.	Voina ní tleng-in rúa a-shúar-ang-ey ...	It will rain all day.
9.	Ni eng-tchengey tní-tá? ...	What time is it?
10.	Tchaw-fút a-hún-tá ...	It is noon.
11.	Bálagh a-hún-in ka-bard ...	I saw him at harvest time.
12.	In pawn í-tavía-loh-chú-na rúa-shúar-loh-vey.	It has not rained since you went out.
13.	Pawn í-tavía hma-chú-na rúa ashúar-loh-vang ey.	It will not rain until you go out.
14.	Pawn í-tavíak-hmé-loh í-dzong-chú-na rúa ashúar-loh-rang-ey.	It will not rain before you go out.
15.	Nungma pá a-rám-tavíak a-lo-haw koy-maní kan-bard.	We saw your uncle when he returned from hunting.
16.	Nungma ai-in rám-tavíak ka-rit-rú-ey.	I like hunting better than you do.
17.	Voi-in ní eng-tingey a-om	What sort of weather is it to-day?
18.	Ni abid-loh, tchúm a-tum-em ...	It is a dirty day, very cloudy.

| 19. | Voina rúa-shúar-túr ni ani-ey | ... | It is a rainy day to-day. |
| 20. | Voina rúa-shúar om-in ka-ring-ey | ... | It seems to me likely to rain to-day. |

Exercise 80.

Tú, wind ; líd, to blow ; htím, dark ; khúa-dúr, a storm ; mái, a drop ; hupai-ei, thunder ; achúr, to growl ; kawl, lightning ; kawl-phú, to lighten ; tdk, thunderbolt ; lei, earth ; lei-diak, mud ; riel, hail ; vúr, snow ; vai-vút, dust ; anál, slippery.

1.	Voina tú atlá-ang ey	...	There will be wind to-day.
2.	Koyma ka-ngai-tita voina ni abiá-angey.		I think it will be a fine day to-day.
3.	Tchúm miuing em, rúa-shúar-aug-in a-om-ey.		There is a heavy mist, it is just like rain.
4.	Ahtím om-ey	...	It is quite dark.
5.	Rúa a-shúar-don-tá	...	It has begun to rain.
6.	Vána tchúm atum ey, khúa adúr-máng-ey.		The sky is very cloudy, there will be a storm.
7.	Rúa atlá koymani kan-bré-máng-loh	...	We did not know that it rained.
8.	Rúa atlá-don-tá	.	Rain has began to fall.
9.	Rúa mái-hnit mái-túm ka-kút-a atlá	...	Two or three drops of rain have fallen on my hand.
10.	Tú atchuk-ey	...	The wind is strong.
11.	Tú tkemtey-ma om-loh	...	There is no wind at all.
12.	Nungma vána-aghúr (-blow-loh-romni?		Are you not afraid of thunder ?
13.	Kapui-ri ka-blow dait	...	I am much afraid of thunder.
14.	Túna kawl a-phú-ey, tók atlá-ey	...	It lightened just now, a thunderbolt has fallen.
15.	Ni abúl atér ka-bré-biel loh-rey	...	The day is variable, there is no dependance on it.
16.	Lei-diak tum-tuk a-om-ey	...	There is much mud.
17.	Riel atlá-ey ; vúr atlá-ang ey	...	It hails ; it will snow.
18.	Vai-vút a-tum-em	...	There is much dust.
19.	Anál em ey ; kul ahret om-ey	...	It is very slippery, difficult to walk.
20.	Koyma ka-blow-rey rúa-shúar-túr	...	I am afraid it will rain.

Exercise 81.

El, to squabble ; khai, to hang ; dzál-búk, guest house ; ding, to stand.

1.	Hé nangma-tá, hey-hi koyma-tá	...	This is yours, that is mine.
2.	Koyma non om-dú-loh-mi-vhú ka-en-htei-loh-vey.		Those who are not with me are against me.
3.	Nangma ni-loh-chú-un am-i-htei-loh-vaag ey.		You were not here therefore you can get nothing.
4.	Nungma al-in koyma ka-deng hmá-ahi-angey.		I shall arrive before you.

5. Nungma chú koyma min ngai-tda-loh-vey.	You do not remember me.
6. Héta nungma far-nd a-om-ey, ama tan engma a-hon-loh-vemai.	Your younger sister is here, have you brought anything for her?
7. Nungma koyma aso nan bid i-ei-fo-vey.	You are always squabbling with my brother.
8. Koya-kul-ngey ...	Where are you going?
9. Koyangey i-kul-ey. ...	Where have you been?
10. Koyangey kul-don? ...	Where are you about to go?
11. Nungma koyismangey i-lo-hon?	From whence do you come?
12. Hé aowpang bi koya-tangey hon? ...	Where does the child come from?
13. Koyangvy mi-don? ...	Whither bound?
14. Koyma tchem koyangey dá? ...	Where have you put my dao?
15. Em tanga a-da-ey tanwta a-khai-ey ...	It is in the basket hanging there.
16. Ko-nao i-ron-hnú-em? ...	Have you seen my brother.
17. Ka-nao i-hnú-em? ...	Do you see my brother?
18. Koyma dzái-ludk kong-kar ding a-om-ka-ron-buú-ey.	I saw him standing at the door of the guest house.
19. Tú vallei ngey a-daú? ...	Whose pipe was he smoking?
20. Nungma i-ril-rún bid i-shoy-emai? ...	Are you saying what you really think?

Exercise 82.

Kongfen, girdle; khal, hip; long, to enter, go in, go over; dawt, false; hàunga, near; abtao, fat; mhriek, oil, grease; pain, belly.

1. Nungma dzáng-bún koyangey? dzúng-a búnrúk.	Where is your ring, put it on your finger.
2. I-dzáng abrol em ey, bún hiel-loh-rang-ey.	Your finger is too large, you will not be able to get it on.
3. Kong-fen khil-a long-luh-vang. ...	The girdle will not come over the hips.
4. La-hrial shrol em, a-long-loh-vang-ey...	The thread is too big, it will not go in.
5. Kúm tachom-ngu a-long-ta-loh.	He will not see fifty again.
6. Koyma in tshnga min kul-pai-tschili, khúta ka-kul-luh-vang.	Do not take me into the house, I will not go there.
7. Nungma nao haéna hril-rúk koyma lo-va ka-hong-ang-ey.	Tell your brother I will come to the *júm*.
8. In tshnga kul-púi-rók-d ...	Take it away into the house.
9. Nungma koyma nen i-om-don-em? ...	Will you stay with me?
10. Koyma haéna om ...	I have it.
11. Nungma koyma nen in-om-lom-ang? ...	Will you play along with me?
12. Ka-mi-angey, ka-om-angey ...	I will lie down, I will remain.
13. Nungma koyma nen hné i-htawk-ang?	Will you work along with me?
14. Tán tkentey om-hri-rúk nungma engey i-du, engey i-dil? Shoy-rók.	Stay then a little; say, what do you wish, what do you want?

15. Húr-deng ina i-kul-loh min ti-a, ka-kul-ey ; ka ta-tecia-loh, dawt ani ey.
You say I did not go to the blacksmith's. I did go, I am not lazy, it is false.

16. Lal kieng-a daoi-tey a-kui-chú ka-hlow vey.
I am afraid to go late before the chief.

17. Nungma búin-láng ahti-loh, engma min pé-loh.
You are uncharitable, you have given me nothing.

18. Nungma pú-un i-tá emai ?   ...
Are you weaving cloth ?

19. Pú-un i-tá-chú-un nungma i-há-loh vemai ?
Are you not tired from weaving ?

20. Ka-hóng-htei-loh, tlomtey ahtao hon-drók.
I cannot open it, bring a little fat.

21. Ahtao i-nei-loh-vin sabrick bondrók ...
If you cannot get any fat bring some grease.

22. Ilná blawk-loh-vin a-om-a ahtao-vey...
He has grown fat from not working.

23. Nungma púm alšeu-dait-ey   ...
You are very corpulent.

Exercise 83.

I'ul. See Ex. 48 ; heaveng, God ; bhduroe, down ; hawaroe, lamp ; bmdrúm, north ; teebiulam, south ; tašk-lam, east ; tháng-lám, west ; mai-eng, flame-light ; mei-al, fire-flame.

1. Koyma min pálrúk   ...   Help me.

2. Nungma púi-a ka-da-ey   ...   I wish to help you.

3. Nungma hném blaw-tlo-vin ka-om-dé-ey.
I wish to stay and serve you.

4. Koyma tieu blaw-tlo-vín akultá ansi-angey maw, nei-loh-vangey maw, ka-hré-htei-loh chítú-chú-un ansi-angey ti-chu-un karii-rú-ey.
My friend has gone to seek for service; whether he will be successful or not I cannot tell, but I hope he will.

5. Kua-vang hném coglo-tul nei-tár ka-rii-rú-ey.
I hope to receive something from providence.

6. Koyinaoi hném nungma farui kul a-dé-ey.
Your sister wishes to accompany us.

7. Koyma engey ka-en ?   ...   What am I looking at.

8. Nungma bé-hi i-bmú-loh vemai ?   ...   Do not you see that ?

9. Koyma engma ka-hmú-loh   ...   I see nothing.

10. I-hmú-loh-chú-un, hta-tuh-in endrók ; en-loh-chú-un engtángey i-hmú-angley ?
If you cannot perceive it, look carefully ; how can you see unless you look ?

11. Nungma ú nímíng ka-hmú-tá   ...   I saw your brother yesterday.

12. Nungma pá koyma min hmú-loh   ...   Your uncle did not see me.

13. Nungma tieu ka-hmú-chú-un béta om-ti-in ka-hril-angey.
If I see your friend I will tell him you are here.

14. Nungma i-hmú-htei-ang em ? nungma mei-tár i-dú-maw ?
Can you see ; do you want a torch ?

15.	Nangma kong i-hmé-ang-eia?	...	Do you see the path?
16.	Ka-hmú-hici-loh-vey.	...	I cannot see it.
17.	Ama tén daong-chi-un i-nci-ang ey adaong-túr engey-tangey i-daak-ey?		Seek and you will find it; why are you ashamed to search?
18.	Koyma Saijvia túa kan-kul-don-in hé-mi-lú ka-hmú.		I saw that man when we went to Saijvia's village.
19.	Ahtim em, dzán onl; khia-var a-huai-loh.		It is very dark, it is night, the dawn is far off.
20.	Kong koy-lâma-agey akul? hmár-lâma-agey, tachím-lâma, tâng lâma, tsák-lâma-agey a-kul?		In what direction does the path go? North, south, west, or east?
21.	Koyma kawarar mei-eng ka-hmú-ey.		I see the light of a lamp.
22.	Khúa avár-don-tá.	...	It has begun to dawn.
23.	Kawarar cui-loh, tsé-ul ani.	...	It is not a lamp; it is fire.

Exercise 84.

1.	Koyma i-hména ka-kul-ong-ey ebití-chú-na hmú-ehá-á kul-tuchúh-ang-tebey.		I will go with you, but you must not go in front of me.
2.	Hú hmá-loh-vin vi-két en abti-ey	...	You should see it once in your life.
3.	Hmána ka-hmú mai-ok-in ahaél ahtá ey.		When I first saw you formerly you were good looking.
4.	Khia-vát hmá-in adang voi-kat tli alá-baur-ló-angey.		It will blow again before the morning.
5.	Nungma, ni engjá-tángey i-kóng-don?..		For how many days are you going out?
6.	Koyma ni-tin dzinga ka-kul-ey	...	I go every day early.
7.	Nungma nimina eng-tchén-a hia-agey i-kul?		How far did you go yesterday?
8.	Koyma pawna kul, ka-nú a-phái-loh-rey.		My mother does not permit me to go out-side.
9.	Eng-ja-rei-agey koy-lâma-agey i-lo-bon?		Whence do you come after so long delay?
10.	Lo vé ka-lo-bongey.		I come from the *jhm.*
11.	Datsailút voin a-kul-loh-vang; apá huéna ram-tsenak-a akul-ey.		Darsailút will not go to-day; he has gone hunting with his father.
12.	Koyma pá voikat-ma a-lo-tleng-loh-vang-ey.		My uncle will not come once even.
13.	Voina ni engtebra ani-in htir-dong-hók alo-tleng-ang?		What time to-day are the blacksmiths coming?
14.	Hmá-ahá-in ni hátí-teben ani-in alo-tleng-tá		They came formerly about this time.
15.	Koyma ú-hók voina Tsa-mat dora-tu alo-tleng-angey.		My sisters will arrive at Kassalong to-day.

16.	Voina lo vé koyma ka-kul-htei-loh, kapé alám-loh-vey,	I cannot go to the *jám* to-day, my father is sick.
17.	Koyma nao voina ak-haw-htei-loh-vangey.	My brother will not be able to come to-day.
18.	Hé tobem koyma-tá ani-chú-na nang-ma ka-pé-htei-angey.	If this *dzo* were mine I could give it to you.
19.	Nimina lo vé ka-kul-htei-loh ...	I could not go to the *jám* yesterday.
20.	Túna koyma hná-htawk-túr a-om-ey, ka-hmán-loh-vey.	I have work to do now, and am not at leisure.
21.	Ka-nao nen a-lo-haw-khá mi ka-hré-loh-vangey,	I do not know my brother's companion.
22.	Nangma nao akul-khá ka-hré-loh-vey	I did not know that your brother had gone.
23.	Nangma tsei-bai-búk i-hré-loh-vemui ?	Do you not know how to salute ?

(*Explanatory*).—The words *tsei-bai-búk* to salute or salaam, and *lei-ahái* writing, with *lei-ahái-tsetsei* reading, are parts of the Lushai speech, but the people themselves have no written character, nor do they employ among themselves any forms of salutation or politeness.

EXERCISE 66.

Líng, a boat ; htem, to send ; tchaw-flín, rice, ready cooked, done up in leaves ; htú-am, things, property ; khúm to hide ; lehl, chan, tribe ; mâ-ai-pat, a mountain.

1.	Nangma eugma i-ril atam loh-vem ? ...	Are you not a bit hungry ?
2.	Vák-tsá tlemtey nen elrók ...	Eat it with a little pork.
3.	Koyma inmiuk ka-ei-tá, túna ka-ril atam-loh.	I have eaten plenty, I am not hungry now.
4.	Adang tsi-tí hrang-kai elrók ...	Eat another bit of meat.
5.	Ilá naopang ni-ieng-in a-ei-ey	That boy eats all day long.
6.	Koymani tún-lai-in tsá-nghák ahtá kan-ei-ey,	We ate a good bit of fish just now.
7.	Tchaw-ei i-tshium-dzaw-tem ...	Have you made ready the dinner.
8.	Tún-tleng-in tshium-dzaw-loh-vey ...	It is not yet ready.
9.	Ka-pá tán tshium-fo-va-tda ahtá-ey ...	It should always be ready for father.
10.	Líng tshium-shá-in darók ...	Make ready the boat.
11.	Lo-vé koyma tán tchaw-fún-in mia htemlrók, tchaw tchúm ka-hman-loh-vey.	Send me my food to the field ready ; I have no time for cooking.
12.	Nuktúka ka-lo-hon-chú-un koyma htú-am tshium-sha-in darók.	Have my things ready by the time I come to-morrow.
13.	Nuktúka ka-lo-hon-chú-un htú-am nei-dzaw-túr-in tshiem-rok-ú.	Let me find everything ready when I come to-morrow.
14.	Nimina-khán-in htú-am tshium-sha-in darók kul-a, eugey-tingey hetiehen i-rei ?	I told you yesterday to have everything ready, how is it you are behind hand ?

E

15.	Tebaw ani-taw-em ?	...	Is the rice ready ?
16.	Túu-tleng-in tchaw a-hmin-loh	...	The rice is not done yet.
17.	Tebaw a-hmin-tem ?	...	Is the rice done ?
18.	I-hman-chó-an tleng-rók	...	Relieve him when you are ready.
19.	Ilé-mi-hi btú shoy-túr a-en-fo-vey	...	That man is always ready to speak.
20.	Nimlm nungma ka-ti-ebey tabiem-aba-in darúk kulf-a tána engtingry í-rei-tagh ?		I told you yesterday, have everything ready I mid, what is the delay now ?
21.	Nungma í-hti-loh-aha-an lal nungma vel-ang-tchey.		If you behave ill the chief will beat you.
22.	Nungma pá-un khdm-in kukhrók, kot ong reng-in, noogmaaí tchí-a bétiang dán a-om-ey.		Hide your face in Bengallm fashion ; it is the custom of your tribe to do so.
23.	Mé-ul-púl ang-in a-om-ey	...	It is like a big hill.

Exercise 86.

Tebel, to grasp ; vai, to row ; tái-hleó, to swim ; tan, to tie ; phol, to unloose ; tlí, to release ; undag, dream ; abawk, a knot ; tak, up ; tlang, down ; tái-haar, up-stream ; tái-mang, down-stream.

1.	Nungma lóng tchel í-tiem-em ?		Do you know how to take hold of a boat ?
2.	Nungma lóng vai í-tiem-em ?	...	Do you know how to row ?
3.	Nungma lóng atút í-tiem-loh-remní ?	...	Don't you know how to sit in a boat ?
4.	Nungma tái-hleo í-tiem-em	...	Do you know how to swim ?
5.	Lóng hrai tondrúk	...	Tie the boat up.
6.	Ilé hrai phehlrok	...	Let go this rope.
7.	Min tlárók	...	Release me.
8.	Túi bol-í-lang mao mldm-angey	...	The water will be about a whole bamboo in depth.
9.	Dzán khó-ai-in ka-mú-loh-rey, nming kanei-ey.		I did not sleep the whole night—I dreamed.
10.	Lóng phim aldm-ey, dzi-an-tlagh in-tabiem-rek-rúk-ú.		The boat is sinking, all be ready to jump.
11.	Nungma tái-hleo tiem-loh-chó-an koy-ma min tebeldrók.		If you do not know how to swim, catch hold of me.
12.	Abrúi abawk-in tondrók	...	Tie the rope in a knot.
13.	Ka-kút bétiang atebel-chú-na nná ey ...		Pressing my hand like that hurts.
14.	Koyma ka-kul-don-aw-ley	...	I am going then.
15.	Tlang-lama-ngey í-kul-ang, tmk-lama ngey í-kul-ang ?		Are you going up or down ?
16.	Túi haat-ang-ey í-kul-doo túi mong-ang-ey í-kul-don ?		Are you going up-stream or down ?
17.	Nungma eng-ey í-ti ?	...	What are you about ?
18.	Nungma btú mí-tiam ka-htawk-ey fey.		I have done what you told me.
19.	Voin thilamn engma ka-tí-loh-vaag-		I shall do nothing this evening.

20. Nungma nao tlan-in a-om-ey engma
hoa-btawk-loh.

Your brother is running about doing nothing.

21. Koyma hna-btawk-dzow-va ka-btawk-
chú-un koyma pakat-ma-in miu hao-
biai-loh-vang-ey.

When I have finished my work no one has
a right to abuse me.

22. Nungma hna-htawk bia-tuk-in i-htawk-
ey.

You have done your work well.

23. Nungma hna-htawk ahtá-ey ti-in ka-
biséna i-shoy koyma chú-nu htá ka-ti-
loh.

You told me the work was good, but it does
not seem so to me.

(*Explanatory*).—Sentences 8 and 10 require explanation. In sentences 15 and 16 the
phraseology is curious—thus : tanklam and tlang-lam here used in the sense of up-country or
down, mean also east and west. The formation of the country is such that in proceeding east
one rises by regular gradation and vice versa in going west. Sentence 16 *tui-daar, up-stream,*
means literally *nose to water,* while *mong* means *buttock or back-side.*

Exercise 87.

Koy, crooked ; tlloh, to snap ; tl.hé, break ; tchim, to break through ; rip, to tread ; fáng, spike ; bé tacoh-ri,
foot-fall; hé-akai, lame ; ktong, a plate.

1. Hé-mi-shoy tak-tuk-tór ani-angey
nungma ang kani-chú-un ka-shoy-
tuk-tuk-tór.

You certainly ought to tell him; were I in
your place I should do so.

2. Ama kút tcheldrok ...

Take hold of his hand.

3. Nungma boi koyma tiang nimina ala-
tá.

Your slave took my stick yesterday.

4. Nungma i-phal-chú-nu tanda-tél kat
kai-pui-angey.

If you permit me I will take a cheroot.

5. Kámina nungmani lo a-htá em? kúm-
ina-chú-un lo-vatrok, nakúma koyma
ka-lá-angey.

Have you good *júm* this year? For this year
go and *júm,* come to me next year and I
will take you.

6. Koyma hnéua hlaw i-tio-vang-em? ...

Will you serve me?

7. Voina artey pahuit ka-man-tá pakat ka-
tchua-tá pakat chú nungma tan ka-
hton-tá.

I caught two birds to-day, one I let go and
one I sent for you.

8. Koymani hadua taing a-dzaiua tchom-
tey a-om-loh chú-vang-in kút-in
hao phel-tagh.

We had no knife to cut the bread, therefore
we brake it with our hands.

9. Hé tiang hétia ti-hoy-chú-un atllok-
angey.

If you bend that stick so it will break.

10. Tiang atllok-in ka-ring-loh ...

I do not believe it will break.

11. Koyma ti-tlia ka-tdm-loh-vey ...

I do not wish to break it.

12. Lo tlaw ka-tdm-loh vey ...

I don't want to work at the *júm.*

13. Hé naopang danno pakat a-ti-ké-tá; ní kat in pahaít atí-ké-tá; ni-tin-in pakat atí-ké-fo-vey.

That boy has broken a cup, he breaks two a day, he always breaks one every day.

14. Nimín-pía danno pahaít atíkétá ...

He broke two the day before yesterday.

15. Nakíípa kleng palí pa-nga ati-ké-ang-ey.

The day after to-morrow he will smash four or five plates.

16. Talakin ráp-rók lúka tchim-angey, í-ilang cy.

Tread carefully, the platform will break through and you will fall.

17. Nungma engey ení-tagh? í-ké alal-ley.

What is the matter with you? you are lame.

18. Hé láma ka-bon-in kong-a fúog ka-ráp-cy.

In coming here I trod on a spike in the road.

19. Dzoi-tak-in kaldrók, í-ké-tœch-rí alicn cy.

Go gently, you tread heavily.

20. Hé mí-bring bí, bíd shoytúr a-ril-ró-cy.

That person is considering what reply to make.

21. Nungma engey íshoy? ...

What do you say?

22. Ka-bril-dzow-tá ...

I have spoken.

23. Nungma táugey dzawt? ...

Who asked you?

Exercise 66.

Awm, breast, chest; bíd-pol grievance; dúm-do-tm, hookah; dœb, to tuck in; bing, to stop, cram; hid-shoy, conversation; tœtal, to offend.

1. Lal alo-tœúia-lob-chu-an engey tangey kan-kul-ang?

What is the use of going when the chief has not come out?

2. Nimína tœw mí-tey, koyma bnúna anshoy-cy, koyma neitúr shtœn an-pal-ey.

They told me yesterday that they had thrown away half what I was to get.

3. Lal bnúna shin-túr shta-loh ...

It is not good to take it before the chief.

4. Ká-kbá peyrók ...

Give it to him.

5. Taaw mí taaw en-tlarók koyma katí-a koyma kashoyey.

I say that I tell that man to stand sentry.

6. Dzoi-tuk-in kaldrók, í-ké-tadh-ri alicn ey

Go gently, your footfall is heavy.

7. Tien pá, awm ati-hí engey-tíngey? ...

Oh friend! what do they mean by "awm"?

8. Ka-awm-a min vún-ey atí ...

He says he beat me on the breast.

9. Ama fœroú ína kulang-in ka-bríor ...

I believe she has gone to her sister's.

10. Hé mí pai-in koymaní kan-kul-tár eaí-angey.

We shall have to go and leave her behind.

11. Taaw mí-tey an-hid-shoy nakin-huía koyma min bril-angey.

I shall be told what they are saying by-and-bye.

12. Hé eny bœn-htawk-túr-in? ...

What is the use of that?

13. Hé engey-taugey? ...

What is that for?

14.	Eng kti-poi-ngey om?	...	What complaint have you to make?
15.	Apei om-chú-un shoytúk-i	...	If you have any complaint to make, speak.
16.	Deo-joug-in bé-hi engey í-ti?	...	What do you call that in Lushai?
17.	Nungma engtingey i-shoy htai?	...	How can you say so?
18.	Tsaw tsaw dúm-do-úm kss-ti	...	We call that "dum-do-im," (a bookah.)
19.	Pawna omtút-in pú-na, tchoy-hng deob-rók.		Raise up the outside cloth a little and tuck it in.
20.	Nungma btú-shoy sbáng-loh	...	Your tongue never stops.
21.	Tih atang-loh	...	The blood is not stopped.
22.	Húa-shuat sbáng tá	...	The rain has stopped.
23.	Tsaw mi-tey htin-úr báag-tirok		Stop those men from quarrelling.
24.	Ka-shoy tsdal-ngey	...	I shall offend by speaking.
25.	Nungma mi-tadal-pá	...	You are an offensive fellow.

EXERCISE 69.

Dsick, colour; hmy, to smear; hin-hnoy, to dye; a-shen, red; a-ngo, white; a-eng, yellow; a-hrïng, blue; a-dum, black; tschám-dawng, merchandise; khám, sleeping-room.

1.	Hé-hi eng daick ngey?	...	What colour is this?
2.	Eng daick ngey om?	...	What colours are there?
3.	Adzick a-om-em?	...	Is it coloured?
4.	Nungma pú-un eng hlo-agey í-hnoy? a-shen-ngey, a-ngo-ngey, a-eng-ngey, a-hrïng-ngey í-hnoy?		What colour is your cloth dyed? Is it red, white, yellow, or blue?
5.	A-dúm em ey	...	It is very black.
6.	Khin-hiim-em, ama pú-un a-dóm-ngey, a-ngo, koyma ka-shoy-htei-loh.		It is so dark I cannot tell whether his cloth is white or black.
7.	Hé bid n-hnok em, koyma ka-shoy htei-loh.		This is very difficult, I cannot say it.
8.	Amak om, amak-ver-ey?	...	It is very wonderful, most wonderful!
9.	Nungma í-hri-oto voina ni a-btá-túr? ...		Do you know if it will be fine to-day?
10.	Koyma ka-agai-túia voina ni a-btá-angey, koyma ti-tuk-in ka-shoy-htei-loh.		I think it will be fine, but I cannot say for certain.
11.	A-haw-loh-vang-ey	...	They will not come.
12.	Koyma púk bétí-ang ka-hlow-vey	...	I also fear the same.
13.	Eng-ti-hangey tschám-dawnga í-kul?		When do you go a trading?
14.	Tdua koyma ka-kul tuk-tuk-don aoi-ang-ey.		Now I really must go.
15.	Nungma í-kul-twni-do-ey [ley?		You wish to go very quickly.
16.	Nungma engey-tingey í-kul-twni-dú-		Why do you wish to go so soon?
17.	Nungma tiemtey om-túr mi-angey ...		You must stay a little.
18.	Nakína ka-hou-ló-chú-un a-rei-tuk om-htei-angey, túua-chú-un rei-tuk ka-ou htei-lok-vey.		When I come again I will stay longer, now I am not able to make a long stay.

19. Xuyma min hril-loh   ...   He did not tell me.
20. A-btd-lob-vin engry ka-ti-ang. Ni-   I cannot help it if it is bad. Let it be.
    rók-tery.
21. Ama a-lo-tleng-chd-on kal-tirók   ...   Send him when he arrives.
22. Koyma kbúm-a lo-haw-tsebdh-ú, pawna   Do not come into my sleeping-room, stay
    on rók-ú.   outside.
23. Engry-lingry koyma nen min hao?   ...   Why are you abusing me?

Exercise 90.

Tcheng, lock of gun; alipal, cock of gun ; a-nghing, lame; atul, excellent.

1. Hé mí ang pakat-ma a-btá an-om-loh.   There is not one so good as he is.
2. Ngol-reng-a om-tdr nungma vol eng-   How often am I to tell you to keep quiet?
   jangry ka-aboy-ang?
3. Hé sillai tcheng ahtái ani ey, alipal a- The lock of this gun is old and the cock loose,
   nghing ey, chiti-chú-on atul em ey ad-   but it carries a long way and shoots
   sawn-tuk a-káp-htei-ey.   straight.
4. Khai! ki atary-ang-chú   ...   Take care the dog may bite.
5. Taaw mi a-dú-loh-chd-no kul-pui-lang   If he does not want it, take it away and throw
   idi-pal-a paitúk-ú.   it into the river.
6. Ka-khda kúl-púi tdn-tleng-in khaw-   I have not yet finished constructing, erecting,
   dsow-lob-rey, teow-dsow-lob-vey.   the village stockade.
7. Hém hmdn btá ani-ey   ...   This is a good place.
8. Ka jong btei-loh ka-aw atacháng-ey ... I am hoarse and cannot speak well.
9. Hé kong pahnit-a koy-ham-angry min   Of these two roads which shall I take?
   kal-pui-don?
10. Hé sillai pahnit-hi khoi-angry ahtá- Which is the best of these two guns?
    daawk?
11. Avéng eng-ti-ang ngry?   ...   How broad is it?
12. Mi khaw-lam ai-chú-on mani khawlam   Of all countries one's own is the best.
    a-btá-daawk.
13. Lal-ahai i-daick emai?   Are you writing?
14. Taaw mi-toy taaw, in tsúnga lu-sirók-n. Forbid them coming into the house.
15. Taaw mi-toy taaw in tsúnga hi-tir-   Do not let them into the house. Let them
    tsebúh-ú. Omrók lacy. Bang-tirúk.   stay. Stop them.
16. Shin-kir-lang, daink   ...   Put it back again.
17. Chitl-ang btd dang-lam shoy tsebdh ... Do not say so again.
18. Fag-tchemgry mdt-ang tow-ta-tchey ?... How long have you been awake?
19. Ka-kul-daow-in. Ka-kul-hmi-in   ... After I am gone. Before I go.
20. Nichúm ka-md-dú, tíma ka-mú-ta-   I wanted to sleep before, but now I am not
    tscuak-loh.   sleepy.
21. Nongmani Dzo pakat-al bé-mi-hi ahul-   Some of your Kookies have broken this.
    tí.

22.	Dám-tieng-in hêta hi-na ka-om-angey.	I shall stay here as long as I am well.
23.	Alá-ei-lé-angey ...	He will eat again.
24.	He latahui-dziak adik-loh nungma dzich-nghil-rúk.	That letter is written wrong, correct it.

---

1. *Story: The Consequences.*

Tehem tadroi kai-knang pán a-kut a-tacrt. A-hila a-úra, ropui kima saha tlagh ; hting varúng akha-ím varúng túka den-suk ; varúng chd-un-in ling-kin báh ahtai bteh ;*   *   *

*   *   *   *

*   *   *   *

*   *   *   *

Aling-kin chd-na tsa-nghui mit atscét suk ; atsa-nghui chd-un-in lág omna hná-tchmg a-bydr-suk ; bag, sai béng-a alút ; asai chd-un-in tátrey in atlaw-taciek-suk ; tátrey in i kút a-va-tlagh ey.

*   *   *   *

*   *   *   *

*   *   *   *

*   *   *   *

Engatangoy tér-tey ini-kút a-va-tlagh? Sai-in ka-in atlaw-taciok tey. Engatangey sai-a mi-in atlaw-taciok? Ani-pót hig ka-béng-a avá-lé-ey. Engatangey lág mi-béng-a va-lé-ey? Anipót hig ka-béng-a va-lé-ey. Tsa-nghui-in ka-omna tahong a-bydr-ey.

A man was sharpening his *dao* (by the river side) and the father of (all) prawns bit him in the hand. The man became angry and (with one stroke of his *dao*) cut down a clump of big bamboos ; a fruit fell from the bamboos and struck a bird on the nape of the neck ; the bird (in his pain) scratched up an ant's nest with his feet ; the ant (irritated) bit a wild boar in the eye, and the boar (rushing off with one toss of his head) bore down a plantain tree where a bat dwelt under a leaf ; the bat (terrified) sought refuge in the ear of an elephant, and the elephant (driven out of his senses by this unwonted intrusion) kicked down the house of an old woman (who lived hard by), the old woman was so frightened that she rushed out and fell into the well.

Why did this old woman thus fall into the well? "Because the elephant kicked down my house." Why did the elephant kick down the house of another person? "So indeed I did, but a bat entered into my ear (and I knew not what I was doing)." Why did the bat go into the ear of another? "Even so (said the elephant) the bat went into my ear." "The wild boar (said the bat) swept down my dwelling place."

Té is sharpen ; kai-knang, a prawn ; ropui, a sort of bamboo ; kim, a clump ; kha-im, a species of fruit ; táh, the nape of neck ; ling-kin, ant ; háh, nest ; ahtai-bteh, to scratch up ; tsa-nghui, wild boar ; bág, a bat ; hna-tchang, plantain ; bydr, to bear away, carry on forehead ; mi, elephant ; lút, to enter ; kur, a hole, cavity ; hná, border ; ch, to excrete ; Vá—see m. sentence 12, Ex. 16.

Engatangey us-nghul-in mi omna hm-tchung
l-bpur-ey?"Ling-kin-inka-mit-a avá-tacé-ey."
Engatangey ling-kin-mi-mit l-tacé? "Var-
úng-in mi-búh vá-hlai htch-ey." Engatangey
ini-búh l-hlai-htch-ey? A-kha-ám-in ka-túk-a
mi va-den-ey." Engatangey kha-úm mi túk-
chú den? "Aul-pak ropui-in mi vá-rd ashagh-
ey." Engatangey ropul mi-chú rú-ak tlagh?
"Tehem tadroh-l-un mi vá-ehá-tlagh-ey."
Engeytangey tchem tadroi mi-chú sha-tlagh?
"Kai-kuang-in ku-kút-a avá-tacé-ey." Engatangey kai-kuang mi kút l-tacé? "Ka-tacó
lrám-hrim."

Why did the boar sweep down the dwelling
place of another? "The ants bit me in the
eye," (said the boar.) Why did the ants
bite the eye of another? "The bird
scratched as up," (replied the ants). Why
did you scratch up the ant's nest? "A
fruit fell on my neck." Why did the
fruit fall on the neck of another." "The
bamboos swept me down." Why did the
bamboos fall down? "The dao-sharpener
cut us down." Why did the dao-sharpener cut down (the bamboos)? "A prawn
bit me in the hand." Why did the prawn
bite another's hand? "I did so, whether
or no," said the prawn-father.

This little story finds a parallel in our own English nursery tale of, how "—— then the
cat began to kill the rat, the rat began to gnaw the rope, the rope began to hang the butcher,
the butcher began to kill the ox, the ox began to drink the water, the water began to quench
the fire, the fire began to burn the stick, the stick began to beat the pig," and thus enabled the
old woman to get home before night-fall.

The above Dzo story was told me by Chamán, a boy of about 14, in the village of the
Lushai chief Rutton Poia. During the narration we were surrounded by a circle of children
who listened with great delight, although they must have heard the tale often before. Like
Squire Hardcastle's story of 'grouse in the gun-room' however the story had not lost flavour
by age or repetition—but the climax was reached when I afterwards read out from my note
book what had been related, and the shouts of laughter brought the chief out of his house
to see what was the matter.

Vá-rú, to eat and cause to fall; llram-hrim, whether or no; with your leave or without.

No. 2.—*Story of Lál Rodnga.*

Rúlpai ngún-tchét angún-chú núlé-in su-hlaw,
chiti-chú-nu núla pakai-in ahilaw-dú-loh:
chiti-chú-un rúlpai húing haul ngúna aichét,
chiti-chú-un rúlpai-in atché, Tui-Roanga i-
tleng-chú-ua jiow-rín nawt-drós, tá-tuk ani-
angey.

The big snake made bracelets, the maidens
did service for these bracelets, but there
was one girl who did not wish to serve.
On this the big snake (cunningly) made a
bracelet using the juice of certain herbs,
and he told (the girl) when you go down
to the Tui Roang rub this bracelet and
clean it with sand; it will be very good.

Rúl, a snake; rúl-pui, a snake of the Python species, to which among all the hill tribes peculiar and magic
attributes are assigned; ngún, a kind of bracelet; haul, jaim, asp; teha, to inform, give news; jiow, sand; ocut,
to clean by rubbing, to scrub; tchét, to be spoiled; mit-tal, tears; shrúk, wipe away with wrist; mit-del, blindness.

Chúl-chú-un anawtá, aichota-rok. Atáptá, mit-tai a-hrúk-in amit adeka; a-htien chú-un apah abril-chú-un, apah-in mí-taeal-nú ati, mí-tin-in agán an-hlaw ama-in ahlaw-dú-loh, mí-tin-in lú-rók-á, ron-daon-drók-ii.

* * * *

Araltá, htien-nú pók a-raitá, chúlchá-un fa a-naitá, an-pahait-in; ahtien-nú afá hmai-tacla ani, amit-del afa mí-pa ani, an-hrol-a ai-in neitá. Chiti-chú-un rúl-pui-in ka-fa-nú i-nei aii amán perók ati-ey. Tú-na péktút a-omloh, ni-dan-ga ka-pé-ang-ichey ati-ey, chitl-chú-an rúlpai atotá mí-del afa, almíng Lamdzára anopul ahútá; kmára a-kaltá, hmara-kal-chú-un hmei-htai lo vá tae-nghul, ngbul-pui-taen, alnitá, bú a-ci-ey.

* * * *

Chúl-chú-un ngbul-pui-taen htí-hlúm-htei an-om-chú-un ka-fa-nú nen ka-nei-úr-angey. Lamdzára chú-un a-ngoi-a in taenga alútá. "Kapl engey in-shoy?" "Engma kan-shoy-loh." "In-shoy-khá ka-briet-kha-ley, shoy rók-ii"—"Koyma lo vá ngbul-pui-taen alútá, bú a-ci-a, ka-naeng ang-in, ahtí-hlám-htei an-om-chú-un ka-fand nen ka-nei-úr-angey ka-tí-ey." "Koyma kanel angey" chiti-chú-un ané-in "Neirók" ati-ey.

* * * *

Koavét chú-un Lamdzára lo vá akultá, htai-pui-in a-tchang-ey; ngul-reng-in a-om-a. Ngbul-pui-taen a-lo hoag-ey, atieng ngem-loh; tae-nghul try a-en-úr-ey chúl-chú-un

---

On her rubbing it it became entirely spoilt. She wept, and in wiping away the tears she became blind. Her friend (who was with her ran and) told her father. Fool girl! said he every one worked for the bracelets but she did not wish to work: Carry her off, any one may do what they like with her.

The girl and her friend both became pregnant and were each delivered of a child; the friend's child was a girl, the blind girl's a boy. They were born quite grown up. On this the snake said "You have got my daughter pay me her price;" she replied, "I have nothing now to give you, some other day I will pay you." After this the snake disappeared. The son of the blind girl, by name Lamdzára, married a wife and she died. He (left home and) went northward, going on (he found) a wild boar who had entered into the joom-field of a widow and was eating the rice; It was a very big boar.

The widow had said, "If there be any one who can slay this boar I will give him my daughter [in marriage"]. Lamdzára heard this and entered into the house. "What were you saying Granny"? "We were saying nothing." "I know what you said, come speak." "A wild boar has entered my field and is eating (all) the grain; (I am) as if in a dream; whoever can slay the beast I will marry my daughter to him; that is what I said." "I am the man for your daughter"said Lamdzára, however, the mother only said "Win her."

At dawn Lamdzára went to the joom, and watched with a big javelin, be stayed very quiet. The wild boar came, he dared not enter (the field) but told a small pig

---

Mi-taai, a quarrelsome foolish person; ron-daon, to carry off; rai, to be pregnant; kmei-htai, a widow; hti-hlúm, to slay; pi, grandmother; máng, a dream; htái, an arrow; tching, to watch; ngám, to dare.

a-en-dú-loh. Tlip puí at-puí tía, haug-tacérúk
atí-ey chití-chú-un akultá: ngbuí-puí-tsen
hnéns abril, " koyma ka-hang-tacé-a atchey
dé-loh, ahíl-ani-ang-ey." Sadzú hang-kaí-
drók, abéng kbing-kat ci-dzow-rók" chití-
chú-nn saúzú ahang-kul-a, abéng kbing-kat
a-ci-dzow vek, atchey-dé-loh. chití-chú-nn
sadzú akultá, ngbuí-puí-tsen hnéns aahoy"
abeng khíng-kat ka-ci-dzow-vek a-tchey dú-
loh, ahíl-ani-angey." Chití-chú-un ngbuí-puí-
tsen ahang-kultá, Lamdzáran btuí-ío akáp-
hlóm-té, akáp-hlóm chú-nn ngbuí-puí-tsen
abtl-té.

*   *   *   *

*   *   *   *

Ahtí-chú-nn, ahí-puí a-té chú-un btem-tleng
tía ani. Chití-chúan Lamdzára ína ahawíá ;
mí hnéns ngbuí-puí-tsen ka-kap-hlóm-té atí,
ahá btem-tleng tía ani tí-in aahoy, chití-chú-
nn kaldrók u atsá í-hpúr-ang atí ; chití-chú-
nn sadzu-ín akuí-a, Kuavang-in tsa-ngbuí
ano-tey-ín aa-tleng-té, tey tuk tey anitá.
" Khoí ! Lamdzára, í-ngbuí-puí-tsen káp-hlam-
chíd tey tuk ani ; ahá btem-tleng tía ani tí-io'
í-ahoy ; tsa-ngbuí tey tuk ani." Chití-chú-un
Lamdzára ahoá adzuí, adzuía Kuavang ín-a
alátá, " Kuavang ín atsher" atí ey ; " lo-lú-
tschúb" atí.   " Ka lát-ang-chú, koyma
ngbuí-puí-tsen káp-ín-la ani lom ley ? ngbuí-
puí-tsen mín pérúk-á." Atí-chú-nn au-prétá ;
Chití-chú-un akuí-puí a-btíru-tey hnéns " Hei
ley !

●

to go before and look about, the small pig
however did not wish to go. Then he
called a hornet as large as a capon and
said " Go, sting him." The hornet went
but (returned and) said to the boar " I
went and hit him, but he would not move,
he must be dead." " Bat, go you, eat
his ear off on one side," so the rat went
and ate the whole of a ear on one side,
but he would not move. So the rat returned, and said to the wild boar " I ate
up the whole of one of his ears, but he
would not move, he is certainly dead."
At last the wild boar went himself, and
Lamdzára smote him with the javelin a
death blow, so he died.

Having killed him he measured his tusks and
they were as big as a weaver's shuttle :
so Lamdzára went home and told the people
that he had killed the wild boar, and that
its tusks was as large as the shuttle of a
weaver. " Go and carry in the flesh" he
said, so everybody went. The Great Spirit
(meanwhile) had changed the big boar for
a small pig, it was a very little pig.
" Hulloa ! Lamdzára your mighty boar
you have killed is rather small ; you said its
teeth were like weaver's shuttles ; it is
indeed a small porker." Lamdzára however (paid no heed to their jeering) but
followed the foot-prints (of the Great Spirit)
and found that they went into the Spirit's
house. " Do not come in here" was said,
"the Great Spirit's house is 'tabú' (sacred)."
" I must come in, shall I not have the wild
boar I killed ? Give me the boar." On
his saying this they gave it to him and he
took it away to his friends. " Here you are,

Tlip, a hornet, or species of stinging fly ; tía, as big as, like ; sadzú, a rat ; tchey, to move, stir ; ahápuí,
tusks ; btem-tleng, a shuttle ; vsn, a cub, young one ; intleng, to exchange ; a-bué, footsteps ; dzuí, to follow ;
Kuaváng, God ; atsher, forbidden ; tabú, in quarantine ; kaí lom ley ? shall I not eat ? ka-eí lom-ioy ? shall I
not eat ? darchúsng, a gong ; tái-rsang-dár, a gong tempered in the magic water of the Tái-rsang stream
(see previous story), and supposed to possess magic properties.

ughol-pui-læn" ali, chiti-chú-un aiał an-
bjár tá. In an-tlêng-chú-un nopul anei-
tá, anei-dzaw-chú-un limat láma akultá,
anopai araitá; hmat-lama kulchá-un tái-
ruang-dat nei-tú hnéna atlêng-tá.

   *   *   *   *

   *   *   *   *

Ná pá tar ani, atar ati chú-un mi tæhom-tú
om-chú-un ka-dér ka-po-tuir. Chiti-chú-un
Lamdzárn in tuúngn aldtá " kopí engey in-
shoy?" "Engma kan-shoy-lob, in-shoy khi-
by, kan-máng-ang-in mi tæhom-tá om-chú-
un dér kan-po-ang, kan-ti-ey." " Keyma ka-
tæhom-mong-tchey-ú." Lamdzárn ati. Chiti-chú-un Lamdzárn chú-un " Lo-vá ka-fé-
angey " ati-ey " Vá férók," an-tí "Blak-lo kol-
drók" an-ti-ey. Chiti-chú-on riak-in akoltá;
lo-vá atlêng-chú-un, eng-lo blo-vin m-va-tsá
a-tachhúm, kusvar-in api-tey ahtou, mvu-tsd
api-tro an-ei-chú-un an-hil-tá.

   *   *   *   *

   *   *   *   *

Ahtí-chú-un adér skal-paith, in-a ahonga a-
nopul hnéna a-tlangtá; atlæng chú-un a-nopul
afá pám tsdnga om-in asong litsi; anl afék-
don-chú-un " Kanł trik-tail khúmrók " ali
" ra anldar-don-ey" chiti-chú-un and-in,
" Nang' apám tsdnga om, om-lo engey l-hriet-
ang" atis akhúm dá-loh. Lo vá atkng chú-
un rus ashdar-ta-tohium-ey, chiti-chú-un in-a
shawtá.

   *   *   *   *

   *   *   *   *

Kúmvár-lé-chú an afé-lé-don-a trik-tail khúm
a-túim, chu-tí chú-un apám tsúnga 'om-in

here is the wild boar," said he, so they
(cut up and) carried off the flesh.
When he reached the house he was married;
after the consummation of this affair he
(again) went northward (leaving) his wife
pregnant; going north he arrived at the
residence of those who possessed the
magic gong.

They were an old couple, (and were crooning
together that) " Had we some one to take
care of us (and cherish us in our old age)
we would learn him the gong." Lamdzárn
stepped into the house " What were you
saying Granny?" " We were not saying
any-thing particular, but were dreaming
as it were, of having some one to take care
of us to whom we could leave our gong."
" Let me take much care of you" said
Lamdzárn. Then Lamdzárn said " I will
go and work at the *júm*." " Go," returned
the old people," Go and stay there a little,"
so he went to stay. When he reached the
júm he cooked up a mess of bird's flesh
with some drugs, and at dawn (next day)
sent it to the old woman. The old couple
ate of the bird's meat and died.

On their death he took the gong, and going
home arrived at his wife's. On his arrival
he found that the child, of which his wife
was pregnant, was able to speak in the
womb. When its mother was going to
work in the *júm* it would say " Mother,
take the umbrella, it is going to rain." His
mother would reply " You unborn thing
what do you know about it?" and she
did not take the umbrella, but at the
júm it rained consumedly so she came
back home again.

Again next morning she was going to *júm*.
" Don't cover yourself with the umbrella"

Tæhom, to cherish, take care of; fék, to eat *júm*; riak, to remain; htao, to send; (example Vá-férók,
go *júm*; lo vát-rók, eat *júm*; lorá vá férók, go work in the *júm*;) trik-tail, a covering for the head, shoulders,
and back, made of leaves and wicker work, as a protection from rain or hail; khúm, to cover oneself.

"Kand teik-tail khém tachúb" ati; chútichú-un
anú in, "Apúm tsúnga om-tu engey i-brief-
ang " ati; ati chú-un lo vá atlengté, ni mahá-
ta-tchfum; chútachúan lo-a ahawta. Kusvár-
lé chú-an tachbún-a dailenga akul-a afá
bringté; in booya apú-tlá-tá; chutichú-un
médeú pahat aron-mun, chutichú-un in-a
ahawta anú-chú-un in "Engtingey i-son-muon-
htri " a-ti, " Ka-man-htei-ang-chú, kám
tachom ni kanitá, ka-hming Lál Rúanga "
ati.

*   *   *   *

A-hming Lál Rúanga ani, chú-tí-chú-un alei
ahpír, apa-in a-lei ahlep-tchhúmtá; ahlep
tchhúm-chú-un-in nula buéna " Ka-lei-hi engey-tingey atchhúm ley" ati, nula-chú-un, " i-
pá-in ahlep-tchhúm ani" ati chutichú-un apá
nen an-in-el-tá; Lál Rúanga chú-un " Kapá"
ati "lo blá-tuk-ngey kan-nei-ang, bnai-tuk-
ngey kan-nei-ang?" chutichú-un apá chú-un
" Il mi-tuk i-nei-ang" ati, Lál Rúanga chú-un
"Illa-tuk i-nei-ang" ati chutichú-un "Kapá lo
blá-a vá férúk" ati, apá chú-an " Riak-in ka-
htawk-angey," ati chú-an akultá; lo vá atleng chú-an kvichála dzán-a chú-un-in,—
keichalan atilyt;

Lál Rúanga pá chú-un a-hlowtá in-a ahaw-lé-tá.
" Khoi ! Lál Rúang auogma lo vá, vá férúk,
riak-in htawk-rúk." Lál Rúanga chú-un
aro-tchem ashín-a akultá, chútichú-an lo vá
atlengté chutichú-an khún ahúm-té, khun
ahúm-chúan krichala lo bawtá, atilyt-tá, chútichúan Lál Rúanga chúan aro-tchem atdm-tá
chuti-ohdan keichala ahlowté Lál Rúanga
chúan "Koyena Lál Rúanga" ati, tin ahnar-
in aro-tchem atdm-a.

said the child, however his mother (paid
no heed saying) " You are still in the
womb, what do you know about it." On
arriving at the *jấm* the son was extremely
hot, so she came home. Next day in the
morning her son was born. (She went out
of the house for a few minutes and) the
child fell (through the flooring) underneath the house, he caught a rat there and
came back to the house; his mother said
" How are you able to catch rats," " I
ought to be able," said he, " I am ten
years old, and my name is Lál Rúang."

His name was Lál Rúanga, but his tongue
was forked; his father had (split it) cut it
so. (One day) he said to a girl "This
tongue of mine, why is it cleft like this?"
the girl replied "Your father cut it," from
this time he and his father disagreed.
Lál Rúang said, " Father, shall we *jấm* far
off or near?" his father said, crar; while
Lál Rúang said, far; so at last they cut two
jấms. (One day) he said to his father
" Father go you and work at the far *jấm*,"
" I will work and stay there" said his
father and went. On arriving at the *jấm*,
at night a man-tiger (Keichala) came and
threatened him,

Lál Rúang's father was afraid and returned
home. "Now Lál Rúang," said he, " you
go and work in the *jấm* and stay there (all
night)." Lál Ruang took his pipes and
went off. He arrived at the *jấm* and it
grew dark, when it was dark Keichala
came and threatened him, but Lál Ruang
played on his pipes and Keichala became
frightened (himself). " I am Lál Ruang,"
said the boy, and then he played the pipes
through his nose.

Túm, to want, wish; tachbúa, day; dzan, night; dal, outskirts of a village; hring, to be born; pú-tla,
to fall through; lei, the tongue; ahpír, forked, double, plaited in two; hlep, to cut; tachúm, to sever, divide; el,
to oppose; keirhala, a man who has the power of transforming himself into a tiger; atilyt, to threaten, to
frighten, startle. Thre:—taw mi-ley vá tilytrúk, go and frighten these men; aro-tchem, reed pipes;
khun-htím, dark, nightfall; tsim, to play on an instrument.

Akút kúanga béng-a keichala chú-un dzasion mi-chú-in vá túen vey, kan túm tay ey, lo haw vairúk aü ey. Keichola chú-un " Ah" ati-a. A-tlém kót-a ldag púin om-a, tin Lál Búangan chútachóan htal a-káp, Kei-chala chúen shong em-a, " Lúng má-má htal-a háp keh, hoy chú mikáp tchela, avana-dou-em ; " mao hi aphút kawm ava-tm tlagh-a, tla " Hong-ang má-má a-tm fi jowra, koy chú mi tmt tchéla avana-don em." Tia Keichala chú-an ati-a " Lál Ruanga, in-gien-ang ? " " Aw " lé aü, " lo hawrúk lé " Lál Búangas ati chuti-chuan lai-ldiain in-tawk-ang ati chutichúan aa-kui vévé an-in-gien-té, Keichalan " Ka-kúa kan-dzin-ang " aü, " Koyma kúa ley " Lál Ruanga aü

*　　*　　*　　*

*　　*　　*　　*

Chutichúan aa-kulté, ankulahdan tm-nghal kul-kong-a alo-om-ey ; Keichala chúan " Hawrok htiran i-kap-ang " aü. Lál Ruanga chúan htal-pai-in akáp-klúmté, chutichúan a-bil-té, chutichúan Keichalan a-bel-in a-citá, Lál Ruanga chúan ahmin-in a-citá. Kún-vát chúan m-hulia, Keichala in-a atleogtá, chutichúan Lál Ruang chú a-mú-dát-té ; chuti-chúan Keichala' apá chúan " I-htien-pu eirók " aü, " kei-chúan a-htia themtey-in ka-ci-angey."

*　　*　　*　　*

Chutichúan Lál Ruanga a-bto-té " Keichala i-nú ley í-pá ka-en-angey " aü, Keichala chúan " Ea-tlágh aai loh " aü, Lal Ruanga chúan " Khoi l ka-en-angey " aü " Endrók " lé aü " en tedage a-om-ey " aü ; Lal Ruanga chúan avá-enté, aaú ley apá chú aaksi ang-in a-om. Chutichúan " Keichal, i-htien-pá khá, vák ei-tirúk " aü. Keichala chúan " Vák té-tak-ngey í-ci-dd ? " aü, " pai-tak-agey í-ci-dd ! "

" Come in the evening," said Lal Ruang, "in your own shape as a man, and we will play the pipes together." "Ah," said Keichala. A little way down was a big stone, at this Lal Ruanga fired an arrow and Keichala came to see—" Can you split rocks in half with a single arrow ? this is beyond me. It is wonderful." He stuck up a slender bamboo, and in the same manner cleft it in twa. " Can you also split reeds, I have to cut them. It is very wonderful." Then Keichala said, " Lal Ruang let us make friends." " Yes," he replied, " Come here then, we will meet in the middle," said Lal Ruanga ; so they went both together and made friends. Keichala said, " let us visit my village." " My village also," said Lal Ruanga.

So they went. In going a wild boar came on to the path. Keichala said, " Come my friend, you shall shoot it." Lal Ruanga shot and killed it with a big arrow, so it died, and Keichala ate it raw, while Lal Ruanga te it cooked. At dawn they went on (again) and arrived at Keichala's home, (where Lal Ruang laid down to rest), he however only pretended to sleep. Presently Keichala's father said, " Eat up your friend. If you (feel disposed to) eat him, I also will take a small piece of his heart." On this Lal Ruang got up, " Keichala," said he, " I should like to see your father and mother." Keichala said, " There is nothing to see." " Ah, but I must see them," said Lal Ruang. " Look then," he rejoined, " they are in the basket there." Lal Ruanga went and looked ; the father and mother were both similar to tigers. They said, " Keichal, my son, make your friend there eat some pig." Keichala asked " woald

Lai, middle ; tawk, to meet ; vé-ré, at once ; dzia, to visit ; zhai, raw ; a-hmin, cooked ; déc, to pretend.

atí. "Té-tuk-tey" lé atí; chutichūan Keichāla chūan poí-tak apétá.

*   *   *   *

Keichāla pā chūan " Hti-pui ka-law-ang-tehey" atí: alūka chūan bli-paí alaw-tá, chutichūan Lal Rūanga chūan " In-a ka-haw-don" atí, bli-paí a-hpuir-tá.

Keichāla kbūa mí-tey, " Keichāla hīern koyangey akultá ;" an-tí ; an-ūm-ta-tebtum-ey chutichū-an Lal Rūanga chū óm phaktá, chutī-chūan Lal Rūanga lei-kua-a alútá, akit chū-an an-haw-tá-veh an-kír-lé-ta-veh. Mi-del pakat-in Lal Rūangan a-ék ahártá, chutichūan mi-del-a chūan " Lal Rūanga ek ka-lài-ey" atí.

Chutichūan Lal Rūanga akbúa atleng-don-tá ; bmáea a-nopai arai akul-ahan ahríng-tá ; afapú adla anitá ; chutī-chū-an túi achoya : Lal Rūanga chū-an, " Hawrók, ka-hti ka-pé-ang-tehey" atí " I-mú-dú-nang ?" atí " Aha I ka-dú-lob-vay ; kapá pók-in hti-paí lawk-túm-in akultá." Atí chūan, Lal Rūanga chūan " Ka-fá aoi-angey" atí " Hawrók,I-kul-ang" atí, chutīchūan an-puhoñ-in an-kultá, in-a atlengta afá-ad ani-tá. " Kapá chūan hawrók I-mú-dú-nang atí" chutichūan Lal Rūanga adzak-tá "Né bli tum-tak peirók" atí, chutichūan lái-a an-tchangtá an-lái-ta-tchūm-ey, kbúa tey tumtak-in an-om-tchium ; in pawna atachúak dú-lob ; ahtá-drit-in an-om-tá. Atawptá.

you like to eat a big pig or a small one?" "A small one," replied Lal Ruang, how-ever Keichala produced a big one. Keichala's father said, " I will reach down the jewels." In the morning early (they went to) reach down the jewels, but Lal Ruang saying, I had better be off home, had carried the jewels off with him. The men of Keichala's village said where is Keichal's friend gone to, so they followed after him hotly, and Lal Ruang found they were overtaking him, so he entered into a cave (and hid there). As soon as he had gone in, they came up and (not finding him) they all returned. One stupid fellow among them, Lal Ruang smeared with filth saying—" It is I, Lal Ruang, who smear you with filth."

So Lal Ruang arrived at his home. His wife, who he had left behind pregnant, had been delivered of a daughter. This girl was fetching water : Lal Ruang said, " Come here and I will give you jewels ; will you be my sweetheart?" " No," said she, " I do not want your jewels—my father has gone to get jewels for me himself." Said Lal Ruang, " This must be my child ! Come," said he, " will you go (up to the village)?" so they both went. On ar-riving at home he found it was his daugh-ter " My father wanted me to be his sweet-heart," said she, but Lal Ruang was much ashamed, and said " Here take these jewels (and be quiet)." Afterwards he became a chief, a most powerful chief, and had many villages ; he had no occasion to stir outside his own door. They lived very happily. It is finished.

Lawk, to reach down ; dzo, to procure ; phák, to catch up, overtake ; lei-kúr or lei hús, a cave or hole in earth ; bús, to smear ; diák, shame, modesty ; tchung, to spring up, to increase from blossom to fruit ; lawp, to conclude, finish.

Note to Story II (Lal Ruang.)

Line 1.—*" Rûli-pûil, the big serpent."*—Throughout the Lushai Hills, among all the tribes with whom I have come in contact, whether ' Toung-tha' or ' Khyoung-tha,' sons of the hill or sons of the river, I have always found that special attributes have been assigned to a certain description of snake or serpent that is found in these forests. I remember once we were camped peacefully beside the border of a small hill stream; the shanties of leaves and grass which form our *trutée d'abri* in this part of the world had been erected, and all the world (our world, some 30 persons) was either smoking the pipe of peace or stirring the pot of rice that was to form the evening meal. Suddenly there arose a shout of " Tchubha-gree! Tchubha-gree!" which is the Hill Arracanese for " the big snake, the king-serpent," and beheld the camp in a ferment, each stalwart young fellow seizing his dao and tightening his waist band. We went forth and indeed the snake was very big. His long sinuous growth was at least 20 feet in length and bulky in proportion; he moved slowly along taking apparently no notice of the turmoil and confusion that soon filled the wood around him. The hillmen swarmed around his length like ants, and in a few moments he was cut in pieces by dao strokes. I noticed that each of my combatants as they ran up to the snake spat at him before striking. On inquiring the reason of this I was informed that in attacking a snake of this description if he spat at you first before you struck him, your fate was sealed, and strangulation was your doom; but if you were speedy in salivation and forestalled his action, that then he was delivered a prey into the hands of his assailants. A similar superstition formerly attached to the basilisk or cockatrice, which was said to be able to fascinate or cause the destruction of man or beast if it first perceived its victim before it was itself perceived. Sir Thomas Browne, in discoursing "Of the Basilisk," says— " that veneration shooteth from the eye, and that this way a basilisk may empoison, is not a thing impossible; but that this destruction should be the effect of the first beholder or depend on priority of aspection is a point not easily to be granted." The flesh of this snake (which is a species of python) is eaten by the hill folk, and the fat of the reptile is held to be a sovereign cure for all cuts and wounds, as well as for more obscure diseases. In the household-tales and fireside-stories of the people " the big snake" holds a prominent place, and is invested with attributes of power and knowledge.

The opening sentence of this story—" the big snake made bracelets and the maidens did service for these bracelets"—opens out the vista of social relation existing between master and servant, between superior and inferior, among the Dzo tribes.

We are acquainted with Plato's Republic, with Sidney's Utopia, with Bacon's New Atlantis, and later, Compte's Philosophic Positif—dreams these, all of them;—the ideas of eminent men as to the conditions which should exist in this world, as to the social relations among their fellows, which are the most conducive to happiness, but here among these hill tribes we find an actual existing system in practical working, which might well be classed among the visions of Utopian philosophy.

Their mode of government may be described as a democracy tempered by despotism. The right of rule is hereditary, that is, only men descended from a certain family can be chiefs. It does not, however, follow that all members of this ruling race should be chiefs, on the contrary, it is only those who are specially gifted and endowed with the capacity of drawing men to them who become so. A chief's power is measured by the number of his followers, and as the people who follow him are perfectly free agents, it is a necessary sequence that the fittest man or sometimes the most fortunate is also the most powerful.

Now as to service or slavery among the Dzo, I use the word 'slavery' for want of a better; "boi" is the term in their dialect, which betokens a person who has lost the right of individual freedom of action, but in all other respects the word 'slave' would be inapplicable. The menial service in a chief's house or in the households of the wealthier persons of the Dzo tribe is performed by two classes, (1) the Boi, (2) the Sul.

(1.) *Boi.*—A man or woman becomes 'boi' for the following reasons: Should any person, lazily neglecting to cultivate rice on his own behalf, surreptitiously take, steal, or attempt to steal the rice of another, he becomes the chief's 'Boi'; should any person commit murder, or commit a fault, the consequences of which he is unable to bear alone or unassisted, he takes refuge in the house of the chief, and he and his family with their descendants become 'Boi.' The chief is responsible for the fault committed, and the avengers of blood will demand restitution at the hands of the chief only. Provided, that in all cases of adultery, killing is no murder.

(2.) *Sul.*—The Sul is simply a man, woman, or child, who has been forcibly taken prisoner in war, who is in fact a captive to the bow and spear of the chief. Such persons in every day life are treated in no way differently to the Boi, but may be redeemed by their relations on a money payment. A Sul lives in the chief's own house, and may be sold from one to another, or treated as a household chattel. The Boi is rather an hereditary retainer, occupying a separate house and not liable to sale or transfer.

A case in point recently came to my own knowledge in reference to the father of one Rowlula, a member of the ruling clan, and brother to the chief Rutton Poia. This man was described by his compatriots as "wanting in wisdom." His father had been a powerful chief, and he had inherited many slaves, gongs, guyals, and all that constitutes the wealth of a Dzo. He, however, being "wanting in wisdom," as the Dzo pithily put it, was unable to curb his desires, and was foolish enough to use force towards several young slave girls of his household; in consequence thereof the whole of his 'Boi' abandoned him and transferred their allegiance to his brother, the chief Rutton Poia. He was consequently reduced to great poverty, having to cultivate for himself; he sold all his gongs, cloths, and guyals, and died finally in a miserable condition—a not uncommon result of a "want of wisdom."

The offices performed by the Sul or such of the Boi as compose the immediate household of the chief is everywhere the same. They have to hew wood and draw water, they cultivate the chief's *jūm*, and in their leisure hours weave cloth, cook the meals of the household, serve the chief's wife, or take care of the children.

The Boi or *clientèle* of the chief, who all occupy houses in his immediate vicinity, are in a word 'his men.' They give him rice or food when he requires it, but if on the one hand all that they have is his, the relations existing between them are reciprocal, and they can draw upon the chief's stores in time of need. I have myself seen, when a considerable present of brass dishes and Manchester cloths had been given on behalf of Government to an influential chief, within an hour he has been left without a single article—everything had been appropriated by, or given to, the Boi.

The Boi are well treated, well fed, and cared for. Orphans find refuge in the chief's house;

it is his care also which provides suitable marriages for the maidens, while if old age or destitution overtake them, they find an unfailing refuge with " the father of the village."

The belief in magic among the Dzo is universal ; it is found throughout their stories and traditions; but they say that no professors of the black art are now to be found among them. "We killed them all," said my informant somewhat naively. They believe, however, that mighty magicians are still to be found among the Burmese and Manipooreans to the north-east. ' *Omne ignotum pro magnifico.*'

In page 73, column 2, lines 13 and 14—" *The snake said, ' you have got my daughter, pay me her price.*'" Human beings, like every thing else, are priced, not in money but in kind. A male slave (Sal) for instance, will, if strong and in good condition, be worth a guyal and a gun, that is about £10, English. Wives vary in price, but must in all cases be paid for, or the marriage would not be legitimate. An ordinary wife will cost some 30 baskets of rice and a guyal; but the chiefs, who in most cases seek wives in the families of their own class, have to pay enormously for their consorts. The wife of Dowlyeyva, brother of our friendly chief Van Hnoya, was purchased by him from her brother, who is an influential chief among the Pois, an eastern tribe. Her price was seven slaves, eight guyals, and ten guns—not to speak of the expenditure involved in the wedding festivities. The life of a man is also priced, but its value varies according to circumstance. This custom is a frequent cause of disagreement among the different village communities of the hills; for, supposing that a traveller dies in a village, it may be by accident or in the course of nature, yet the price of his head (" goung-hpo," as the Burmese call it,) must be paid by the village in which he died, and as this price has no definitely defined limit, a powerful chief seeking a quarrel with a weaker community has only to declare that one of his men has died in their limits and to demand an exorbitant price for his life, and behold a lawful ground of quarrel ready to his hand.

MARRIAGE RELATIONS.—If a husband and wife separate by mutual agreement, the father takes all the children save those under three years of age, and for these latter also, as they grow older, the mother has to pay a stated price, otherwise they go to the father. In the event however of a man putting away his wife for no fault at all, the custom is strict and beneficially rigorous; such man is entitled to go forth from his house with one dao and the body cloth he wears: all the rest of the property—the children, the homestead, the cattle, everything—goes to the wife. Cases of separation are not common among the Lushais.

Adultery is rare. The language contains the word ' adulteress' (uirey,) but has no masculine denomination. In cases of adultery the husband has the right to kill his wife's seducer wherever and whenever he may find him; no penalty attaches to this taking of life. The woman is liable to be put away, and a certain amount of stigma seems attached to the crime as on her side. She is however not subjected to fine or any other specific punishment.

In page 74, column 2, lines 33 and 34—" GOD.—*The Great Spirit's house is sacred.*" The Dzo recognise two deities, Kusvang, the good spirit, and Patien, the evil spirit. The former is said to reside in a village among the hills, which is often seen indistinctly, far away amid the clouds which hide the blue hill-tops, but which, like the Fata Morgana, possesses the property of vanishing as it is approached. A chief told me in all good faith, how his father, who was a mighty man, had for a long time seen in the distance a village which no one could identify ; he had said " Who is this chief, his people do not come to us, they hold aloof—this is not good," so he collected his young men and they travelled east, travelled and travelled ; as they mounted each range of hills the chief said " Surely this is the last, we shall reach the village after the next valley ;" but as fast as they advanced the village receded. At last they topped a lofty hill, the eastern side of which was a precipice, and they looked towards the sun which was rising, and there was the village, quite close. They heard the roar of the war-gongs and the houses were decked in red cloth, and as they looked a cloud came over the sun and over the village, and when it lifted there was no longer any village to be seen—' Then,' said the narrator, " my father knew that the village belonged to Kuavang and he was afraid. None of our young men came back, they had gone so far. My father only, who was very strong, reached home, and he told our people and then he died."

There is something almost pathetic in this wild story. The simple people seeing God's village in the clouds far away towards the rising sun, and then the sudden awakening to the knowledge that they were fighting against a supernatural power, and the solitary return of the old chief to die.

Kuavang, the good spirit, has to this day, and in almost every village of the Dzo, certain special favorites (male or female) who are known by the name of " Kuavang Dzawl," possessed or inspired by Kuavang. The Dzawl are subject to long trances or ecstacies when they are thought to be present only in body, the soul (*tlarao*) having gone to visit its master at Kuavang's village. This power or property is by no means hereditary ; it is however held in high consideration among the Dzo, and is supposed to carry with it an inherent knowledge of medicines, simples, &c. A Dzawl is also able to cure barrenness in women, and the ill-will of a Dzawl is sure to bring evil consequences. Last year the husband of a female Dzawl at Rattan Pois's village quarrelled with his wife and spoke evil of her office. Lo ! next day he dislocated his jaw in yawning and died miserably of starvation. Provoke not the Dzawl !

It is believed, moreover, among the Dzo that Kuavang's young men occasionally become enamoured of fair mortal maidens. The result, however, is fatal, for the girl must die and that quickly. Hence if a young woman pines away, or is consumptive, the people say "One of Kuavang's young men has lain with her." This belief will bring to mind a still older one, " and the sons of God came in unto the daughters of men." Patien, the evil one, is a restless spirit ; he roams about in the forest seeking what evil he may do. Sometimes he steals children away, and he always has in wait at a death to appropriate the soul of the deceased, which, if he catches it, he straightway eats. He sometimes causes death by eating the heart of a live man or woman whom he specially fancies. Those honest Dzo who are not eaten by Patien (the souls of them, that is) go to a dark and dismal abiding place under the earth known as "Deadman's village," here those who have done well will be born again in some other human body. The Dzo are frequent in offering sacrifice of animals, some to Kuavang, some to Patien, some to the minor spirits of the trees and rocks, which latter are supposed to be able to exercise a malign influence in their own immediate vicinity. Those beasts which are sacrificed during life time to Kuavang will after death be found and possessed by the sacrificer in Deadman's village.

Another common functionary among the Dzo is the exorcist, *pái-liem*, which signifies literally ' the great knower.' This office requires merely knowledge, not inspiration. The *pái-liem* is really a man cunning in sacrifice—a priest who knows when and how to make offerings and is able to interpret the omens. The *pái-liem* possesses but small influence, save in respect to the actual performance of his office. Those who employ him remunerate his services. For the rest he earns his bread by cultivation, as the rest of his world do.

In page 74, column 1, lines 35 and 36—"*Túi-rüang-dar*," a gong tempered in the water of the stream called Túi-Rüang, and supposed to possess magical qualities. This Túi-Rüang is frequently mentioned in Dzo stories, Túi means water or stream, Rüang is the proper name, and this we find also borne by the hero of the story Lál (or chief) Rüang. The Dzo say that originally they came from the north-east, and that it is there, in the cradle of their race, that is found this magic stream. The scene of action of this story is evidently in the far-away-land referred to, for at the opening, it is to the Túi-Rüang that the big snake cunningly sends the girl to clean the bracelet he has made.

In page 76, column 2, lines 6, 7, and 8—"*She went out of the house for a few moments, and the child fell through the flooring underneath the house, and there he caught a rat.*" This exemplifies the universal structure of all hill-houses, which are raised a foot or so off the ground. The house floor consists merely of loose pieces of bamboo beaten out flat, which can be easily removed, and the sweepings and refuse of the house thrown below. Here, underneath, is the haunt of pigs and fowls, while numberless rats burrow in warmth and safety from the rain and furious blasts of wind which sweep the hill-tops.

In page 76, column 2, lines 14, 15, and 16—"*His name was Lál Rüanga, but his tongue was forked; his father had cut it so.*" This has evident reference to the original snake origin of the father. It would be curious to trace by a comparison of legends whether there is any connection between the Dzo and the Nagas, and again what relation exists between these people and the semi-royal families in Central India, who claim descent from a snake; interesting, moreover, in its bearing upon the much-discussed question of the serpent worship of old.

In page 76, column 2, line 27 and 28—"*At night a man-tiger (Keichala) came and threatened him.*" The word Keichala does not absolutely mean man-tiger, 'Kei' is the abbreviation of 'Sakei,' a tiger, while *chal* or *chala* is a common termination of nouns proper, masculine. We shall see the same thing in the next story, where we meet really with Kei-mi, the tiger man. This belief in the ability of certain human creatures to transform themselves into wild beasts is curiously met with in this out-of-the-way corner of the world.

The German wēhr-wolf, and the belief in lycanthropy are but different forms of the same superstition. Even in England it was prevalent in the 16th century. We find, in an old play of John Webster's, a dramatist of that period, the following passage:—

Ferd.—"Pray thee, what's his disease?

Doctor—A very pestilent disease, my lord, they call it lycanthropia."

In page 76, column 2, lines 36 and 37—"*He had no occasion to stir outside his own door.*" Can a phrase be found more expressive of peace and quiet?

3. The Story of Kúngóri.

Apé chú nopai ansiloh; kiáugrú baang a-blais a-kúta bling atachúna, ahling chú nowté-a atchöng-tá. Chutichúan nowté apieng-tá nú ansiloh a-bainga chúan Kúngóri antí. Bú-tún mul khat ley an-ei-tíra, bú-fäng khat té an-ei-tíra, alien déo-déo-vey. Chú-tichúan kúm bnít kúm túm ani obúan ttíla ntling-tá; ahméi ahlá dzit; chútichúan an-khúa rol-btár-tey in-mei an-túm-a; tú-má apé-in aphal-loh. Chutichúan Kei-mí rol-btár a-hoiak a-fún-a arapú arépa: chútichúan Kúngóri adám-loh-tá.

```
*    *    *    *
*    *    *    *
*    *    *    *
*    *    *    *
```

Kúngóri pa chúan " Atahiöm-htei an-om-chúan kaíáuú kamei-tí-angey atí. Akhúa mí-tey-in antahiöm, tahiöm tú-má-in an-tí-dám-htei-loh. Chutichúan Keimi rolbtár alo-benga, "Koyma ka-tahiöm angey" atí "adám chúan koyma kanei angey" atí; Kúngóri pá chúan "Tahiöm rok" lé atí "adám chúan í-uei-ang-tchey."

Chitichúan an-tahiöm-tá, ahoiak-fún arapá arép-chú a-bpel-a, apai-a. Kúngóri-chú adam-tá, chutichúan Keimi rol-btár chúan aweitá-"Hawrúk Kúngóri, koyma ín-a í-kui-ang," atí, chutichúan an-kultá, akoi obúan-in Keimí rol-btár chú saksi-a a-tchung-tá; Kúngóri chúan amei-a avú-no-a atlán-ta-tchiom-ey. Kúngóri pá tey khua hmei-tchia bling bpdr-in an-hmú, chutichúan ahúng bpár chú in-a ahonga Kúngóri pá badna, " Ifánú chú

Her father, who was unmarried, was splitting bamboos to make a winnowing basket when he ran a splinter into his hand; the splinter grew into a little child; (after a time) the child was brought forth motherless and they called her Kúngóri. Even as a grain of rice swells in the cooking so little by little she grew big. Two or three years passed by and she became a maiden; she was very pretty, and all the young men of the village were rivals for her favour, but her father kept her close and permitted no one to approach her. There was one young man named Keimi, he took up the impression of her foot (from the ground) and placed it on the bamboo grating over the house fire (there to dry and shrivel up), and so it fell out that Kúngóri became ill.

Kúngóri's father said, " If there be any one that can cure her, he shall have my daughter." All the villagers tried, but not one of them could do any good, however (at last) Keimi came " I will cure her, and I will marry her afterwards," said he. Her father said, " Cure the girl first and you may then have her."

So she was cured, the foot print which he had placed to dry on the fireshelf he opened out and scattered (to the wind). Kúngóri became well and Keimi married her. " Come Kúngóri," said he, " will you go to my house"? So they went; on the road Keimi turned himself into a tiger, Kúngóri caught hold of his tail, and they ran like the wind. (It so happened) that some women of the village were gathering wood and

Kúngóri, a winnowing basket; baang, thin slips of bamboo used in basket work; blai, to split; tschän, to spear. pierce; ahling, a thorn, splinter; nowté, a little child; pleng, to bring forth; bd-fäng, a sort of rice called 'kungyu'; mal, a grain; bd-fäng, cooked rice; dao-deo, little by little; keimi or mhei-mi, a man-tiger; a-hoiak, f-ot-print; tña, to gather up; arep, bamboo shelf over the hearth used to dry meat; rép, to dry; tahiöm, to make ready; to curv; phal, to loose, open out; pai, to throw away; amei, tail; arti-an, to mixn; hpér, to carry;

apmal mkei nuri" an-ti, chutichúan Kúngóri
pá chúan alá-htai in-om-chú-an Kúngóri nei-
aag-tchey-ú.

   *   *   *   *

Chutichúan tú-ma-in an-lá-ngum-loh, chutichú-an Hpohtíra ley Hrangahála an-htisa-dún
in "Koymani kan-lá-angey" "anti; chutichúan Kúngóri pá chúan "In-lagh-htsi-chú-an
nei-ang-tchey-ú," ati, chutichuan Hpohtíra
ley Hrangubála an-kulté, an-kui-chúan Keimí khúa atleng-ta, Keimí ráhtár chá aram-
tacuak; in-a atleng hmá-in Hpohtír ley Hrangchal Kúngóri húma akaltá. "Kúngóri"
anti "I-pasái koyangey?" "Aram tacúak-
tá" ati; ati-chúan "atleng-don-tá," ati;
chutichúan an-hlow-va, rápúi tchúog-chánga
Hpohtíra ley Hrangchal an-lawa-tá; Kúngóri pasal alo-tlengta. "Mi-hríng rim anam"
ati; Kúngóri chúan "Koyma rim nui-angey"
ati, chutichuan khúa ablim-tá, tchaw an-ci-a,
an-mú-tá; khuaver lé chúan Kúngóri pasal
aram-tacuak-lé-tá; chutiehúan hmei-htai-in
"Kúngóri in-lagh-don chúan mei-tchi shindrok-ú, bling-tehí shindrok-ú, túi-tchí shin-
drók-ú." An-tí chutichú-an amei-tchí, ahling-
tehí, atái-tchí an-china, Kúngóri an-lé-tá
an-kui-púi-tá.

   *   *   *   *

Kúngóri pasal alo-tlengtá fo-a, a-en-chúan
Kúngóri a-om-ta-loh. Kúngóri pasal chúan
a-úm-ta-tchium; savatay in Hrangchala,
"Tlandrók, tlandrók" ati "Kúngóri pasal
atleng-don-tá" ati. Chútichúan mei-tchi
an-vor-a, rim skang-ta-tchium, chuti-chúan
Kúngóri pasal a-baw-htsi-loh; mei adai
chúan a-úm-lé-tchíum-ey.

   *   *   *   *

they saw all this, so they went back home
to Kúngóri's father and said, "Your daughter has got a tiger for a husband." Kúngóri's father said, "Whoever can go and take
Kúngóri may have her," but no one had
the courage to take her. However, Hpohtír and Hrangchal, two friends, said, "We
will go and try our fortune." Kúngóri's
father said, "If you are able to take her
you may have her," so Hpohtír and Hrangchál set off. Going on they came to
Keimí's village. The young man Keimí
had gone out hunting; before going in to
the house Hpohtír and Hrangchal went to
Kúngóri. "Kúngóri," said they, "where
is your husband?" "He is gone out hunting," she said, "but will be home directly."
On this they became afraid, and Hpohtír and
Hrangchal climbed up on to the top of the
high shenshelf. Kúngóri's husband arrived,
"I smell the smell of a man," said
he. "It must be me who you smell" said
Kúngóri. Night fell, everyone ate their
dinners and lay down to rest. In the
morning Kúngóri's husband again went
out to hunt. A widow came and said (to
the two friends) "If you are going to run
away with Kúngóri take fire-seed, thorn-
seed, and water-seed (with you)," so they
took fire-seed, thorn-seed, and water-seed,
and they took Kúngóri also and carried
her off.

Kúngóri's husband returned home, he looked
and found Kungori was gone, so he followed after them in hot haste. A little
bird called to Hrangchal, "Run! run!
Kúngóri's husband will catch you," said
the bird. So (the friends) scattered the fire
seed, and (the fire spring up and) the
jungle and undergrowth burnt furiously, so
that Kúngóri's husband could not come

Ngrum, to dare; tehdung, on top; cháng, high; rim, a small; cum, to stink; ver, to matter, now; adai, quench, burn out.

*　　*　　*　　*

*　　*　　*　　*

Chutichuan savatey in, Hrangchala-té "Um-phak-ló-don-ta" ati, chutichuan tui-tebi an-vór-a, tüi-pui alien-ta tchium, chutichuan Kungóri pasél-in angbak-kama, aidi-chú akamta Kungóri pasél chuan a-um-lé-tá, chutichuan " Aphak-lé-don" savatey chuan Hrangchala-té " a-um-phak-lé-don-ta" ati ; chutichuan " Hling tebi vórók-á," ati : hling-tebi au-vór-lé-ta, chutichuan hling ajob-ta-tchium, Kungóri pasél akui htei-ta-loh.

*　　*　　*　　*

Ahling chú ated-chúma akui-lé-htei-ta, a-um-phak-lé-don-ta. Chutichuan-in Hrang-chala-té an-mang-ang-ta ; hpai-bpeng buia atchanga. Hpobtiran sakei chú tchem-in achát-hhim-ta. " Koyma Hpobtira" ati, chutichuan sakei chú ahti-ta. Hrangchala-té chúan kul-lé-ta, Khoavang lam-htwam-htúm-a an-rick-ta. Hpobtira ley Hrangchala an-in-mem-tawk.

Hrangchala amú hma-aha chutichuan Hpob-tira aveng-a.

*　　*　　*　　*

*　　*　　*　　*

*　　*　　*　　*

Dzana chúan Kaavang alo-hongs "Tú maw ka-lam-htwom ariak" atia : Hpobtira chuan " Hpobtira ley Hrangchala" ati " hpai-bpeng bdi-a kam, kei lú kan shá tchawt tchawt" chutichuan Kuavang-in abrier, ahlow-ta, atléa-ta ; chutichuan Hpobtira "Hrangchal htorók, nuug vengrók, koyma ka-mú-ta-tacnak-ey ; ka-mú-angvy. Kuavang alo-hong chúan, hlow tachuh-ang-tchey." Atia a-mú-ta, Hrang-chala avengta ; chutichuan Kua-vang ahaw-

any further. When the fire subsided he again resumed the pursuit.

The little bird cried to Hrangchal " He is catching you up," so they scattered the water-seed, and a great river greatened (between them and their pursuer.) However Kungóri's husband waited for the water to go down, and when the water went down he followed after them as before. The bird said to Hrangchal, " He is after you again, he is fast gaining on you, sprinkle the thorn-seed" said the bird. So they sprinkled the thorn-seed and thorns sprouted in thickets, so that Kun-gori's husband could not get on ; by biting and tearing the thorns he at length made a way and again he followed after them. Hrangchala became dazed, as one in a dream, (at this persistence of pursuit), and crouching down among the roots of some reeds, watched. Hpobtir cut the tiger down dead with a blow of his dao. " I am Hpobtira" said he, so the tiger died.

Hrangchal and the others went on again until they came to the three cross roads of " Kaavang," and there they stopped. Hpobtir and Hrangchal were to keep guard turn about. Hrangchala went to sleep first while Hpobtir stayed awake (watching.)

At night 'Kaavang' came " Who is staying at my cross roads" he said. Hpobtira (spoke out boldly) " Hpobtira and Hrangchala (are here) " said he " crouching under the reeds, we cut off the tiger's head without much ado." On this Kuavang understood (who he had to deal with) and becoming afraid he ran off. So Hpobtira (woke up Hrang-chal saying) "Hrangchal get up, you stay awake now, I am very sleepy, I will lie

Ngtak, to wait ; kam, to subside ; jok, spring up, sprout ; tawk, to bite ; hpai-bpeng, reeds ; bil bill, root ; lam-btwom, cross roads ; mú-tawk, to guard ; veng, to be awake ; Kaavang—See Explanatory Notes at the end of story No. 1 (Lei Eney).

lé-tá "Tú-maw ka-lam-btwum ariak?" atla.
Hrángchála chúan ahlow-vá "Hpohtíra ley
Hráng chála,bpai-bpeng bdla-kam, kai lá kan-
aha tchawt tchawt" atla Kúavang-in ahllow-
dú-loh, chutichúan Kúngóri, Kúavang in aláiá.
Kúngori chúan la-dzai a-dzám aog, lel kdra
alútá ; Kúavang kda atlengtá, alei-kór chú
láng-púi-in a-tchhíua. Chutichúan kuavár
chúan Hpohtíra ley Hrángchála an-in-haotá.

    *   *   *   *

    *   *   *   *

    *   *   *   *

    *   *   *   *

Hpohtíran Hrángchála chú "Mí-tadal-pá l"
atí "koyangey Kúngóri, akultá? [-blow-
vang-in Kuavang-in an-kul-púi-ta. Kaldrók
Kuavang kúa [-kul-ang " ati. Kúngóri la-dzai
dzám an-dzuia láng-púi tedugan la-dzai
alútá, aldng-púi chú an-bpawk-a, Kuavang
kúa an-dzók-hmú-ta; chutichdan Hpohtíra
chú-an "Khoi l koyma Kúng-óri min pé-ló-
rók-ú" atí ; chutichúan Kuavang-in " Nungmani Kúngori kan-bré-loh-vey" ati, "in-kul-
púi-kha" atí. Hpohtíra chúau " Kuagori
min pók-loh-chúan ka-tehem ka-tlagh-doa
atí;" chutichdan Kuavang-in "Tlagh-rók" atí.
Allagh-chúan véug khat an-htí-dzow-tá.
Chutichuan Hpohtíran "Koyma Kúngóri min
pérók-ú" atí. Kúavang-in " nungma Kungóri a-om-loh" atí, atichdan Hpohtíra ley
Hrangchalan " Kan-lo-kul-aogey" atí. Kúavang-in " Lo-hawrok-ú" atí, chutichuan ankul-
tá, Kuavang [na antleng-tá, Kúavang laud
hmél abtá-dait "Hai-ki Kúngori" antí. Hpohtíra chúan. " Ilé-ki sui-loh-vey, Kúngóri
toh-ink min pérók-ú" atí, chutichúan an pútá.

down. If Kuavang comes you must not
be afraid." Having said this he lay down
(and went to sleep), Hrangchala stayed
awake, presently Kuavang returned " Who
is this staying at my cross-roads?" he
said. Hrangchala was frightened, (however) he replied " Hpohtíra and Hrangchala (are here), they killed the tiger that
followed them among the reed-roots."
But Kuavang was not to be frightened by
this, so he took Kúngóri (and carried her
off) Kúngóri marked the road, trailing behind her a line of cotton thread; they entered
into a hole in the earth and so arrived at
Kuavang's village. The hole in the earth
by which they entered was stopped up by
a great stone. In the morning Hpohtír
and Hrangchala began to abuse each other.
Said Hpohtíra to Hrangchal " Fool man,"
said he, " where has Kúngori gone to? on
account of your faintheartedness Kuavang
has carried her off. Away I you will have to
go to Kuavang's village." So they
followed Kúngori's line of white thread
and found that the thread entered (the
earth) under a big rock : they moved away
the rock and there lay Kuavang's village
before them. Hpohtíra called out " Hoy I
give me back my Kúngori" Kuavang
replied. " We know nothing about your
Kúngori, they have taken her away."
" If you do not (immediately) give me
Kúngori I will use my *dao*" said Hpohtír.
" Hit away" answered Kuavang. With
one cut of the *dao* a whole village died
right off. Again Hpohtír cried " Give
me my Kúngori," Kuavang said " Your
Kúngori is not here." On this Hpohtír
and Hrangchal said " We will come in"
" Come along ' said Kuavang, so they
went in and came to Kuavang's house ;

La-dzai, cotton-thread ; dzam, a line, clue ; húr, a cavity ; lei, earth ; láng, a stone, rock ; tchhia, to block
up, close ; hao or how, to abuse ; hprok, to remove, roll away ; véug, a hamlet, small village.

<table>
<tr><td>¶</td><td>◆</td><td>◆</td><td>◆</td></tr>
<tr><td>◆</td><td>◆</td><td>◆</td><td>¶</td></tr>
<tr><td>◆</td><td>*</td><td>◆</td><td>◆</td></tr>
</table>

An-kul-púi-a : Kángóri chúan. "Tsum-khui ka-bté-nghíl-ey" atí. Hpohtíra chd-an "Hrangchál, dzú-lá-rók." Hrángchalá chdan "Ka-la-ngnm-loh, ka-hlow-vey" atí. Chúti-chuan Hpohtíra akul-a adzú-la : a-lágh hlán-la Hrángohálan Kángóri akul-púi-tá, alei-kúr chú lúng-pul-in an-tchhín-tá. Chuti-chuan Hrángchala-tó Kúngori pá badna an-tlerg-ta. "Nongma, ka-fanú í-lá-btsi-a, nangma ocirdk" atí ; Kúngori chúan a-dú-loh. Kúngori pá chúan "Koyangey Hpohtíra?" atí, "Hrangchala chúan aoi." "Hpohtíra omta kan-bré-loh-vey" atí.

Hrángchala ley Kúngori an-ín-tsmítá, adú-loh-tchdug-tchúhg, anci-hrum. Hpohtíra-chú Kúavang nála sncíta ; a-ín shára chúan koy atí-a ; aloh-vá abrúí alawntá. Hpohtíra chd Kuávang nen fá anci-a ; háng-tey atschhúm a, Kuávang núla om-loh-bían-ín, afí alóng-tey tachhúm chd "Eiruk" atí ; a-ei-hlan-ín Hpohtíra chd koy brsí-a alawn-a a-kul-tchtuk-tá. Akulté Kúngóri pá ín-a alleugté Kúngóri tey sciel an-tschdn khdang an-tcboy-a, an-lám-a, Hpohtíran Hrangohéla alú atun-tá.

<table>
<tr><td>◆</td><td>◆</td><td>◆</td><td>◆</td></tr>
<tr><td>¶</td><td>◆</td><td>¶</td><td>¶</td></tr>
<tr><td>¶</td><td>¶</td><td>◆</td><td>◆</td></tr>
</table>

Kaavang's daughter, who was a very pretty girl, was pointed out as Kúngori. "Here is Kúngori" said they, "This is not she" said Hpohtír "really now, give me Kúngóri," so (at last) they gave her to him.

They took her away. Kúngori said "I have forgotten my comb." "Go Hrangchal and fetch it" said Hpohtír, but Hrangchala dared not venture. "I am afraid" said he. So Hpohtír went (himself) to fetch (the comb), while he was gone Hrangchal took Kúngori out and closed the hole with the great stone. After this they arrived at the house of Kúngori's father. "You have been able to release my daughter" said he "so take her." Kúngóri however did not wish to be taken. Said Kúngóri's father "Hrangchal is here, but where is Hpohtíra ?" "We do not know Hpohtíra's dwelling-place" was the reply.

So Hrangchala and Kúngori were united. Kúngori was altogether averse to the marriage, but she was coupled with Hrangchal whether she would or no.

Hpohtíra was married to Kaavang's daughter. Beside the house he sowed a koy-seed, it sprouted and a creeper sprang (upwards like a ladder). Hpohtíra when he was at Kúavang's had a child (born to him), and he cooked some small stones (in place of rice), and when his wife was absent he gave the stones which he had cooked to the child saying "Eat." While it was eating Hpohtír climbed up the stalks of the creeper (that had sprung up near the house), and got out (into the upper world). He went on and arrived at the house of Kúngori's father ; they had killed a goyal, and were dancing and making merry. With one

Kúngóri pá chúan "Engey-tingey Hpohtír Hrángebúla lé í-tan?" atí "Ka-tuo-ang-chú, Keimi kúa ka-lagh-pók-in ani, Hrangebala a-lé-ngum-loh. Kuavang-in a-lagh-pók-in Hrángchála chú ablow-va, a-oi-ngum-loh; atúka chúan Kúngóri la-dzai dzam kao-dzai-a Kúavang kúm alútá; koyma ka-dai-lagh anl. Kúngóri chúao ka-taom-khúi ka-blé-aghíl atí. Hrangebala dzú-lnrók kao-lí-a, kol a-ngum-loh atí, ka-blow-vey, atí; chutichuan koyma ka-dzé-lá-a. Kúngóri ley Hrangebala mia kul-shao-a, a-lei-kúr-chú lúngpúli-in ao-tchhhbisa—ankeltá; chutichúan Kúavang núla kuaci-a, a-kua-vang núla chú aknl-blau-in koy brúi-a ka-lawn-a, ka-lo-kul ani." Chutichúan "Ani lé, onngma in-neirók" lé antl Hrángchála chú ahtútá, Kúngóri lé Hpohtírn an-ío-nei-a; tuk-tuk-in an-om-a; mial-tey an-tachúna; kúa-tey tamtak-in an-om-a; an-blé-ta-tchíum-oy; chútichúan atowptá.

*   *   *   *

*   *   *   *

*   *   *   *

blow Hpohtíra cut off the head of Hrang-chal!

Kúngóri's father cried, "Why Hpohtíra do you cut off Hrangchala's head?" "I was obliged to decapitate him" said Hpohtír "It was I who released Kúngóri from Keimi's village, Hrangchala dared not do it; when Kúavang carried off Kúngóri also, Hrangchala dared not say him nay, he was afraid; afterwards we followed Kúngóri's line of cotton thread which led us to Kúavang's village. Kúngóri (after we had released her from there) forgot her comb, we told Hrangchal to go and fetch it, but he dared not, I am afraid, said he, so I went to get it. He then took Kúngóri and left me behind, shutting the hole in the earth with a great stone. They went away. I married Kúavang's daughter, and while she was absent I climbed up the stalks of the creeper and came here." On this "Is it so," said they, "then you shall be united." So Hrangchala died, and Hpohtíra and Kúngóri were married; they were very comfortable together, and killed many gayal; they possessed many villages, and lived happy ever after. Thus the story is concluded.

Lám, to dance; tachúa, to stab, spear; tú, to cut.

Note to Story III (*Kúngóri.*)

This story is the more interesting from the connection which can be traced between it and many of our English children's stories.

In page 84, column 2, lines 13 and 14—"*There was one young man, named Keimi, &c.*" "'Kei' or "Sakei-mi" is literally the tiger man. Here we again touch upon the belief analogous to the ancient lycanthropy which was met with in the last tale. We also see the agenda of Dzo magic, and it is worthy of remark how closely the practice in question approaches to the ancient mode of destroying an enemy by a waxen image slowly melting before a fire. The course taken by Kúngóri's father to facilitate his daughter's cure is as old as the Arabian nights, where Prince Caralzaman wins his wife in much the same fashion. The said father, however, seems somewhat barren in device, for having fallen into the error of marrying his child to a tiger, he has to resort to an exactly similar expedient to get her out of the beast's clutches.

In page 85, column 2, lines 20, 21, and 22—"*Kángóri's husband arrived, I smell the smell of a man,*" *said he.* This reminds one strongly of "Fee I faw I fum I I smell the blood of an Englishman" in the case of our ever memorable Jack the Giant Killer. Again, the thorn-seed, fire-seed, and water-seed, with which the fugitives ineffectually endeavour to stay their pursuer, and the friendly little bird who advises them, have their parallel in some of our own stories—the tales of the Genii, I think, but I have no opportunity for reference and my memory fails me.

In page 85, column 2, lines 15—"*Hrangchala became dazed, &c.*" We here have the first intimation of the difference in character of the two friends. The killing of the tiger and the exclamation "I am Hpohtira" is almost Homeric. It has a smack of savage chivalry—a waft as it were from the middle ages, tempered by an after puff, me-meniment of Cooper's Red Indians.

In page 86, column 2, lines 24, 25, and 26—'*Hrangchal and the others went on again until they came to the three cross roads of Kúavang.*" It is curious to meet here with the same superstition as to the cross-roads which was formerly so prevalent in Europe.

In page 87, column 2, lines 12 and 13—*Kángóri marked the road, trailing behind her a line of cotton thread.*" From Theseus with his clue to the labyrinth, down to that small person of nursery story who filled his pockets with stones or beans, and dropped them one by one to enable him to find his way home again, after his wicked uncle should have abandoned him in the forest, we find the same expedient resorted to by heroes and heroines of story. Note here, however, that Kúavang's village is said to be underground. This is not in accordance with general belief at the present day. Kúavang, both in this story and the last, is represented as a rather humourous and trickey deity, and certainly is no malign or malicious spirit.

The forgetting by Kángóri of her comb a little farther on is essentially feminine, natural, and amusing.

In page 88, column 2, lines 33, 34, 35, and 36—"*While it (the child) was eating, Hpohtir climbed up the stalks of the creeper and got out.*" The object of cooking stones for the child in place of rice was, I suppose, to make the eating of the mess a difficult and lengthy task, and so give the father time to carry out his purpose of escape. It brings to mind the passage from Scripture, "we asked for bread and he gave us a stone."

The escape of Hpohtir up the stalks of the koy-bean is in exact parallel with the familiar adventures of Jack and the Bean Stalk, save that the direction of going and coming is reversed. It might seem, from the manner of Hpohtir's exit, that Kúavang's village was not situated underground but lay in a deep valley, the entrance to which was by a subterraneous passage.

The end of Hrangchala is strictly according to poetic justice, and the story ends in a most orthodox manner, even down to the memorable phrase, "and they lived happy ever afterwards."

VOCABULARY.

DZO-ENGLISH.

A.

Ahai	...	lame.
Ahawk	...	a knot.
Abi-ni	...	round.
Aho	...	loss.
Ahowk	...	bark (of dog.)
Abul	...	dirty.
Abul-hlo	...	to dirty.
Abúl alér	...	anyhow, disorder.
Abing	...	half, a portion.
Achir	...	to find.
Achúar	...	to frown.
Adai	...	cool.
Adám	...	well.
Adám-loh	...	ill, sick.
Adáng	...	other, different.
Adik	...	proper, fit.
Adúm	...	dark blue.
Adáng	...	length.
Adzá	...	all.
Adzáng	...	light (in weight.)
Adzawn	...	exactly.
Adzim	...	narrow.
Adzik	...	pith.
Adzir	...	flabby, loose.
Adzow	...	large, extensive.
Adziek	...	variegation, colour.
Aeng	...	yellow.
Afá	...	a child.
Afa-pá	...	a son.
Afa-nú	...	a daughter.
Afing	...	wisdom.
Ah	...	foolishness.
Ah	...	to reap.

Abá	...	fatigue.
Abat	...	difficult.
Abang	...	black.
Abel	...	raw.
Abol	...	easy.
Abúl	...	dry.
Abd	...	wet.
Abún	...	time, season.
Abain	...	equal.
Abling	...	a splinter.
Ablo	...	loss, accident.
Ablow	...	fear.
Abhui	...	old.
Ablogh	...	expensive, dear.
Ahmél	...	appearance.
Ahmnn	...	me.
Ahnd	...	footstep.
Ahniak	...	footprint.
Ahnok	...	confused, difficult.
Abnai	...	near.
Ahow	...	abuse.
Abrang	...	alone.
Ahrui	...	troublesome.
Ahrol	...	large.
Ahzap	...	rough.
A-htien	...	friend.
Ablá	...	good.
Ahtá-loh	...	bad.
Ablar	...	new.
Ahtá-toh	...	diligent.
Abino	...	fat, grease.
Ahten	...	half.
A-htak	...	an itching.
Ahúm	...	dark.

Ahtal	...	upright, topside up.	A-ong	... a hole.
A-htawk-lek	...	fitting, even.	Apán	... a wound.
A-htawk-fúng	...	about.	Apáng	... the body.
Ai-la ⎫			Apíang	... as.
Ai-chn-un ⎬	...	than.	Apíeng	... birth.
Ai-shon ⎭			Apúi	... big.
Akím	...	entire, complete.	Apím	... the whole.
Akoy	...	crooked.	Apol	... vexation, damage.
Akul	...	going.	At	... chicken, fowl.
Akul-akír	...	go and return.	Arautchom	... pipes (musical).
Akhá	...	bitter.	Arim	... odour, smell.
Akhaop	...	hard, coarse.	Arít	... weight, heaviness.
Aklan	...	sweat, perspiration.	A-rdál-in	... together.
Akún	...	a nod.	Ardk	... stealthily, theft.
Alal	...	middle, the navel.	Arpg	... bone.
Alám	...	a dance.	Ariak-in	... naked.
Alet	...	topsy-turvy.	Aro	... dry.
Alét	...	sinking.	Arúl	... an egg.
Alei	...	purchase.	Ashang	... tall, high.
Alien	...	big.	Ashá	... hot.
Alom	...	joy, happiness.	Ashong	... gathered, collected.
Aldin	...	warm.	Ashen	... red.
Alo-kír	...	return.	Ashei	... length.
Ama	...	he, she.	Ashik	... cold.
Ams ⎫			Alát	... old.
Ama-tá ⎬	...	his, hers.	Atán	... for.
Amán	...	price.	Atawb	... last.
Amak	...	wonderful.	Alal	... waist, the reins.
Amal	...	a drop.	Aley	... little.
Amák	...	a divorce.	Atel	... along with.
Amel	...	tail.	Aten	... mire, mud.
Aman	...	profit.	Atchnk	... strength, hardness.
Amur	...	tight, stretched.	Atchí	... seed, clan.
Aná	...	pain.	Atchín	... had.
Anál	...	slippery, smooth.	Atchang	... alone, motionless.
Anem	...	fine in texture, soft.	Atchanvey	... half (of liquid).
Ang	...	like, resemble.	Atí-ké	... to break.
Anghing	...	to move.	Atí-lol	... rape.
Angú	...	straight.	Atí	... flesh.
Ango	...	white.	Atíao	... mislaid.
Angúr	...	a growl.	Atíeng	... to arrive.
Angúl	...	lonely.	Atíck	... to break, snap.
Anum	...	a stink.	Atlú	... to fall.

Adăm	...	sweet.
Atoi	...	breadth.
Atol	...	arm.
Atoy	...	short.
Atoy	...	rot.
Aishet	...	quarantine.
Atser	...	a scar.
Atschang	...	inside.
A-tscét	...	a bite.
Atdi	...	excellent.
Atúr	...	strong (as spirits).
Avér	...	white, light.
Aráng	...	breadth, broad.
Avang	...	scanty.
Averg	...	awake, watchful.
Arui	...	chilly, cold as steel.
Ardt	...	ashes.
Avual	...	flabby.
Avon	...	skin.
Aw	...	noise, voice.
Awm	...	the breast, chest.
Awr	...	to wear round neck.

B.

Bái	...	potatoes, yam.
Bénárei	...	the wrist.
Bán	...	the arms.
Bán	...	to cuddle, encircle with the arms.
Bang	...	stop, cease.
Bang-ú	...	cause to stop.
Bák-tchai-jé	...	scissors.
Bág	...	a hat.
Bai	...	to stuff in.
Bári	...	parting of hair.
Ben	...	to clap, pat.
Beng	...	the ear.
Beng bay	...	earrings.
Beng-etchey	...	deaf.
Beng	...	to wear in the ear.
Bél	...	an earthen pot.
Bél vúa	...	a potter.
Búrán	...	sheep.

Bi-ung	...	cheek.
Bol	...	houseman, retainer.
Bol-nú	...	maid servant.
Bá	...	rice.
Bú-tchi	...	rice seed.
Bá-fang	...	cooked rice.
Bá-fai	...	husked rice.
Bú-tán	...	a species of rice.
Dan	...	to arrive.
Bunglai	...	a compartment, room.
Bún	...	to wear, as shoes, ring, &c., to encircle.
Bni-hie	...	to dirty.
Dúm-rúa	...	a load.
Búh	...	a nest.
Búi	...	root.
Bui-blá	...	war-song.

C.

Chútachúan Chútichúan } Chitlchúan	...	thus, this being so.
Chútl-ja	...	so much.
Chil	...	to button.
Chai	...	dance of young people.
Chá-váng-in	...	because, on that account.
Chútl-váng-in	...	therefore.
Chán	...	to prick.
Chú	...	thus.
Chú	...	a particle used as particle, ed in Hindi.
Ching	...	to plant.
Chen	...	since.

D.

Dár	...	brass.
Dé	...	to place, put.
Dár-tchem-btei	...	a telescope.
Dár-blá-ebatai	...	musical box.
Dár-klá-lang	...	a mirror, looking glass.
Dát-kleng	...	a brass plate or dish.
Dár-húang	...	a gong.
Dát-loy	...	a bugle.

Dát-loy-túm	...	a bugler.
Dim	...	well, health.
Dim-loh	...	unwell, sickness.
Din	...	custom.
Ding	...	other, different.
Dái-paí	...	fort, stockade.
Dai	...	outskirts, environs.
Dao	...	enmity.
Dawt	...	lies, falsehood.
Deng	...	to hammer, pound.
Deo-deo	...	little-by-little.
Dèr	...	to pretend, make believe.
Dèer	...	turban.
Di	...	sun-grass.
Dil	...	to want, demand.
Ding	...	to stand.
Ding	...	the right.
Dot	...	bazaar.
Donkon	...	a syphon.
Doy	...	magic, sorcery.
Dó	...	to wish.
Dúm	...	black.
Dúm-lo-úm	...	a hookah.
Durrun	...	a sort of basket.
Dung-ek	...	a dye.
Dua	...	to tickle (passive form).
Dzáng-rók	...	back-bone.
Dzák	...	arm-pit.
Dzák	...	shame, modesty.
Dzai	...	single.
Dzai	...	to cut.
Dzai-tchúm	...	cut with scissors.
Dzál-bák	...	guest-house.
Dzawl	...	inspired, possessed.
Dzawt	...	to ask, inquire.
Dzawk	...	much.
Dzawtey	...	a cat.
Dzán	...	night.
Dzanína	...	at night.
Dzán-khú-ai-in	...	all night.
Dzang	...	the sides.
Dzeb	...	to tuck in.
Dzen	...	gunpowder.

Dzick	...	to read.
Dziok	...	colour, variegation.
Dzlak	...	to tickle (active form).
Dzit	...	very.
Dzinga	...	early.
Dzír	...	to learn.
Dzír-tí	...	to teach.
Dzingan	...	among.
Dzong-kri	...	small-pox.
Dzong	...	affix of multitude.
Dzong	...	to search.
Dzong	...	a monkey.
Dzo	...	Kookie.
Dzol	...	slow, easy, gentle.
Dzol-in	...	by degrees.
Dzow	...	to finish.
Dzow-tí	...	to complete.
Dzúng-pal	...	the thumb or big finger.
Dzúng-tchul	...	the fore-finger.
Dzúng-lai	...	the middle-finger.
Dzúng-té-á	...	the third finger or the elder brother of the little finger.
Dzúng-tey	...	the little finger.
Dzúng	...	to make water.
Dzú	...	beer.
Dzú	...	to imbibe, to smoke.
Dzú-dzú	...	a feast.
Dzú-bél	...	a beer pot.
Dzú-er	...	to sell.
Dzúang	...	leap.
Dzui	...	to follow, track.
Dzung	...	the vulva.
Dzúno	...	a beer-cup.
Dzing	...	finger.
Dzú-ul-kow	...	message, news.
Dzúng	...	root.
Dzúng-bún	...	a finger ring.

E.

El-pal	...	the thigh.
El	...	the lower part of leg.
El-sawp	...	to wash ditto.

El	...	to oppose, disagree.
Em	...	a kind of basket.
Em	...	interrogative affix.
Em	...	very.
Eng	...	what.
Eng-jung-ey	...	how many.
Eng-tcheng-ey	...	how much.
Eng-ma	...	nothing.
Eng-jok	...	anything, any.
Eng-li-ka	...	when.
Enga-tang-ey	...	what for, why.
Eng-thgey	...	how.
Eng-kim	...	everything.
Eng-li-kema	...	any time.
Eng-lo-tui	...	something.
Eng-hmun	...	nothing.
Eng-lo	...	whatever.
Eng	...	grave.
Eo	...	to look.
Eo-tlá	...	a scout.
Ey	...	! (exclamation).
E-hi	...	this.

F.

Fáng-bná	...	pumpkin.
Fánd	...	daughter.
Fátná	...	sister.
Fát	...	a leak.
Fára	...	an orphan.
Fai-fúk	...	whistle.
Fa-ib	...	advice.
Fang-hmír	...	small black ant.
Fawb	...	to him.
Féi	...	a spear.
Feng	...	much*
Fi-an	...	a spoon.
Fo	...	always (affix).
Fúng	...	a spike.
Fúr-hána	...	rainy season, monsoon.
Fúk	...	to stand erect, stiffness.

* Ka-then-feng-lah-vey. I don't know much about it.

H.

Ná	...	fire.
Hé	...	tooth.
Ná-bní	...	gums.
Ná ti	...	to give trouble, annoy.
Núl	...	to burn, set on fire.
Nám	...	to gape, yawn.
Ham	...	to scratch, claw.
Náng	...	blue-black.
Háng tuk	...	jet-black.
Hát	...	lead (metal).
Hát	...	difficult.
Há	...	this.
Né-hí	...	this, here.
Héta	...	here.
Hé	...	lip.
Hé-mí	...	he, this man.
Netí-chen	...	so many.
Netí-ang } Netí-a }	...	like this.
Hér	...	slanting.
Hét	...	to turn round.
Hem	...	to roast.
Hé-láma	...	this road.
Hli-un	...	lo.
Hí	...	that.
Hli-et	...	to scratch.
Hlá	...	far.
Hlá	...	a song.
Hlá-aá	...	to sing.
Hlal	...	to split.
Hlam	...	to measure.
Hlaw	...	to serve.
Hlaw-nei	...	wages.
Hlaw-tlo	...	service.
Hlo	...	to be lost, mislaid.
Hlo	...	medicine, to dye.
Hlow	...	to fear.
Hlop	...	to pare the nails.
Hlim	...	shade, shadow.
Hlm	...	to expose.
Hlúng	...	a thorn.
Hldm	...	to slay.

Hluf	...	old.
Hmei-tchim }		
Hmai-tchin }	...	woman.
Hma-sha	...	in front, before.
Hmai	...	face.
Hmai-bpfh	...	to wash face.
Hmát	...	north.
Hman	...	leisure.
Hmél	...	aspect, appearance.
Hmél-briet	...	acquaintance, know by sight.
Hmei-htai	...	widow.
Hmét	...	to shampoo.
Hmin	...	to cook, to ripen, mature.
Hming	...	name.
Hmu	...	to see.
Hmot	...	border.
Hmu-tí	...	to show.
Hmún	...	part, portion, kind, sort.
Hmún-hat	...	one sort, alike.
Hmún	...	a place.
Hmúu-kat-al	...	in one place.
Hmun	...	use.*
Hmun-tlágh	...	useful.
Hmun-tlágh-loh	...	useless.
Hmui	...	the mouth.
Hmui-hmdl	...	moustache.
Hná	...	a leaf.
Hná-blawk	...	work.
Hnai	...	near.
Hnai	...	juice, sap.
Hnám-tachom	...	poor.
Hnam	...	sort, kind.
Hnár	...	nose.
Hnat	...	up-stream.
Hnár	...	border, bank.
Hnek-in	...	than.
Hnéua	...	with.
Hné	...	to win.
Hné-loh	...	to lose.
Hnep-bsel	...	penis.
Hnim	...	to smell (active form).

* Engángey hmun ang. what use is it.

Hnoya	...	under.
Hnoy	...	to smear.
Hnúng	...	the back.
Hnúng lama }		
Hnúnga }	...	behind.
Hnúnga }		
Hnún }	...	presently.
Hnú-tey	...	the breasts.
Hnú-tey bmúr	...	the nipples.
Hnú-tey-túi	...	milk.
Hong }		
Hun }	...	to come.
Hong	...	to open.
Hon	...	to bring.
Hon-mi	...	open.
Hao-va }		
How }	...	to abuse.
Hpá	...	to spread.
Hpai	..	rorda.
Hpawk	...	remove, roll away.
Hpé	...	toe.
Hpé-pal	...	big toe.
Hpé-tchul	...	first toe.
Hpé-lai	...	middle toe.
Hpé-tey-ú	...	third toe.
Hpé-ley	...	little toe.
Hpé-mit	...	ankle.
Hpé-khoong	...	heel.
Hpúr	...	to carry on head.
Hpft	...	to crouch.
Hrál	...	to sell.
Hrai	...	a kind of basket.
Hrong	...	a morsel, a bit.
Hram	...	to mew.
Hram-hram	...	whether or no.
Hré	...	to know.
Hren	...	dhoti, waist cloth.
Hré	...	to bear, understand.
Hrier	...	to know.
Hril	...	to speak.
Hril-fia	...	to prove.
Hri-ow	...	needle.
Hrik	...	a louse.

Hri-tlang	...	to catch cold.
Hri	...	any particular disorder.
Hriog	...	to bring forth, produce.
Hrui	...	rope, string, cord.
Hruik	...	to wipe away.
Hrui-vai	...	a loop.
Htá	...	good.
Htá-tuk-in	...	carefully.
Htak	...	to lick, horn.
Htái	...	to pour.
Htat	...	new.
Htawk	...	to blow with mouth.
Htá-tuk	...	to take care.
Htáh	...	strength.
Htei	...	to be able, can.
Htá-nghil	...	to forget.
Htúk	...	thunder-bolt.
Htgen	...	to separate.
Htin	...	heart.
Htin lúng	...	heart, memory.
Htin-htá	...	happy, good-natured.
Htin-eichia } Htin-ahtá-loh }	...	ill-natured.
Htú	...	beads.
Htú-bná	...	amber beads.
Htú-ley	...	small beads.
Htí	...	to die.
Htí-tá	...	dead.
Htin-ur	...	to be angry.
Htir	...	iron.
Htir-tek	...	steel.
Htí-tír	...	to cause to die, to extinguish.
Htih	...	blood.
Htit-deng } Htit-tachar-tiem }	...	a blacksmith, worker in iron.
Hting	...	a tree.
Htíng-hná	...	tree leaves.
Hting	...	to shake.
Htip	...	to pain, ache.
Htil	...	to thread.
Htim	...	dark.
Htieng	...	customary.

Hhing-htin	...	to kneel.
Hto	...	a fly.
Hto } Htao }	...	to rise, get up.
Hton	...	to send.
Htowk } Htawk }	...	the breath.
Htd	...	words.
Htd-em	...	everything.
Htú-rdat	...	advice.
Htú-hpoi	...	a case (judicial).
Htoy	...	to sacrifice.
Htúr	...	acid.
Htul	...	an arrow.
Htul-ngúl	...	a bow.
Húm	...	to clench, grasp.
Húp	...	to hide.

I.

Itey	...	bag.
I-long } I-ta }	...	if.
In	...	a house.
In	...	to drink.
In-btan	...	to wrestle.
In-bú-ol	...	to bathe.
In-ei	...	to disagree.
In-kót	...	house platform.
In-tchúng	...	house-top.
In-lom-kem	...	to play, sport together.
In-tsiem	...	to prepare, be ready.
In-taw	...	to visit.
In-tadai	...	to quarrel.
In-bgen	...	to separate.
It	...	to belch.
It-fiak	...	to hiccup.

J.

Já	...	one hundred.
Já	...	much.

K.

Ka	...	my, I, (nominative prefix).
Ka-pú	...	my grandfather.

Ka-túh	...	my grandson.
Ká-púp	...	pop-gun.
Kapai rí	...	thunder.
Kai-knang	...	a prawn.
Kai	...	to pull.
Kai-tao	...	to waken.
Kai	...	to wear, put on.
Kao	...	to call.
Kap	...	to fire gun.
Kát	...	to shut.
Káng	...	to burn.
Kát	...	sulphur.
Kawu-vat	...	a lamp.
Kang	...	to raise.
Kao-kí	...	the shoulder.
Kawnbul	...	deputy, agent.
Kawlai-on	...	underneath.
Kawl-phoy	...	to lighten.
Kawl	...	lightning.
Kawláng	...	flint.
Kól	...	a goat.
Ké	...	to break.
Ké-pá	...	the foot.
Ké-abai	...	to halt, be lame.
Ké-tail	...	to wash feet.
Ké-taréb-rí	...	footfall.
Krima	...	I.
Khá	...	that.
Khabey	...	the chin.
Khabey-bmúl	...	the beard.
Khai-tawk	...	enough.
Khaop	...	coarse, hard.
Khaw	...	village.
Khátá	...	there.
Khawlám	...	place, country.
Khai	...	to hang.
Kha-pui	...	to assist, help.
Kbél	...	the hips.
Khin	...	to measure.
Khiang-kat	...	one side.
Khím	...	to wear.
Khoingoy	...	which?
Kho-ngai	...	to love.

Kho-vát	...	daybreak.
Khú-ai-la	...	always.
Kbúi	...	to comb.
Khúk	...	the knee.
Khup	...	to wink.
Khóm	...	sleeping place.
Khák	...	to cough.
Khám	...	to cover, hide.
Khúong	...	a drum.
Khwai	...	a wasp.
Kí	...	to cut down, fell.
Kin	...	a seer, two pounds weight.
Kim	...	to suffice.
Kír	...	again (affix).
Kili	...	square.
Kil-tam	...	three cornered.
Kil	...	a corner.
Kiew	...	the elbow.
Kinga	...	near.
Kleng	...	a plate.
Klán	...	perspiration, sweat.
Klán-tacmk	...	to perspire.
Koi-ndr	...	amber necklace.
Koag	...	a path.
Koag	...	the loins.
Koag-fen	...	a girdle.
Korh	...	a coat.
Korh	...	a Bengalee or coat-wearing person.
Korh-shen	...	a policeman—literally a red coat, from the first red-coated soldiers seen by the Dzo in 1861.
Korh-chil-an	...	button.
Korh-ani-na	...	a button.
Koy	...	the seed of a creeper, used in boy's games.
Koyma	...	I.
Koya		
Koya-ngoy }	...	where.
Koya-la-ngoy	...	whence.
Koy-la-mangoy	...	from where.
Koyma-tá	...	mine.

Koya-bmna }	...	nowhere.
Koya-má }		
Koya-pók	...	anywhere.
Kong-hat	...	a door.
Kul	...	to go.
Kul-tír	...	to send, make go.
Kul-pal	...	to take.
Kul-kong	...	pathway.
Kul-ahan	...	to abandon, leave behind.
Kul-huia	...	a prisoner.
Kút-pal	...	a stockade.
Kúm	...	a year.
Kúm	...	the month.
Kúmína	...	this year.
Kúa	...	a village.
Kúa-vang	...	God, the good spirit.
Kúa-vár	...	dawn.
Kúa dúr	...	a storm.
Kuavang-tchim-tchor		a spot, mole.
Kuavang-dzawl	...	a prophet, one inspired.
Kúr	...	a hole.
Kúr-tchis	...	an unlucky cavity in the earth, which prohibits cultivation.
Kúrh	...	to tremble.
Kúrkyi	...	arm.
Kút	...	the hand.
Kút-pá	...	the palm.
Kút-tchang	...	the knuckles.
Kút-tail	...	to wash hands.

L.

Lá	...	to take.
Lá	...	cotton.
Lá-dzai	...	cotton thread.
Lá-bér	...	a cotton gin.
Lá-pat	...	cotton flower.
Lá-mú	...	cotton seed.
Lá-kyt	...	cotton winder.
Lá-húng	...	cotton plant.
Lai	...	time.
Lai-ahai	...	a writing, a book.
Lai-tchi	...	relations, kindred.

Lál	...	a chief.
Lám	...	to dance.
Lám	...	a road.
Lám-hwam	...	cross-roads.
Lawn	...	to climb, ascend.
Lákdr.	...	the tribe of Shendús.
Ld	...	again (affix).
Ld-abey	...	to invert, turn inside out.
Leng	...	to stroll.
Leng	...	to penetrate.
Lei	...	earth, land.
Lai-lié	...	tax, tribute.
Lei	...	the tongue.
Lal	...	to buy.
Len-lai-dzai	...	a love song.
Len	...	a net.
Lei-diak	...	mud.
Lei-thang	...	dust.
Lét	...	to sink.
Lér-lawn	...	to climb.
Ley	...	also, and.
Ling-hia	...	a species of ant.
Ling-kin-búh	...	ant's nest.
Lo	...	a jalm, cultivated field.
Lo }		
Lo-ak }	...	to vomit.
Lo-vát	...	to jhm, to cultivate.
Lo-bang	...	to come.
Lo-kal	...	to go or come.
Lo-tsouak	...	to come out.
Lo-kír	...	to return.
Lóng	...	a boat.
Loh	...	not (negative affix).
Loh-chú	...	except, but.
Lóng-tchel	...	the management of a boat.
Lóng-val	...	to row a boat.
Lom	...	to play, sport.
Lúng	...	heart.
Lú	...	the head.
Lú-hai	...	giddy.
Lú-vá	...	headache.
Lú-húm	...	a cap.
Lú	...	to enter.

4

Lā-bŭl	...	crop-head.
Lúkha	...	platform.
Lŭm	...	warm, hot, (as water).
Lúng	...	a rock, stone.
Lúng-ngui	...	to be anxious, sorrowful.
Lúng-oi	...	to be content.

M.

Mái	...	only, is rain.
Mái-méi } Ma-ma }	...	uselessly.
Mak	...	to divorce.
Man	...	to seize.
Manl	...	his or her own, such.
Máng	...	a dream.
Mao	...	bamboo.
Matd	...	Kúmí tribe.
Matei-lovin	...	surely, certainly.
Mé } Méi }	...	fire.
Méi-koh	...	smoke.
Méi-eng	...	fire-light.
Mé-ol	...	flame.
Mé-tarr	...	a torch.
Méi-tú	...	to light fire.
Méi-tarm	...	to blow fire.
Mei-bol	...	charcoal.
Mei-ling	...	embers.
Mei-váp	...	ashes of pipe.
Mei-btei	...	Manipores.
Mei-tal	...	a steel used to strike fire.
Mei-tul-bam	...	a tinder box.
Méi-boh	...	tinder.
Meng	...	to wake (active form).
Mi	...	man.
Mí-pá	...	a male.
Mi-bring	—	a person.
Mí-toúal-pa (masc.) } Mí-toúal-nú (fem.) }	...	a quarrelsome or foolish person.
Mi-ah	...	a fool.
Mi-dawt	...	a liar.

Mi-dmb	...	a prevaricator.
Mi-hlep	...	a cheat.
Mi-búm	...	a knave.
Mi-rúk	...	a thief.
Mi-dang-pakai-al	...	any other person.
Mi-rún	...	rain, destruction.
Min	...	me.
Mit	...	the eye.
Mi-ko	...	the eyebrow.
Mit-vun	...	the eyelid.
Mit-kow-tlang	...	the brow.
Mit-del	...	blind.
Mit-mú	...	the eyeball.
Mit-bmúl	...	the eyelash.
Mirang	...	a Mugh, Burman.
Moy	...	pretty, fit.
Mong	...	much.
Mong	...	down-stream.
Mong	—	the buttocks, rear part.
Mun	...	to seize, catch hold.
Mú	...	to repose, lie-down.
Mú-ol-pal	...	a mountain.
Mú-tacnak	...	sleepy.
Mút	...	sleep.
Mú-ngbil	...	to be asleep.
Mú	...	kernel, stone.
Mút-bmún	...	sleeping place.
Mún-piah	...	a besom, broom.
Mún-piah	...	to sweep.
Múr	...	face, mouth.
Mal	...	a grain.
Mul-pal	...	the thigh.

N.

Naopang	...	child.
Naopang-lai	...	childhood.
Nao	...	younger brother.
Ná	...	to hurt, pain.
Nát	...	snow.
Nang-rung-in	...	together.
Nahiua	...	presently.
Nukin-hrua	...	by-and-bye.
Nawt	...	to rub, scrub.

Nam	...	soft, fine in texture.
Nen	...	with.
Nel	...	to get, obtain.
Ngá	...	to possess.
Ngáb	...	fish.
Ngáb-aha	...	fish-flesh.
Ngáb-kwai	...	fish-hook.
Ngab-kwai-ngúl	...	fishing rod.
Ngbak	...	to wait.
Nghawng	...	the neck.
Ngai-túa	...	to consider, think, remember.
Ngai	...	desire, pleasure.
Ngui	...	a sweetheart.
Ngai-loh-vey	...	never.
Ngul	...	to listen.
Ngoi-rung	...	to remain silent, attentive.
Ngo	...	white.
Ngúr	...	to growl.
Ngún	...	a sort of bracelet.
Ngúk	...	to grunt.
Ngam	...	to dare.
Ni	...	day, the sun.
Ni } Ni-ey }	...	you (abbr. enf.).
Ni-loh	...	no.
Ni } Nin }	...	aunt.
Nimin	...	yesterday.
Ni-tmri	...	a week.
Ni-tin	...	daily.
Ni-long	...	all day.
Nimin-duan	...	yesterday night.
Nimin-pia	...	the day before yesterday.
Ni-tlagh	...	sun-set.
Ni-blirp	...	an umbrella, sun-shade.
Nikúm	...	last year.
Nichim	...	before.
Nilovin	...	annoyed, angry.
Nopui	...	a wife.
Ne	...	a cup.
Nú	...	mother, feminine affix.
Núh	...	a young girl, a maiden.
Nú-tloy	...	a married woman.
Núta	...	brother-in-law.
Núl	...	to laugh.
Naktipa	...	day after to-morrow.
Naktúka	...	to-morrow.
Nukúma	...	next year.
Nungma	...	you.
Nungma-tá	...	yours.
Nung	...	to awake.
Nuk-duan	...	to-night.
Nuktúp-duan	...	to-morrow night.
Nam	...	to push.
Nam	...	to stink.
Nú-al	...	to brush, rub.
Nwam	...	to wish.

O.

Oi	...	to believe.
Om	...	to be, have, remain.
Om-loh	...	is not, have not.
Om-brí	...	stop, stay.
Omaa	...	residence, abiding place.
Om-dai	...	meaning.
Ong-púar	...	goitre.

P.

Pá	...	father.
Pá-tloy	...	a married man.
Paral	...	husband.
Pa-tchia	...	poor.
Pakat	...	one.
Pahnlj	...	two.
Patúm	...	three.
Palí	...	four.
Pa-ngá	...	five.
Parúk	...	six.
Pamri	...	seven.
Parich	...	eight.
Pa-kon	...	nine.
Pai-lung	...	a sort of basket.
Pai	...	to throw away, abandon.
Pai-hol	...	cowries.
Pakat-al	...	anyone.

Pán-dam-aá	...	wound healing.
Pán	...	a wound.
Pang	...	body.
Pat	...	a flower.
Par-vá	...	a pigeon.
Patien	...	evil spirit.
Pawna	...	outside.
Pawlai	...	interpreter.
Paw-tcha	...	to explain.
Pé	...	to give.
Pé-kír	...	to give back, return.
Pem	...	to migrate.
Pbák	...	overtake.
Phai	...	to permit, allow.
Phar-vai	...	an oar.
Phel	...	to loose, let go.
Phûm	...	to capsize, overturn.
Phûm	...	a grave; to bury.
Phûn	...	to plant.
Phût	...	scurf.
Pi	...	a grandmother.
Ping	...	to close.
Pilang	...	a bottle.
Poi	...	the tribes that wear their hair in a knot on the forehead.
Pol	...	to spoil.
Pul	...	to mix, mingle.
Pom	...	to embrace, take hold of.
Pom	...	to obey, observe.
Potet	...	to tear.
Pûi	...	big.
Púi	...	to help, assist.
Púk	...	to borrow.
Púi-tiem	...	an exorcist.
Pùm	...	the stomach.
Pún } Púng }	...	an assembly.
Pún-tír	...	to assemble.
Púk-tle	...	to lead.
Púrbin	...	the pulse.
Pú-an	...	cloth.
Pú-an-fen	...	petticoat.

Pú-an-hpa	...	a bed.
Pun	...	thin.
Pang-tchang	...	pettish.

R.

Bá	...	fruit.
Rai	...	pregnant.
Bák-dzu	...	spirits, alcohol.
Rái	...	war, enmity.
Rái-bía	...	to fight.
Rái	...	side.*
Rái-vsng	...	a sentry.
Rsm	...	jungle, country.
Rsm-tsrtsak	...	hunting.
Ráuáng	...	insect.
Ráp	...	the shelf over the fire.
Ráp	...	to tread.
Rei	...	delay, slowness.
Rsm	...	friendship, peace, agreement.
Reng	...	to remain.
Reng-tok	...	the beginning.
Reng-htín	...	always.
Rep	...	to dry.
Rá-ei	...	hail.
Risk	...	to stay.
Rûh	...	noise.
Ril	...	entrails, bowels.
Ril-tam-bak	...	to hunger.
Bil-rú	...	to ponder, have a mind.
Ring	...	to think, believe.
Ring-tuk	...	loudly, beginning.
Ring	...	throat.
Rim	...	smell.
Rol-htar	...	young.
Ron-hou	...	to bring.
Roo-dzun	...	to carry off.
Rûa	...	rain.
Rûa-ahím	...	to rain.
Rûak	...	to empty, discharge.
Rûa-mái	...	rain-drop.
Rûk	...	to whisper, to steal.

* Tsaw rái, on that side.

Rúi	... to be drunk.	Sillal-hlo	... gunpowder.
Rúl	... a snake.	Sakkut	... a horse.
Rúm	... to groan.	Suk	... to seem.
Rom	... to attack, war.	Sul	... a captive, a slave.

S.		**T.**	
Sá	... to sing.	Tá	... (possessive affix).
Sa-drú	... a rat.	Tá	... to cut, hack.
Sa-brick	... grease, oil.	Tá	... to wear.
Sá-káp	... game (wild).	Táh	... a vein.
Sadnik	... a stag.	Tám	... to claw.
Sakí	... a deer.	Taima	... diligence.
Sadrúk-shuar.	... The stag's fall; Ulan Chatra.	Táukanga	... rich, wealthy.
		Tún	... for.
Samai-dot	... Kassaloong bazaar.	Tél	... to kill.
Sakúp	... a porcupine.	Táp	... to weep.
Savom	... a bear (large species).	Tát	... old.
Samong	... a bear (small species).	Tát	... to sharpen.
Sapherik	... a tick.	Tatobla	... lazy.
Savé	... a bird.	Taut	... light, close-fitting.
Sara-bab	... a bird's nest.	Tawg-lck	... moderately.
Sara-hmúl	... feathers.	Tawg	... to meet.
Sakzi	... a tiger.	Tawp	... to conclude.
Sai	... an elephant.	Tchá	... to give news, to inform.
Sai-húl	... big beads (large bead necklace.)	Tchábet	... a burr.
		Tchakai	... a crab.
Sai-taik	... to whistle.	Tchang-khen	... a popgun.
Scid	... a gayal, bos-gaurus.	Tchán	... equal.
Seybong	... a cow.	Tchát	... to break (as rope).
Shag	... to gather up.	Tchang	... watching.
Shá	... to fell, cut, build.	Tchaw	... food, cooked rice.
Shey	... to bite.	Tchaw-fák	... a meal.
Sha-ngbah	... fish-flesh.	Tchaw-fák-hmá	... morning.
Sha-doi-úm	... a bottle.	Tchaw-fák-bún	... noon.
Shla	... to bring, take away.	Tchaw-fún	... cooked rice gathered up in a leaf.
Shin } Shil }	... to put on, wear, to rub.	Tchaw-ei	... a dinner, repast.
Shey	... to say.	Tchaw-hmet	... the vegetables, meat, &c., accessory to the main staple, rice.
Shoy-ngil	... to correct.		
Shon	... inkle.		
Shá	... to wash.	Tchaw-tchám	... to cook food.
Sik	... to pinch.	Tebét	... to spoil.
Silki	... a gun.	Tchép-tchám	... to cut with scissors.

Tcherm	...	a knife, a dao.
Tcherm-tey	...	a small knife.
Tchóp	...	to cut.
Tchel	...	to take hold, grasp.
Tcheng	...	lock of gun.
Tchir	...	to count, reckon.
Tchí	...	seed, clan.
Tchim	...	to break through.
Tchbla	...	to close.
Tchlam	...	inordinately, extremely.
Tchik	...	pitted, dented.
Tchblim-bal	...	rainbow.
Tchoy	...	to lift, raise.
Tchok	...	to stir, move.
Tchol	...	a radish.
Tchóm	...	a cloud, mist.
Tchúk	...	to peck.
Tchúm-dzing	...	morning mist.
Tchúk-tua	...	a joint.
Tchúng	...	on top.
Tchhúm	...	to sever.
Tchúa	...	free.
Tchúa-tir	...	to release.
Tchjul	...	forehead.
Tchúng-tchúng	...	altogether, entirely.
Tchún	...	to cast (metal).
Tchwut	...	the floor.
Td	...	to measure crosswise.
Tek	...	a thunderbolt.
Túp	...	to co-habit.
Tet	...	to tear.
Tí	...	to do, say.
Tikoi	...	to bend.
Tikám	...	Chulam tribe.
Ti-tuk	...	exactly.
Ti-búr	...	woman's pipe.
Tíom	...	promise.
Ti-ung	...	a stick, staff.
Tiem	...	to know, be acquainted with.
Tía	...	like, as.
Tilret	...	India-rubber.
Tio	...	nail of the hand.

Tíh	...	blood.
Tim	...	a needle.
Til	...	testicle.
Tiow	...	sand.
Ti-lé-tak	...	to squeeze.
Tiá	...	the moon, a month.
Tiá } Tia-tek	...	to let go.
Tiá-ráo	...	the soul.
Tiá } Tiagh	...	to fall.
Tiáng	...	a hill.
Tiangval	...	a youth, bachelor.
Tíán	...	to run.
Tiág	...	edge.
Tiáng	...	underneath, below, down.
Tiáng-lam	...	downwards.
Tiáng-lam	...	the west.
Tián	...	after.
Tiágh-tieng	...	exchange.
Tiáp	...	to fold.
Tiaw-rák	...	kick.
Tiabúnga	...	Demagree.
Tiai-lama	—	evening.
Tiem	...	a little.
Tiemtey	...	very little.
Tieng	...	to arrive.
Tieng	...	exchange.
Tieng	...	during.
Tió	...	to blow (as wind).
Tieng	...	a plate.
Tiep-tchúm	...	to cut, saw.
Til	...	wind.
Tiip	...	a stinging fly, horse-fly.
Tliak	...	to break.
Tio	...	to weed, clear.
Tong	...	language, speech.
Ton	...	to tie, bind.
Ton-btú	...	a tale, story.
Tong	...	a cubit, to measure by cubits.
Toh	...	to sprout.
Tuá	...	an animal.

Taa-nghal	...	wild boar.
Tsada-tel	...	a cigar.
Tait	...	to chop.
Taik-lam	...	east, above, up.
Tsamat-dor	...	Kawalong.
Taaw	...	that.
Taaw-hting	...	ginger.
Tamg	...	bread.
Taci-lai-luk	...	to salute.
Tsci	...	salt.
Tschūm	...	goods, merchandise.
Tschūm-dawog	...	merchandise, to trade.
Tschier	...	an oath.
Tschier-tsdm	...	to swear.
Tschūm-pūk	...	to borrow.
Tscúak	...	out.
Tscúak-ti	...	to put out, eject.
Tschūm	...	to cook, distil.
Tschnh	...	not.
Tschūm	...	day as opposed to night.
Tschū-nga	...	within.
Tschom	...	ten.
Tschang	...	a thousand.
Tschem	...	to blow with the mouth.
Tschim	...	the south.
Tschúng	...	to pour.
Tschūm	...	to spear, stab.
Tschung	...	to grow.
Tscér	...	lime, lemon.
Tscét-tlúm	...	orange.
Tscrn	...	to divide.
Tshinm	...	to make ready.
Tshinm-sha	...	ready.
Tshiém	...	to prepare, cure.
Tsbá	...	flesh, meat.
Tshat	...	to find.
Tsbé	...	to seek.
Tscy	...	to shake.
Tsam	...	hair.
Tsam-dziel	...	to knot the hair.
Tsam-tdak	...	to become grey-haired.
Tsam-khui	...	a comb.
Tsih-tail	...	a sort of umbrella.
Tail	...	to wash face.
Tsam-tdm	...	hair-knot.
Tsam-dzai	...	a single hair (compare La-dzai and dzai).
Tsú-al	...	fault.
Tsúk	...	to wash.
Tsúk	...	a pestle.
Tsdm	...	a mortar.
Tú	...	who.
Túak	...	to breathe.
Tú-má	...	no one.
Tú-hmon	...	nobody.
Tú-pók	...	any one.
Tú-lia	...	every one.
Túh	...	to sit.
Tóktna	...	to-day, just now.
Túi	...	water.
Túi-pui	...	a river.
Túi-hal-buk	...	to thirst.
Túi-abdar	...	waterfall.
Túi-m-tél	...	a turtle.
Túi-kúr	...	a well.
Túi-hal	...	thirst.
Túi-ek	...	rust.
Túi	...	excellent.
Túi-hléo	...	to swim.
Túi-krk	...	Tipra tribe.
Tuk	...	true.
Tukmeo	...	faithful.
Túkvér	...	a window.
Túk-lin	...	every day.
Túkim	...	nape of the neck.
Tum	...	much.
Tún-tleng-in	...	at the present time.
Túna	...	now.
Túm	...	to play on an instrument.
Túm	...	to want, wish.
Tul	...	even.
Tup	...	fireplace.
Tú-pók	...	any one.
Túp	...	to sow.
Ton	...	to decapitate.
Témbdog	...	half (cloth.)

Twei-twai	...	quickly.	Vák	...	a pig.
Twíb	...	mend, sew.	Vai-vút	...	dust.
			Van	...	the sky, heavens.
	U.		Vandú-ai	...	unlucky.
U	...	elder brother or sister.	Vanei	...	fortunate.
U-nso	...	relative.	Vana-dael	...	unfortunate.
Uí	...	a dog.	Vana-nghúr	...	thunder.
Uí-púm	...	Obeepuom, (name of a hill,	Vang	...	on account of, because.
		the dog's grave.)	Vang-vúai	...	a leech.
Ul	...	to be salt.	Vó-ré	...	together.
Ui	...	to forbid.	Val	...	to beat.
Um	...	to hunt, pursue.	Vai	...	the left.
Ur	...	anger.	Vek (affix)	...	all.
Uírey	...	adulteress.	Veng	...	to watch.
Upá	...	elder.	Véng	...	a small village, hamlet.
			Vér	...	very.
	V.		Vir	...	to revolve.
Vá	...	to go (anx.)	Vil	...	to bore the ears, to cut.
Vá-lá	...	go bring.	Vol	...	a time.
Vá-lút	...	go enter.	Voi-kat	...	once.
Vaibél	...	a tobacco pipe.	Voína	...	to-day.
Vai-hlo	...	tobacco.	Voi-dsana	...	this night.
Val	...	foreign.	Von	...	the belly.
Vai-mim	...	Indian corn.	Von-aahúar	...	diarrhœa, purging.
Vai-tawk-tlá	...	a goose quill.	Vor	...	to scatter.
Vai-hto-lru	...	a mosquito curtain.	Vos	...	to beat.
Vai-túng	...	a puddle.	Vúr	...	to snow.

A.

Abandon	... kol-shan; pal.
Abore	... tadklém.
Abuse, to	... bow.
About	... shtawk-fung.
Acid	... bidr.
Acquainted, to be	... tiem; hmél-hrist-sndi.
Acquaintance	... hmél-hrist.
Account of	... váng-lo.
Accurate	... adik, mlmawn-tuk.
Ache	... htlp.
Adulterем	... nlrey, (no mass.)
Advice	... fai-ib; bid-rú-ot.
After	... tlán.
Again	... kir; ld (affixes).
Agent	... hawnbul.
Ague	... tlún.
Alike	... hmún-kat; ang.
All	... adzá; vek (aff.); dzong (aff.)
All day	... ni-krug.
All night	... dzún-khd-al-im.
Allow	... phál.
Alone	... aichang; shrung; mai.
Along with	... aidi; baéna.
Altogether	... tchúng-tchúng.
Always	... khú-ai-in; lo (aff.); rong; rrog-hiín.
Amber	... koé-núr.
Amber necklace	... hti-hué.
Among	... dxing-us.
Anxiety	... láng-ngai.
Animal	... tad.
Ant (small black)	... fang-bmir.
Ant	... ling-kin.
Ant's nest	... ling-kin-bdh.

Angry	... hífn-dr; nilovin.
Ankle	... hpé-coil.
Annoy	... bé-lir.
Any	... engam.
Any other person	... ml-ddng pahát-al.
Anywhere	... koya-puk.
Anyhow	... abúl alér.
Anything	... eng-púk.
Anytime	... eng-ti-ká-má.
Anyone	... tú-pók.
Ape	... dzong.
Appearance	... ahmél.
Arm	... bán; hdrhyt.
Arm-pit	... dzsh.
Arrive	... tleng; hun.
Arrow	... btsl.
As	... spúng; tís.
Ascend	... lawn.
Ashes	... avút.
Ashes (of pipe)	... mel-váp.
Ask	... dzawt; dil.
Aspect	... ahmel.
Assemble	... pdn-lír.
Assist	... khá-puf; puf; tchan.
Assembly	... apdn.
Aunt	... ai; nln.
Awaken s. o.	... kai-tao.
Awake	... aveng, ameng.
Awake, to	... nung, meng.

B.

Bachelor	... tlángvél.
Backbone (the)	... dzáng rúk.
Back, the	... hnúng.
Bad	... a-htá-loh; sichis.
Bamboo	... mao.

Bauk (above)	... badf.	Boar (wild)	...	tm-nghal.
Bag	... fútey.	Bone	...	a-rúk.
Bazar	... dot.	Border (edge)	...	bmot tláng.
Basket	... { brul; pai-láng; dorrun; em.	Borrow	...	tmbúm-púk; pdk.
		Bore (the ears)	...	vit.
Bathe	... la-búal.	Bosom	...	bná-tey.
Bat	... ldg.	Bottle	...	ahadoi-ám; piláng.
Bear, s. (large)	... aavom.	Bow	...	btul-ngúl.
Boar, s. (small)	... aamoug.	Dowels	...	ríl.
Bear (bring forth)	... bring.	Box (musical)	...	dar-bla-abatai.
Beard	... khabey-bmill.	Bracelet	...	btí; ngún.
Bent	... vel; rúa.	Brass	...	dar.
Because	... rung-in; chú-vang-in.	Bread	...	taáng.
Beckon	... dzap.	Breadth	...	atol.
Bed	... pá-an-phá.	Break (shatter)	...	ké; tí-ké.
Bed-room	... khúm.	Break (as rope)	...	tchát.
Beer	... dzú.	Break (snap as stick)	...	atlíck.
Beer-pot	... dzú bel.	Break through	...	tchlm.
Before	... ni-hina.	Breast	...	awm.
Before (in front)	... bmd-shá.	Breathe	...	techem; tdak.
Belly	... vam.	Breath	...	blowk.
Belch	... it.	Breadth	...	arang. [tachin.
Behind	... hodng-láma.	Bring	...	vúlé; bon; ron-bon;
Believe	... oi; ring.	Bring forth	...	spieng.
Below	... tking; baoy.	Broad	...	aráng.
Bend	... tí-koy.	Brother (elder)	...	d.
Beneath	... kaw-lai-on.	Brother (younger)	...	nan.
Bungalow	... korb.	Brow	...	mit-kow-tlang.
Besom	... mda-plab.	Brother-in-law	...	ndta.
Bind	... ton.	Brush	...	ná-ai.
Bird	... mvá.	Build	...	abá.
Bite	... she; ata-cég.	Dunjoges	...	Pol.
Bitter	... akhá (Burmese.)	Durn	...	hal; kang.
Big	... pol.	Borr	...	tchalat.
Blacksmith	... biír-techer-tlem; biír-dewg.	Bugle	...	dar-koy.
		Bugler	...	dar-loy-túm.
Black	... abáng; báng-tak.	But	...	loh-chú.
Blood	... tib.	Boy	...	lei.
Blind	... mlt-del.	Button	... { korb-chil-ná. korb-sci-na.
Blow	... blawk; thé; tacem.			
Blue	... adúm.	Button, to	...	chil.
Boat	... kóng (Burmese.)	By degrees	...	dzoi-in; deow-deow.
Body	... páng.			

C.

Call ... kao.
Can ... hlei.
Carry ... hpúr.
Carefully ... bia-tuk-ia.
Cast away ... pai.
Captive ... sul.
Case (judicial) ... bid-phoi.
Capsize ... phám.
Cap ... lú-khám.
Cat ... daawtey.
Catch held ... mn.
Cast (metal) ... tchún.
Certainly ... matei-lo-vin.
Cease ... báng.
Cavity ... khot; kúr.
Charcoal ... mei-hol.
Cheat s. ... mi-blep; mi-búm.
Cheek ... bi-ung.
Chief ... lai.
Child ... nao-pang.
Chilly ... avut; avaw.
Chin ... khabey.
Chop ... tchát.
Clear v. a. ... lo-rát; tle.
Clip ... tchep.
Chicken ... ar.
Chukma (tribe of) ... Tikám.
Cigar ... tsada-túl.
Clan ... aichi.
Clap ... ben.
Clamber ... lawn.
Claw, to ... ham; tmn.
Clench (the hand) ... búm.
Climb ... lér-lawn.
Cloud ... tchám.
Claw v. a. ... taúm; ping; tebhin
Cloth ... pú-nn.   [del
Coat ... koth.
Comb ... tsum-khál.
Complete ... skim; dzow.   [kuL
Come ... hawng; lo-hawng; lo-

Cold ... asbik.
Cold (as steel) ... avut; avaw.
Cold (to catch) ... bri-tling.
Comb v. ... kbaL
Come out ... lo-tsoúak.
Conclude ... dsow-tir; tawp.
Content ... alom; lúng-ol.
Conceal ... khám.
Cook ... hmin; tschlóm.
Cough ... khák.
Count ... tchir.
Correct ... shoy-agil.
Crouch ... hpek.
Cross roads ... lám-hlwum.
Cotton ... lá.
Cotton-thread ... lá-dzai.
Cotton-gin ... lá-lair.
Cotton-spindle ... bmui-htnl.
Cotton-flower ... lá-pár.
Cotton seed ... lá-má.
Cotton winder ... lá-kyg.
Cotton shrub ... lá-kúng.
Cool ... adai.
Coarse ... kbadp.
Cock crow ... ar-kúong.
Cock ... ar-pd.
Cock (of gun) ... allpul.
Cock's comb ... ar-cháong.
Cow ... acy-boug.
Cowries ... pai-hol.
Cohabit ... tép.
Cramp v. ... kbúm.
Crow s. ... cho-ák.
Cover ... kbúm.
Crooked ... akoy.
Cut ... dzai; tá; tchép; vál.
Cut down (as tree) ... shá; kL
Cut (with scissors) ... tchép-tcbám; dzai-tcbam.
Custom ... dán.
Cap ... no; dzmno.
Cobit ... toug.
Customary ... hlieng.

D.

Dance	...	lom, lám.
Dare	...	ngom.
Darkness	...	ahtlm.
Daughter	...	fánú, afánd.
Day	...	ni, tœbún.
Dawn	...	káavár.
Daybreak	...	khovár.
Dead	...	hti-tá.
Dance (of young people)	chai.
Decapitate	...	ion.
Deer	...	sakt.
Delay	...	rei.
Deaf	...	leng-atebey.
Demagree	...	Tlabánga.
Destruction	...	mi-rua.
Desire	...	ngai.
Devil	...	patico.
Dhotee	...	brea.
Diligence	...	talma.
Diarrhœa	...	voo-sobdar.
Diligent	...	a-hta-bto.
Difficult	...	ahár.
Die	...	htl.
Disagree	...	in-el.
Different	...	alaáng.
Dirty	...	abal ; bal-hla.
Distil	...	tœbhóm.
Divide	...	tœem ; in-tœm.
Divorce	...	smák.
Do	...	ti : tabiam.
Dog	...	di.
Dog's bark	...	alowk.
Dog's grave	...	U'i-phám.
Door	...	kong-kár.
Down	...	tláng ; tlang-lam.
Down-stream	...	mong.
Dream	...	máng.
Drunk, to be	...	rui.
Drink	...	in ; drd.
Drop	...	amál.
Dry	...	ahúl ; aro.

Drum	...	khúong.
Dust	...	val-vil.
Dye	...	blo ; dong-ck.

E.

Ear	...	léng.
Earring	...	téng-bey.
Earth	...	lei.
Easy	...	ahol.
Eat	...	ci.
Early	...	dainga.
East	...	bák-lám.
Egg	...	artá.
Eight	...	parish.
Eighty	...	tœloom-risk.
Elbow	...	kiew.
Edge (of knife)	...	hmá.
Edge	...	hmow ; tlang.
Elder	...	ú-pá.
Elephant	...	sai.
Eleven	...	tœboom ley pakát.
Embers	...	mei-lung.
Empty	...	rúak.
Embrace	...	pœm ; lán.
Enceinte	...	rai.
Enough	...	khai-tawk.
Enmity	...	dao.
Enter	...	ld ; avéld.
Entire	...	ahim.
Entrails	...	ril.
Evening	...	tlai-lána.
Even	...	tal.
Everything	...	eng-him ; hta-am.
Except	...	lob-chá.
Exchange	...	tlong ; tlagh-tlong.
Everyone	...	tú-tio.
Every day	...	túk-tin.
Extensive	...	aluow.
Exorcist	...	pái-tiom.
Expensive	...	a-logh.
Extinguish	...	htf-tír.
Explain	...	paw-tcha ; briet-tir.
Equal	...	tchaa.

Exactly	...	ti-tuk ; sdzawn.
Expose	...	lilfm.
Excellent	...	atái.
Eye	...	mít.
Eye-ball	...	mít- md.
Eye-brow	...	mít-ko.
Eyelash	...	mí-bmúl.
Eyelid	...	mít-vún.

F.

Face	...	hrml.
Fall	...	atlú ; tlágh.
Faithful	...	tuk ; tuk-meo.
Far	...	hlá.
Fat	...	ahtao.
Fatigue	...	ahá.
Fank	...	tsú-ul.
Female	...	uí (affix).
Fear	...	blow.
Feather	...	sava hsmíl.
Festival	...	dzú-dzú.
Fell	...	hí ; shá.
Find	...	tshar.
Five	...	pangá.
Fifteen	...	tschom ley pa-ngá.
Fifty	...	tschom-ngá.
Fight	...	rái-htá.
Fine (in texture)	...	aném.
Finger	...	dudng.
Finger-nail	...	tin.
Finish	...	dzow.
Fire v. a. (a gun)	...	káp.
Fireplace	...	tup.
Firebell	...	ráp.
Fire v. a. (a jdm or grass)	hál.
Fire v. a. (to light)	...	mé-td.
Fire, to blow the	...	mei-tsoem.
Fire-light	...	mei-eng.
Fire s.	...	mei.
Fish	...	ngah ; sha-ngháh.
Fit	...	moy.
Fish-hook	...	ngah-kwai.

Fishing-rod	...	ngah-kwai-ngúl.
Flame	...	mé-ul.
Flabby (loose)	...	avwai ; adzár.
Flesh	...	aúí ; shá.
Flint	...	kawhíng.
Floor	...	tchwut.
Flower	...	púr.
Fly s.	...	hto.
Fog	...	tchúm ; tchúm-dzing.
Foot-base	...	ké-almi.
Food	...	tchaw ; tchaw-fák.
Fool	...	mí-ah ; mí-taúal.
Foot	...	ké-pá.
Footstep	...	ahná.
Footprint	...	ahniak.
Footfall	...	ké-tsech-rí.
For	...	atán ; tán.
Forbid	...	ní.
Follow	...	dzuí.
Foreign	...	vai.
Fold	...	tlep.
Fort	...	dai-pul.
Forefinger	...	dzúng-tchnl.
Forehead	...	tchul.
Forget	...	hté-nghit.
Forge (iron)	...	tschér.
Forty	...	tschom-lí.
Four	...	pali.
Fourteen	...	tschom-ley-pali.
Fowl	...	at.
Formerly	...	hmáoa.
Fortunate	...	vanel.
Free v. a.	...	tchua-tír.
Friend	...	a-htion.
Frown	...	achdar.
Fruit	...	rí.
Front (in)	...	hmá-bí.
Friendship	...	ram.

G.

Game (wild)	...	sukáp.
Gape	...	hám.
Gather up	...	aekeng.

Gently	... dzoi-in.		Hair	... trom.
Gecko (lizard)	... tchoh-ey.		Hair-knot	... tanm-dziel; trum-tám.
Get	... nei.		Half	... abung.
Get-up	... bto.		Half (equal shares)	... atchaavoy.
Give	... pé.		Half (of cloth)	... tám-búng.
Give back	... pé-kir.		Hand	... kút.
Ginger	... taaw-bling.		Hang	... khal.
Girdle	... kong-ien.		Happy	... alom; búo-btá.
Giddy	... hi-hai.		Hard	... atchnk; akhaop.
Go	... kul.		Have	... om; nei.
Goat	... kel.		He	... ama; ba-bl; bó-ml.
Gold	... Kuaváng.		Head	... lá.
Good	... a-htá.		Headache	... lá-ol.
Go and return	... akul-akir.		Hear	... liré.
Gold	... slóns (hind).		Heart	... btio; klag.
Gong	... darkúang.		Heavy	... arit.
Gourd	... tachúm.		Heaven	... ván.
Grain (single)	... mal.		Heel	... bpé-khong.
Grandmother	... pi.		Help	... kha-pui; pui; tchan.
Grasp	... mun; tchel; húm.		Here	... héta; bd-láma.
Great	... alien.		Her	... ama.
Grey, to become	... tanm-tdak.		Hide	... khúm; bóp.
Grass (big)	... dl.		Hiccup	... ir-fiak.
Grandfather	... pú.		High	... mhóng.
Grandson	... táh.		His	... ama-tá.
Goose	... vátawh.		Hip	... khel.
Green	... eng.		Horse	... sakbut.
Groan	... rúm.		Hookah	... dám-do-tm.
Grieve	... abtao.		Hot	... akim; aahá.
Growl	... angúr.		House	... io.
Grow	... taebung; toh.		How	... engtlogey.
Grunt	... agdk.		How much	... engtchengey.
Gums, the	... bá-bul.		How many	... engjongry.
Gun	... silai.		House platform	... in-kót; lákhd.
Gunpowder	... silai-blo.		Housetop	... in-tebdng.
Guest-house	... dzál-ldk.		Hole	... a-ong; khor; kár.
Gayal (bos Gaurus)	... swieL		Hundred	... já.
Goitre	... ong-pdar.		Hold	... tchel.
			Hunger	... ril-tam-bnk.
H.			Hurt	... sé.
Hail	... rial.		Hunt	... tim; rum-terdak.
Hammer, to	... deng.		Husband	... pasi.

I.

I	—	keima; koyma.
If	...	fla; tchfla.
Ill	...	dnm-loh.
Ill-natured	...	hiln-aichla.
Ill-fortune	...	apoi; vanddal.
In	...	bi-on.
Insect	...	rauang.
India-rubber	...	tilret.
Inside	...	n-tachd-nga; abda.
Inform	...	tchá.
Interpreter	...	yawhal.
Intoxicate	...	rub-tir.
In vain	...	mai-mal.
Indian corn	...	vai-mim.
Invent	...	ke-shey.
Iron	...	htír.
Itch v.	...	htak.
Idiot	...	mi-ah.

J.

Joint	...	tchük-tia.
Joy	...	lom.
Joom	...	lo.
Juice	...	abnal.
Just now	...	ldkica.

K.

Kamalong n. p.	...	Sámai-dot.
Karbaree	...	kawnbal.
Kick	...	tiaw-vak.
Kill	...	btí-tir; tál; hlúm.
Kind (sort)	...	hmdn.
Kiss	...	fawb.
Knee	...	khúp.
Kneel	...	bjing-hgit.
Knife	...	tchem-toy.
Knot	...	abawk.
Know	...	tiem.
Knuckle	...	kúl-tchang.

Kookie	...	Dao.
Kümi	...	Maid.

L.

Lame	...	abai; ké-búl.
Lamp	...	kawnvát.
Land	...	lal.
Language	...	gong.
Large	...	ahral.
Last	...	atawia.
Laugh	...	nal.
Lazy	...	tá-tchla.
Load	...	búm-rúa.
Loud s.	...	kár.
Leaf	...	hoá.
Leak	...	fár.
Leap	...	dzáang.
Learn	...	dzír.
Leech	...	váng-vúai.
Leg (lower part)	...	al.
Leisure	...	hmáa.
Lend	...	púk-tír.
Let go	...	tchúa-tír; tlá-tch; phel.
Lemons	...	taér.
Left, the	...	vei.
Length	...	nalmi; alúng.
Liar	...	mi-dawt.
Lie v.	...	dawt; dzah.
Lie (to recline)	...	mi.
Little	...	atey.
Little by little	...	déo-déo.
Lift	...	tchoy.
Light (not heavy)	...	adzang.
Light v. a.	...	mei-tú.
Light s.	...	avár; mai-ong.
Lighten (flash)	...	kawl-phé.
Lightning	...	kawl.
Like	...	ang.
Like this	...	béti-ang.
Lip	...	ké.
Listen	...	ngoi.
Lime (fruit)	...	taér-hlúm.

English	Dro	English	Dro
Little (quantity)	... them.	Message	... drú-al-kow.
Loins	... kong.	Mew	... bram.
Lung	... aahet.	Middle	... alaj.
Lonely	... angul.	Migrate	... pem.
Look	... en.	Milk	... hnú-tey-tul.
Looking-glass	... dat-kla-lang.	Mine	... koyma-ta.
Loop	... hrui-ral.	Mirror	... dat-kla-lang.
Loose r. a.	... phél.	Mire	... alen.
Loeo	... bo ; blo ; hné-loh.	Mist	... tchism.
Lost	... abotá ; ahlotá.	Mix	... pol.
Loss	... abo.	Modest	... dzak.
Louse	... brik.	Monkey	... dzong.
Loudly	... ring-toh.	Monsoon	... fúr-bún.
Love	... kho-ngai.	Month	... tla.
Lover	... ngai.	Mislaid	... ahlo.
Love-song	... len-lui-dzal.	Misfortune	... apoi.
Lock (of gun)	... tcheng.	Moon	... tlá.
		Mole (a spot)	... huarang tchin-tchér.
M.		Morning	... tchaw-fák-hmá.
Maiden	... núla.	Morsel	... hráug.
Maize	... vaimim.	Mother	... ni.
Magic	... doy.	Motionless	... atchang.
Matron	... nd-tloy.	Mountain	... tlaug ; mú-al.
Married man	... pé-tloy.	Moustache	... hmal-hmúl.
Married woman	... nú-tloy.	Mouth	... knm ; mdr ; hmuí.
Marry	... paaal-nei ; noyui-nei.	Move	... angbiug.
Mar	... tchet ; bpoi.	Much	... dmwk ; tnm ; mong ; tchium.
Make water	... dzúng.		
Make ready	... tabíum.	Mud	... lel-diak.
Male	... mi-pá ; pá (affix).	Mortar (for pounding)	... talm.
Man	... mí.		
Manage	... tchél.	**N.**	
Market	... dor.	Nail	... tin.
Mature	... hmin.	Naked	... armk-in.
Meaning	... om-dzL	Name	... ahming.
Measure v. a.	... khin ; tong ; hlám ; té.	Navel	... alai.
Me	... min.	Nape of neck	... tákúm.
Meal	... tchaw-fak.	Narrow	... adzim.
Meat	... tahá.	Nasty	... atchia.
Medicine	... hlo.	Near	... ahnai ; kivnga.
Meet	... tawg.	Neck	... nglawng ; ring.
Merchandise	... tchúm-dawng.	Necklace	... aai-hti ; hti-ley.
Mend	... twih.	Needle	... brí-ow ; tim.

Nest ... bulb.
Net ... len.
Never ... ngai-loh-vey.
New ... a-bidr.
News ... tcha; dzial-kow.
Night ... dzin.
Night (to-night) ... nuk-dzan; dzanlm.
Night (last) ... ni-dzan.
Night (yesterday) ... nimin-dzán.
Night (day before yesterday) ... nimin-pia-dzán.
Night (to-morrow) ... nuktip dzán.
Nine ... pahon.
Ninety ... tschom-kon.

O.

Obey ... pom.
Obtain ... noi.
Observe ... pom; dzni.
Oar ... parrai.
Oath ... tachier.
Odour ... arim.
Offer sacrifice ... btoy.
Oil ... mbrisk.
Old (person) ... tat.
Old (thing) ... ablal.
Once ... voikat.
One ... pakat.
Only ... mai.
Open, v. ... hong.
Open, to be ... hemmai.
Orange ... tafr-tlúm.
Orphan ... fára.
Out ... tacuak.
Outskirts ... dai.
Outside ... pawna.
Overturn ... phúm.
Overtake ... phák.

P.

Paddle, s. ... vai-fúng
Pain ... ani.
Palm ... kúl-pá.

Paper ... laisbui.
Part ... hmún.
Parting (of hair) ... bárf.
Path ... kul-koug.
Pare (the nails) ... hlep.
Peace ... rem.
Penetrate ... leng.
People ... mi-hring.
Penis ... dzang; heep-hool.
Perspiration ... aklán.
Permit ... phil.
Pestle ... tadk.
Pen ... vá-tawk-tlé.
Petticoat ... pi-au-fen.
Pettish ... pung-chang.
Piece ... abúng.
Pierce (the ears) ... vi.
Pigeon ... parvú.
Pig ... vák.
Pimple ... ahawk; pan-tawk.
Pinch ... sik.
Pipe (man's) ... vailel.
Pipe (woman's) ... libúr.
Pipes (musical) ... arau-tchem.
Pith ... adzik.
Pitted ... tchik.
Place, v. ... dá.
Place, s. ... emoa; hmún.
Plate ... darkleng; kleng.
Plant, v ... chíng; phún.
Play (to sport) ... lom; in-lom-lem.
Play (to make music) ... túm.
Policeman ... kotwhen.
Ponder ... rik-rú.
Popgun ... tchang-khen; ka-pdp.
Possess ... ogá.
Porcupine ... sakúp.
Poor ... hoam-tschom; pa-tch-
Portion ... hmún. [in.
Possessed (by a spirit) ... dmwl.
Potatoe ... bál.
Potter ... bdl-vna.
Pot (earthen) ... bál.

d

Pour	... btal ; tchúng.		Race	... béram-pú.
Pound, v.	... deng.		Read	... dziek.
Powder	... dzem.		Ready (to be)	... in-tsiem ; tshlvm-ebs.
Prawn	... kai-klang.		Ready (to make)	... tsbiem.
Pregnant	... raí. [bnús ; bnóngu.		Reap	... k.
Presently	... nakina ; nakin-bnds ;		Reckon	... tcbír.
Pretty	... hmól-btá ; moy,		Recollect	... ril-rú ; agai-tún.
Pretend	... dót.		Red	... asben.
Prevaricator	... mí-dseb.		Reeds	... hpai.
Price	... amán.		Relation	... únno ; lai-tcbí.
Prick	... tschdn.		Release	... tchús-tír.
Prophet	... kuarang-dzawl.		Remain	... om ; reng ; riek.
Prisoner	... kul-buin ; sal,		Remembrance	... búin-ldng.
Profit	... smun.		Remember	... -agai-tún.
Promise	... tlam		Repose	... mú.
Proper	... adik.		Return	... alokír.
Prove	... brll-fia.		Revolve	... vír ; bét.
Pull	... kai.		Rice	... bú.
Pulse	... púrhin.		Rice (husked)	... bú-fai.
Purchase	... alei.		Rice (cooked)	... bó-fang.
Purge	... von-achdar.		Rice (as seed)	... bú-tchí.
Purvue	... úm.		Rice (in a parcel)	... tchaw-fún.
Push	... onmo.		Rice (a meal of)	... tchaw-fák.
Put	... dé.		Rich	... tankanga.
Pumkin	... fang-bmú.		Right (the)	... ading.
Put on	... kai ; sbil ; chln.		Ring (for the finger)	... dzúng-búo.
Put out (eject)	... tscnak-tér.		Ring v. (to put on)	... bún.
			Ripe	... abmin.
Q.			Rise	... bto.
Quarrel	... in-trúal.		River	... tuí-pal.
Quick	... twai-twái.		Road	... kul-kong ; kās.
Quarantine	... a-tsbet.		Roast	... bem.
			Roll	... brú-al.
R.			Roof	... fu-tchdng.
Radish	... tchol.		Room	... bungial.
Rainbow	... tchblm-bál.		Root	... dzúng ; búl.
Rain, s.	... rús.		Rope	... bral.
Rain, v.	... rús-abúal.		Rot	... atoy.
Rain-drop	... rús-múl.		Rough	... a-bkap.
Raise	... kang ; tchoy.		Round	... abí-al.
Rape	... all-loi.		Rob	... nomi ; sawt ; chll.
Rat	... aadsú.		Ron	... llan.
Raw	... abel.		Rusty	... tuí-ok.

S.

English	Dao		English	Dao
Salt, s.	taví.		Shot	hát.
Salt (to be)	ul.		Short	atoy.
Solute	taví-bal-búk.		Sick	dám-loh.
Sand	tíow.		Sides	dzáng.
Sacrifice (to offer)	htoy.		Side	hhing; ral.
Sap	huai.		Silent (to be)	ngui-reng.
Saw	blep-tchhúm.		Sing	hlú-sl.
Say	sboy.		Since	chon.
Scanty	avaug.		Sister	fatoú; ú.
Scatter	vot.		Single	dmi.
Scissors	bák-tchai-jé.		Sink	lét.
Scar	pún-dum-mú; alur.		Sit	túh.
Scout	euilú.		Six	parúk.
Scratch	ld-ot.		Sixty	tchhom-rúk.
Scurf	phút.		Sixteen	tchhom-ley-parúk.
Search	dzong.		Skin	avún.
Season	shún.		Sky	ván.
Seam	atol.		Slanting	hét.
Seem	suk.		Slave	sul.
Sear	kin.		Sleep	mú-nghil.
Seed	tchi; ml.		Sleepy	mú-tachiak.
Seize	mun.		Slippery	snail.
Sell	hrul; dsú-ur.		Slow	rel; dzoi.
Sentry	rál-reng.		Slowly	dzoi-in; rei-tch.
Send	kul-ti; htoo.		Sleeping-place	khdœ; mút-hmún.
Separate	htjen; iu-htjen.		Small	atey; tey-tuk.
Sew	túib.		Small-pox	dzong-bri.
Sever	tchhúm.		Smear	huoy.
Service	hlaw-tlo.		Smell s.	haim.
Servo	hlaw.		Smell t.	arim.
Seven	pasarí.		Smoke (tobacco)	dzn.
Seventy	tchhom-mrl.		Smoke, s.	mei-koh.
Seventeen	tchom-ley-pasarí.		Smooth	snail.
Sheep	béram.		Snake	rúl.
Shampoo	huct.		Snow	vút.
Shade	blim; bmong-ber.		Snow, v.	nat.
Shadow	bmong-lér.		Sow, a.	túp.
Sbcudú (tribe of)	Lahér.		Soft	ancm.
Shake	hting; twy.		So	hotiang.
Shoulder	kaoki.		So many	heti-chon.
Show	bmú-ti.		So much	chn-ti-ja.
Sharpen	tét.		Something	cuglo-tul.
			Son	afú-pá.

Song	... blé.
Sorrowful	... hing-ngai.
Sort	... haam ; bmún.
South	... tschim.
Soul	... llaroo.
Speak	... bril.
Spear, s.	... lai.
Spear, v.	... tschún.
Spike	... fúng.
Spirits	... rák-dnú.
Speech	... tong.
Spoil v.	... bpol.
Split	... hlai.
Splinter	... ahling.
Spread	... bpá.
Sprout, v.	... sok.
Spoon	... fi-un.
Squeeze	... tí-lé-tek.
Square	... ki-lk.
Staff	... li-uag.
Stand	... ding.
Stand erect	... fák.
Stab	... tschún.
Staunch (to stop)	... bang.
Stay	... om ; om-brí.
Steel	... blír-tek ; mai-tal.
Sting	... m-dzúk.
Steal	... rók.
Stick	... li-ung.
Stir	... tschók.
Stink	... anem.
Storm	... kús-dúr.
Story	... hton-htú.
Stockade	... kil-pal.
Stone	... hing.
Straight	... angil.
Strike	... tchám ; vá.
String	... hrai.
Strong (as liquor)	... sidr.
Strength	... htáb ; alchak.
Stroll	... lrug.
Surely	... matai-lovin.
Sufficient	... kim.

Stuff in	... lait.
Sulphur	... kát.
Swear (an oath)	... tchiet-tsám.
Swear, v.	... taam.
Sweet	... atlám.
Sweetheart	... agai.
Sweat	... aklda.
Swim	... táí-bleo.
Syphon	... don-kon.

T.

Tail	... amei.
Take	... lá ; kulpal.
Take away	... shin ; kal-pal.
Take hold	... pom ; tchol.
Tall	... achang.
Tax	... kiba.
Tear (to rend)	... tat ; potet.
Tear s. (of the eye)	... mit-tal.
Teach	... dale-tir.
Teeth	... bá.
Telescope	... dát-tchem-htai.
Testicle	... til.
Than	... ai-in ; back-in ; ai-cho-an ; ai-chón.
That	... bí ; khá ; taaw.
There	... taawiá ; kbátá.
Therefore	... ché-vaag-in ; cball-[vaug-in.
This	... bé ; ha-bi.
This road	... bé láma.
This year	... kúmina.
Thing	... tschém ; htá-nm.
Think	... ngai-tua.
Thin	... pon.
Thirsty	... tái-hal.
Thirst	... hal.
Thigh	... el-pal ; mul-pal.
Thousand	... tschaag.
Thorn	... bling.
Thief	... mi-rik.
Thread, v.	... btil.
Thread, s.	... pot ; ladeai

Throw away	...	pai.	Trouble (to give)	... ba-tír.
Thumb	...	dzúng pai.	Tribute	... lei-bé.
Thunder	...	ka-puí-rí; rán-anghér.	Turban	... dír.
Thunderbolt	...	tek.	Tuck in	... dzsb.
Tickle (active form)	...	dziak.	Turn round	... hér; vi.
Tickle (passive form)	...	dzá.	Turtle	... tui-ea-tíl.
Tie	...	too.		
Tick (bug)	...	saphrrik.	**U.**	
Tight	...	tant; amut.	Umbrella	... ni-bliep; tsik-tríl.
Tir	...	há-tír.	Unlucky	... vandú-ai.
Thus	...	chú.	Unfortunate	... vans-dziel.
Thus being	...	chátí-chdan.	Underneath	... tlánga; hnoya.
Thus much	...	há-dza.	Under	... hnoy; kaw-lai-un.
Tinder-box	...	mel-tsl-bom.	Understand	... hré.
Tinder	...	msri-boh.	Up	... tssk-lam.
Tiger	...	sskei.	Use, s.	... hmum.
Time (at present)	...	tún-tleng-ia.	Upside down	... alul-aler; akíl.
Time (season)	...	ahún; lai; voi.	Upright	... abtul; fúk.
Tipra (tribe of)	...	Tui-kúk.	Useless	... hmun-tlsgb-loh.
To-day	...	tukina; voina.	Utan chutra, a. p.	... Ssdruik-ahular.
Tobacco	...	vai-blo.		
Toe (big)	...	dzúng or bpé-pai.	**V.**	
Toe (second)	...	dzúng or bpé-tchal.	Vein	... tsb.
Toe (third)	...	dzúng or bpé-lai.	Very	... dsil; em.
Toe (fourth)	...	dzúng or bpé-tey-d.	Visit, n.	... in-taw.
Toe (little)	...	dzúng or bpé-tey.	Voice	... aw.
Together	...	aríwul-ia; nang-rang-	Vomit	... lo; lo-ak.
Tongue	...	lei. [in; vé-vé.	Variegation	... sdsiek.
Top	...	tchdng.	Village	... kús; rung.
Torch, s.	...	mé-tsdr.	Valva	... dzung.
Topside up	...	ahtol.		
Topsy-turvy	...	alet.	**W.**	
To-morrow	...	nuktska.	Wages	... hhaw-sei.
To-morrow (the day after)		nuktipa.	Waist	... stai.
To-night	...	nuk-dzán.	Waist cloth (dhoti)	... hren.
Trade	...	tschúm-dawng.	Wake	... nang; meug
Track	...	dzsi.	Wait	... ngbák.
Tread	...	rép.	Want, v.	... dil; tús.
Tremble	...	hárb.	War	... rél; rún.
Tree	...	búag.	Warm	... sldn.
Trouble	...	abrot; ahnok.	Wasp	... khwsi.
True	...	tak.	Wash	... teák; tsswb.
Tribe	...	atchí.	Wash (feet, hands)	... tsi.

Wash (face, body)	... bpí ; in-bú-uL	Wildboar	... tsa-ngbul.
Watch	... veng.	Wind	... .lìL
Waterfall	... túi-abúar.	Window	... túk-vát.
Water	... túi.	Wink	... khop.
Wear	... kai; khim.	Wisdom	... afing.
Wear (round neck)	... awr.	Wish, v.	... dú; awum; túm.
Weak	... chao.	Within	... tachú-nga.
Weave, v.	... tá.	Woman	... hanci-tchín.
Weed, v.	... tlo.	Wonderful	... amak.
Weep, v.	... tap.	Word	... htú.
Week	... ní-mrí.	Work, s.	... haa-htawk.
Weight	... arít.	Work, v.	... llo; thaw.
Well (water-hole)	... túi-kúrh.	Wound	... pán.
Well (not ill)	... mláns.	Writing	... lai sbúi.
West	... tláng-láns.	Wrist	... bándrel.
Wet	... nhú.	With	... nen ; hsésa.
Whatever	... englo.	Wrestle	... in-bú-an.
What	... eng.		
What for	... enga-tangey.	**Y.**	
When	... engtikaugey.	Yea	... ní; ní-ey.
Whence	... koylamaugey ; koya-tangey.	Yet	... tún-tleng-in.
		Year	... kúm.
Where	... koyangey.	Year (last)	... nikuma.
Which	... khoi-ngey.	Year (this)	... kumfna.
Whisper	... ardk.	Year (next)	... nakdma.
Whistle	... fai-fúk ; sai-sík.	Yellow	... a-eng.
White	... awsr; ango.	Yesterday	... nimjno.
Who	... tú.	Yesterday (the day before)	... nimin-pia.
Whole	... akina ; npúma.		
Why	... engaiya.	You	... nungma.
Widow	... hmei-htai.	Your	... nungma-tá.
Wife	... nopuí.	Young	... rol-btar.
Win	... haé.	Youth, s.	... túngvál.

www.ingramcontent.com/pod-product-compliance
Lightning Source LLC
Chambersburg PA
CBHW020758020726
47495CB00008B/2493